For Nick

I think you would have liked this one

Poker Night

Chapter One

Eric was wandering the aisles of BigMart, killing time until his shift was over. A young woman approached him somewhat hesitantly. She looked lost and confused.

"Excuse me," she said softly. "Can you tell me where hardware is? I'm looking for stuff to hang some paintings and photos."

"Sure, follow me," Eric replied.

Eric walked the woman over to the picture hanging hardware. She thanked him and he went on his way. As he rounded the corner, he ran into his buddy Deandre.

"Dude, did you get her info?" Deandre asked.

"Shit, no," Eric replied. "I ain't going down that road anymore. I'm not askin' customers out ever again!"

"Oh, yeah, cus of what happened with Jolene?" Deandre said with a chuckle. "Bro, that shit blew up in your face bad!"

"Yeah, no shit, it did. She came in here and went off on me in front of the whole store. Never again, man."

"Dude, that shit was epic!" Deandre laughed. "We still playin' cards at Aaron's tonight?"

"Hell yeah, man!" Eric replied. "Lookin' forward to a night of poker and way too much booze!"

"Yo! Dre! Eric!" Ozzy yelled from the back aisle as the two walked by.

"Hey, Ozzy! Whatcha up to?" Deandre asked.

"Just got some girl's number! She was trying to find hardware to hang paintings and shit in her new apartment. I'm gonna text her later. We might get some drinks!" Ozzy replied with a shit-eating grin on his baby face.

"Tonight's poker night, dude," Eric said.

"Hey, bro, chicks before dicks, ya know?" Ozzy chuckled.

"Dude, you're so lame sometimes," Eric laughed.

"Bro, I'm with my boy here," Deandre said. "You gotta get the dates when ya can."

"Well, have fun," Eric said. "Aaron's gonna be pissed though."

"Shit if I care!" Ozzy said. "That dude bails on us for chicks all the time."

"Never on poker night though," Eric said. "That shit's sacred to him."

"He'll survive," Ozzy said. "Oh, shit, that's her! See ya guys later."

Ozzy rushed off after the woman Eric had walked to the hardware section. Deandre and Eric looked at each other, shook their heads and laughed. They wandered off into the back room of the store. Aaron was back there scanning in new merchandise.

"No Ozzy tonight," Eric said to Aaron.

"What? Why the hell not?" Aaron asked, setting down his scan gun.

Aaron pulled out a pack of cigarettes and motioned to the back door. The three men headed outside to smoke.

"He's got a date," Deandre said, lighting a cigarette. "Well, at least a potential date."

"Yeah, I'm pretty sure he's scaring her away as we speak," Eric laughed.

"That fuckin' guy is a piece of work. He thinks he's so cool cus he goes by Ozzy. If people knew his real name was Oswald, he'd be a lot less cool," Aaron laughed.

Deandre pulled a joint from his shirt pocket, "Ya'all want some of this?"

"Hell yeah, I do!" Eric exclaimed. "That'll get me through the last two hours of this long-ass day!"

"Shit yeah, bro, I'll have some too," Aaron replied.

Deandre lit the joint and took a long drag. He handed it to Eric, who hit it hard and passed it to Aaron. The three of them killed that joint in no time. Now, slightly high, the three men went back to work. Deandre headed over the lawn and garden section where he was supposed to be stocking shelves. Aaron went back to receiving freight. Eric went off to automotive where he was supposed to be building a windshield wiper display.

Before Eric could even start on his project, his work phone rang. He pulled the phone from its holster and answered, "Automotive, this is Brent." He never gave his real name on phone calls.

"Eric, you always do that," Rachel chuckled. "You answer with a different name every time."

"People don't need to know I work here," Eric replied with a laugh.

"You been here six years, I think everyone knows by now," Rachel giggled.

"Maybe, but I ain't giving out my real name. What's up Rachel?"

"Nothin' much," she replied. "I was just wondering what you're doing after work tonight. I was wondering if you wanna get some drinks with me over at the Bigfoot."

5

"Tonight's poker night," Eric replied.

"Oh, shit, it is Friday," Rachel said, sounding less chipper. "Days run together 'round this place."

"Yeah, they do," Eric agreed. "What time are you off?"

"Nine," she replied.

"Me too. We're not meeting at Aaron's 'til ten-thirty. Wanna have a couple drinks before I go over to his place?"

"Yes!" she practically shrieked. "That'd be great!"

"Okay, cool. Meet ya at the time clock at nine."

"Sounds good!"

They hung up and Eric started on his project. He felt like he was being watched. He knew one of his buddies was about to mess with him. They were all constantly playing pranks on one another. Eric was expecting anything at that point. What he didn't expect was for a little girl to walk toward him. She was crying and looked frightened.

"You, okay?" Eric asked, leaning down to get on her level.

The little girl shook her head, no.

"Are you lost?"

She nodded.

"Come with me," Eric said softly and kindly.

He put his hand out and she took it.

"What's your mommy's name?" Eric asked as he led her up front.

"Tina," the little girl sobbed.

"Is she in the store somewhere?"

The little girl nodded.

"Okay, we will go up front and page your mommy."

Rachel was standing at the customer service desk. She perked up when she saw Eric approaching. Then she noticed the crying little girl.

"My little friend here is lost," Eric said to Rachel. "Her mommy's name is Tina."

Rachel picked up the PA mic and paged Tina to customer service. A frantic woman soon rushed up front. The little girl wiggled her hand free from Eric's and ran to her mom. Tina scooped the girl up and thanked Rachel profusely. Eric quietly ducked away and let Rachel take the glory.

*****

Eric was standing in front of the time clock waiting for it to hit 9:01. He never punched out exactly at nine. Rachel was standing next to him, bouncing her right leg in anticipation. She kept looking at Eric and smiling.

"This is the best part of the day, huh?" she said to him with a grin.

"Oh, yeah, no doubt," he replied with a smile. "Lunch and quittin' time!"

The clock hit 9:01 and they both punched out. Aaron was still receiving freight back there and told Eric he'd see him later. Eric shouted goodbye to his friend as he and Rachel walked out. They hurried through the store and out to their vehicles. Rachel followed Eric across the street to the Bigfoot tavern.

"Whatcha all having tonight?" Terry, the bartender, asked as they sat down at the bar.

"Jack and Coke for me," Eric replied.

"I'll do a vodka cran, please," Rachel said.

"Comin' right up," Terry said and started on their drinks. He set the drinks in front of them and wandered off.

Eric took a sip of his drink and sighed, "ah, nothin' beats a drink after a late shift."

"No kidding," Rachel replied with a satisfied sigh of her own.

"How's your brother doin'?" Eric asked.

"He's okay," she replied, "they say he'll make a full recovery. He will never walk the same again, but at least he will walk again."

"That's good to hear," Eric said. He could tell he had bummed her out bringing up her little brother.

"Yeah, we are all glad he's okay," Rachel paused and looked over at Eric, "thank you for being there for me when it all went down. You helped me through a lot of shit."

"You bet," Eric replied. "You're one of my best friends. I've always got your back."

"Thanks, you're a good friend," she said, somewhat deflated.

Rachel and Eric had briefly dated years ago. Both of them had wanted to be more than just friends at one time or the other since they broke up. Eric had fallen deep down the rabbit hole of alcohol and drugs. Rachel loved him but found it hard to respect him a lot of the time. He was selfish and clueless. His life revolved around his many vices. They both knew deep down they were meant for each other, but the timing always seemed to be off. Rachel wasn't the type of person to sit around and wait for a stubborn fool to come around. She had a life to live, and she believed things would work out how they were meant to. She believed deep down that they would eventually get back together and live out their lives together. They would rekindle their love for each other before they died.

"You're welcome," Eric said with a smile. "How was your day?"

"Long!" she chuckled. "Jesus, I don't know how much longer I can take working customer service. People are fuckin' assholes!"

"Ain't that the truth!" he replied, motioning to Terry for a refill. "How many times did you get yelled at today?"

"Oh, shit, like, a million," she chuckled. "You?"

"Not quite a million," he laughed. "We don't get yelled at as much on the floor. Most people need our help so they're somewhat nice to us."

"I'm jealous. Seems like every person I deal with is pissed off. They're pissed off at us because they bought the wrong size of whatever and had to come back to the store. Or they think one of you all gave em attitude, so they're pissed at us."

"That's probably mostly a true occurrence," Eric laughed. "We can be dicks!"

"People exaggerate though," Rachel said. "It pisses me off that these people think they can yell and curse at us. Just cus we work there doesn't mean we don't have feelings too. It's getting to me."

"Apply for a floor position," Eric suggested.

"I don't know shit about any of that," she said.

"Bullshit you don't," Eric said. "You could work in clothing, or grocery, or shit, anywhere. You know how much I knew about automotive before they moved me over there?"

"No."

"Nothin'. Not a damn thing. Know how much I know about it now?"

"Still nothin'?" she replied with a smile.

"Exactly! The system does all the work for us. Some dude comes in for a Ford battery and all I do is punch the info into the computer and it tells me what battery to sell him. It's so easy. And we make more money than you guys. You should just apply."

"Maybe I will," she said, truly contemplating it.

"Do it! Do it! Do it!" Eric chanted and laughed. "Seriously, you don't deserve to be yelled at every day. Come work out on the floor with us."

"I will!" she smiled. "Thanks, Eric."

"Of course! I think you'd like it. Grocery is the best in my opinion, but that's why it's hard to get a spot there. I know they're looking for people for sporting goods and men's clothing. I think lawn and garden too."

"I don't know anything about any of those," she said.

"It doesn't matter. Like I said, the system does all the work. You could totally do men's clothing. It's just folding and hanging clothes. Dudes don't need help picking' out clothes."

"Hey guys!" Karissa said from behind them.

Rachel looked away and rolled her eyes. She couldn't stand Karissa, but she played nice to her face.

"Oh hey!" Eric replied and stood up to hug Karissa.

Karissa threw her arms around Eric and squeezed him tight. She looked at Rachel as she did it. Karissa gave Rachel a smug look.

"What are you two up to tonight?" Karissa asked as Eric released her.

"Just having a couple drinks," Eric said. "Wanna join us?"

"I sure do!" Karissa giggled and took the stool next to Eric.

Rachel felt her stomach turn. Karissa was as basic bitch as they come. She hung every bit and piece of her body out that she could. She wore way too much makeup and had bleach-blonde hair. Rachel watched as Karissa scooted her stool as close to Eric as possible. Rachel gagged as Karissa's cheap perfume filled her nostrils.

Karissa pulled out her phone and took a selfie. She pounded away on the screen as she either sent it to someone or posted it somewhere on social media. Karissa looked at Eric and said, "take a photo with me!" He leaned over and she snapped a photo of them. Karissa then said, "give me your number so I can you send you this photo." Rachel couldn't take it anymore and got up.

She didn't say anything, she just walked to the bathroom.

      Rachel went to the bathroom sink and washed her hands. She didn't have to go to the bathroom, she just wanted to step away from Karissa, obviously throwing herself at Eric. Karissa was a cashier, which meant her and Rachel both worked on the front end. Rachel hadn't liked Karissa from day one. The bitch had strolled into her first shift like she owned the place. Rachel had the unfortunate pleasure of training Karissa. Karissa acted like she already knew everything and wouldn't let Rachel teach her anything. Karissa didn't learn anything and then had to constantly call on Rachel to show her how to do the most basic of things. Everything about that woman drove Rachel nuts.

      Rachel took in a deep breath, a mistake considering she was in a nasty bar bathroom. She looked at herself in the mirror and smiled. She was a beautiful woman, and she knew it. She shouldn't let the Karissa's of the world get to her. Rachel knew these kinds of women were not truly happy. They put on a show, but deep down they hated themselves. That's why they spent so much time on their outfits, hair, makeup, and photo filters. They tried so hard to be "hot" that it made most people think the opposite of them. Rachel knew Eric well enough to know he wasn't the kind of man to fall for Karissa's shenanigans. It just disgusted her to see Karissa blatantly flirting and throwing herself at him.

The bathroom door swung open and startled Rachel. She turned to the door and there was Karissa strolling in with a smirk on her face.

"Oh, Eric is so dreamy, huh?" Karissa said as she floated past Rachel to the far stall.

What was this dumb bitch up to? Why would she say such a thing to Rachel? They weren't friends. They weren't confidantes. Rachel said as little to Karissa as possible and what she did say to her was, and always had been, work related. She had never shared anything personal with Karissa. Rachel knew far more about Karissa than she had ever wanted to because the woman never shut her goddamn mouth.

"You guys are friends, right?" Karissa asked from the stall after Rachel didn't respond to her.

"Yeah," Rachel replied.

"Has he ever talked about me?"

"No," Rachel said as she walked toward the door.

Karissa let her bowels go loudly and Rachel didn't know if she should laugh or run for her life. It was horribly disgusting.

"He's so cute!" Karissa said from the stall as if she hadn't just done what she did.

"Uh-huh," Rachel said and pulled open the door. "Later," she added and left the bathroom.

Rachel burst into laughter as she walked back to the bar. Eric was scrolling his Facebook feed and sipping his third drink. He lit up and put his phone down when he saw Rachel.

"I thought you fell in or something," he giggled. Old joke but still kinda funny.

"No, I just had to get away from Karissa. She drives me nuts," Rachel said as she sat down.

"She is a piece of work," Eric said. "I ordered you another vodka cran."

"Thanks!" Rachel replied and took a healthy sip. "She's a nut job. She has a crush on you!"

"Ugh, fuck, I know," Eric said and rolled his eyes. "It's always the crazy bitches like her that do. Normal chicks don't show any interest in me."

"Oh, they do, they're just not as obvious about it. Normal chicks, as you put it, aren't hoes. They don't attract guys by flaunting their tits and asses or by being all touchy feely. Self-respecting women show interest by having conversations with men and actually trying to get to know them."

"Someday I hope to find a chick like that," Eric said with a soft sigh.

"You will," Rachel said and patted him on the shoulder.

Eric's phone dinged and he picked it up.

"Shit, I'm late to poker night," he said to Rachel. "I wanna finish these drinks with you first though." He replied to the message on his phone and set it back onto the bar.

"I'd like that," Rachel said. "I'd really like to leave at the same time as you. I don't wanna be stuck here with Karissa."

"Where is she?" Eric asked looking around the bar.

"She's taking a big ol nasty shit," Rachel laughed.

"No way, chicks don't shit!" Eric said and laughed way too hard at his own dumb joke.

"You're a dork," Rachel chuckled.

"Hell yeah, I am and I'm damn proud of it! Cheers!" Eric raised his mostly empty glass to Rachel.

"Cheers!" Rachel replied and clinked glasses.

"I got the tab. You ready to get outta here?" Eric asked.

Rachel sucked down the rest of her drink and said, "yeah, I am. Thanks for the drinks, man. I appreciate it."

"My pleasure! We gotta make this a regular thing again."

"I'd love that!" Rachel said with a big smile.

"Just not on poker nights, so we're not so rushed," Eric said as he signed the credit card slip. "Let's go."

They walked out of the bar. As Eric pulled open the front door for Rachel, he saw Karissa walk out of the lady's room. She was looking around the bar with a confused look. He quickly ducked out the door behind Rachel. Eric walked Rachel to her car and gave her a big hug.

"Text me when you get home," he told her.

"I will," she replied with a smile. "Have fun playing cards with the guys."

"Thanks, I will," Eric said with a smile. "Hey, if it's not too late when we're done, can I call you?"

"Yes! Of course!" Rachel replied excitedly. "I work a late shift again tomorrow, so I'll be up late tonight. Call anytime."

"Okay, cool! I will," Eric said. "Talk to you later, then."

"Yeah, talk soon."

Eric turned and walked to his truck. He felt almost giddy inside and didn't quite know why. He was probably just excited about poker night. It was one of his favorite things. No Ozzy that night, but the rest of them would still have a blast.

*****

Eric walked into Aaron's house and could hear the guys chatting in the kitchen. He went into the kitchen and said hello to the guys. To his surprise, Ozzy was there.

"What happened to your hot date? Did you scare her off already?" Eric asked Ozzy.

"No. She gave me a fake number!" Ozzy replied, and Eric burst out laughing.

"No shit? Again?" Eric chuckled.

"Yeah, man, I fuckin' messaged her like six times and then I called the number. Some dude answered and said to quit messaging him. Dude was like, 'I ain't Becky, she gave you a fake number.' Then he laughed at me and hung up."

"Oh-my-fuckin' God that's too funny!" Eric cried with laughter. "We'll never see that chick shopping at our store again."

"Nope," Aaron agreed. "Hey, Ozzy, how many chicks you think quit shopping at our store cus of you?"

"Dozens probably," Ozzy replied and chuckled. "All worth it though! At least I'm out there trying to get dates. You fools are just happy slinking by week to week waiting on poker nights."

"Dude, I'm happy with my life right now," Deandre said. "I am glad to be single again. After dating Luna for so many years, it feels nice to be on my own."

"I hear that!" Aaron said and raised his beer bottle to Deandre. "Dre's right, it's nice to be single for a bit."

"You guys are just making the best of it," Eric said. "You're trying to convince yourselves you like it."

"Hey, man, you're single too," Deandre said.

"Yeah, but I'm looking for the right girl. I'm not trying to convince myself I like being single. I want love and companionship," Eric explained.

"Um, dumbass you have that right now!" Aaron said. "Pull your drunken head out of your ass and ask Rachel out already. She adores you for some unknown reason. She's a great girl."

"Naw, man, she doesn't like me like that anymore," Eric said and shook his head.

"The fuck she doesn't!" Aaron said.

"Dude, me and Rachel been through some shit. We tried the dating thing, remember? It ended horribly."

"That's cus you fucked it up! You panicked when she said she loved you and you fuckin' bailed!" Aaron said, sitting down at the table. The other guys followed his lead and all sat down.

"Look man, I was only twenty-two at the time. I didn't know what the fuck love was. I've known Rachel since junior high, we go way back. Fuckin' Dre's the only person I've known longer than her. It's too late now, I blew my chance with her years ago."

"Bro, it's not too late," Deandre said. "I've known you two forever and I promise she loves you, dude. She always has and I think she always will."

"Yeah, she does, as a friend. Same way you fools love me," Eric said.

"Shuffle up and deal," Ozzy told Aaron.

"Okay, game's Texas Hold 'em, as usual," Aaron said and shuffled. He looked at Eric as he started to deal the cards, "Rachel loves you more than just a friend. Think about it. How many guys has she dated since you?"

"Like one, maybe two, but that one guy Brad for sure," Eric replied.

"And how many women have you dated since then?" Aaron asked.

"Shit, I don't know, a lot," Eric replied, studying his cards.

"That right there should tell you something," Aaron said.

"Tell me what?" Eric asked.

"That she still loves you," Aaron replied.

"How? What's that gotta do with it? What does how many dudes she's dated matter?"

"'Cus, she wants to be with you," Aaron replied. "One, maybe two, relationships since you all broke up doesn't seem odd to you? She's a hot and fun chick; any dude would want to date her. I think she's waiting to see if you ever pull your head out of your ass. But she ain't gonna wait forever, man."

"You all believe that?" Eric asked looking around the table. They all nodded.

"You're all nuts," Eric said. "Rachel and I are friends. We had a couple drinks tonight before I came over here and nothin' happened. She messaged when she got home and just said thanks again for the drinks. No different than if I went for drinks with any of you."

"Except you never buy us any fuckin' drinks," Deandre said with a chuckle.

"It's cus we don't have tits," Ozzy laughed.

"And we haven't fucked you before," Harvey added.

"Shut up, all of you," Eric said.

"Just ask her out and see what happens," Aaron said.

"I'm not sure I like her that way anymore," Eric said. "I used to. And we've hooked up a few times since at parties and shit, but I don't think I have romantic feelings for her anymore."

"Bullshit you don't!" Deandre said. "I see the way you look at her. The way you light up and your voice changes when you talk to her. She calls you on your work phone all the time to just bullshit and you fuckin' light up every time! You so love that girl, bro."

"I care deeply about her and her well-being. I enjoy talking to her and hanging out. I am there for her when she needs a friend," Eric said. "But none of that means I'm in love with her. None of that means we should be an item."

"Dude, she's gorgeous, she's cool as fuck, and she's so into you," Harvey said. "Quit being a fool and snatch that girl up before she moves on."

"Harvey's right, dude, you'll hate yourself if she gives up waiting on you and meets someone else. Don't wait 'til it's too late," Aaron said and dealt the flop.

"Look, guys, I appreciate your little pep-talk or whatever this is, but I can't ask her out. It's too late already. I blew it and I don't think I'll ever regain her full trust."

"It's worth a chance, bro," Deandre said.

"Yeah, what's the worst that could happen?" Harvey asked.

"It could all go down in flames, and I'd lose her in my life forever," Eric said with a tone of sadness. "I can't risk losing her friendship. I can't imagine not being her friend."

"Well, don't fuck it up this time," Ozzy said.

"You're going to lose her if you don't ask her out," Deandre said. "She's not going to keep hanging around watching you date other chicks and party with your boys. She's a smart girl. She knows what she wants in life. She's not getting any younger. She'll eventually date another dude, and he probably won't like her having a dude best friend. You'll get faded out."

"Our friendship is stronger than any of that," Eric said. "I believe it'd survive anything, except for another breakup."

"Let me ask you this," Aaron started, "how would you feel if she did start dating someone else again?"

Eric thought about that for a moment. He looked at his cards and the cards on the table. He had a horrible hand, so he folded. As the other guys played their cards, Eric imagined seeing Rachel dating someone else. He didn't like how that made him feel. Jealousy and irritation were the emotions he felt most.

"So, how'd you feel?" Aaron asked.

"I dunno," Eric said. He didn't want to admit it'd make him jealous. It would only prove his buddies right. "I think I'd be cool with it. As long as she was happy, and he treated her right." He could barely spit the words out. He didn't believe a word of it.

"Oh, bullshit, bro!" Deandre said, throwing his cards in.

"You're so full of shit!" Aaron said. "We can see it all over your face! You'd be so jealous, just fuckin' admit it already."

Eric took a deep breath and stood up. He went to the counter and made himself a new drink.

"I'm gonna have a smoke," Eric said and headed for the back door.

Deandre and Aaron stood up. They followed Eric out back. The three lit cigarettes.

"Can we just drop the Rachel thing for the night?" Eric asked.

"No, not yet. You never answered my question." Aaron said.

"I did answer it," Eric said.

"Okay, then, you never answered my question honestly," Aaron replied.

"Fuck, you're annoying," Eric chuckled, shaking his head. "You all are like a fuckin' broken record. 'Ask Rachel out.' 'She fuckin' loves you.' Blah blah blah!"

"Look, bro, I'm good friends with her too," Deandre said. "You're my boy and I always got your back first, but I care about her too. We ain't tryin' to make you do anything. We just know you'd both be so happy together."

"What's she doing tonight?" Aaron asked.

"I dunno," Eric replied. "I think she's just chilling at home."

"Call her and ask her out," Aaron said.

"Right now?" Eric asked, surprised.

"Yeah, right now," Aaron said. "Take her to a movie then drinks or somethin'."

"What about poker night? That shit's sacred to you."

"Fuck it, man," Aaron replied. "We ain't even really playing anyhow. Ozzy's already half blitzed; he'll be passed out in under an hour. Harvey has to get home to his old lady by midnight. Me and Dre can kick it without you."

"Seriously? You think I should just call her out of the blue and ask her out?" Eric was shocked that they were pushing it so hard. They razzed him about it a lot but never pushed him this hard.

"What would it hurt?" Aaron asked. "Worst case scenario, she just thinks you're hanging as friends."

"She'll know something's up if I ask her to hang on poker night. She knows how important that is to us," Eric said and lit another cigarette. He felt nervous.

"Good, then she'll know she's that important to you," Aaron said. "You don't need to tell her poker night was basically a bust. Let her believe you would rather spend time with her than us tonight."

"Oh, yeah, bro, I like that shit," Deandre said, pointing at Aaron in agreeance.

"You guys are fuckin' serious?" Eric said and took a long sip of his drink.

"Totally serious," Deandre said. "Just do it, bro. It's time."

Eric stared at his two best friends and sighed. A smile crept across his face. He said he wanted to go home first to change. He thanked the guys and took off.

Chapter Two

Eric's alarm clock scared him awake. He had slept until eleven am. He almost never did that, even after a late night of drinking. He rolled over and turned the alarm off. He kicked the covers off and stretched. Eric sat up and looked at his date lying next to him. She was awake and smiling at him.

"Good morning, Eric," she said.

"Good morning, Lucy," he replied. "How'd you sleep?"

"Oh, fuck, after what we did last night, I slept like a rock!" Lucy replied and sat up. "How about you?"

"Fairly well," he replied. "I'm gonna piss and then go make coffee."

"Okay, I'll meet you in the kitchen in a bit," Lucy smiled and laid back down.

Eric stood in front of the toilet draining his bladder. The feeling of guilt filled his entire body. Why did he feel so guilty? He was a single guy; he was allowed to date anyone he wanted to. Did he feel guilty because he lied to the guys and called Lucy instead of Rachel? Was it because he had told Rachel he'd call and never did? Knowing her, she probably stayed up way too late waiting for him to call. He felt like a dick for that.

Eric and Lucy had been flirting and chatting for weeks. He met her on a dating app and was instantly attracted to her. He had never met anyone on one of those apps before and it was all honestly very exciting. It all felt naughty to him. Lucy liked him immediately too and did not hide that fact at all. Although she never said so, Eric got the feeling she was no stranger to dating apps.

Eric heard his phone notification go off several times in a row. He washed up and went back into the bedroom. Lucy watched him with a sly smile as he walked around the bed to the nightstand. It was Aaron and Deandre blowing him up asking about his hot date with Rachel. They were going to be so pissed at him when he told them what he had really done the night before. When they were younger the guys would've applauded him for hooking up with a new girl on the first date. Now they were so intent on him dating Rachel again that no other woman was ever good enough anymore. They would just bring everything back around to how he was wasting his time with all these other women. How Rachel was his one and he was an idiot for not seeing it.

Having life-long friends was great, but shit, they were always up in his business. He knew they only had his best interests in mind and appreciated that, but sometimes he just wished he could live his life without constant criticism and advice.

"What is it, Eric?" Lucy asked, shaking him free from his thoughts. "You look concerned."

"Oh, everything's fine," Eric answered with a forced smile. "It's just my buddies asking what time I work today."

Eric got dressed and put his phone in his pocket. He went out to the kitchen and started a pot of coffee. He looked out the kitchen window and drummed on the countertop as he waited for the coffee.

"Did I do or say something to offend you?" Lucy asked from behind him. She was dressed and had her bag in her hand.

"No, no, not at all," Eric said and turned to face her.

"Look, we don't know each other super well yet, but I can tell something is clearly bothering you this morning. Last night you were so fun, flirty, kinda dirty, and so easy-going. This morning you're all quiet and you seem almost sad."

"It's nothin'," Eric insisted. "I'm just not a morning person. It takes a while for me to perk up in the morning."

"Are you dating someone? Am I your dirty little secret?" Lucy asked with a look of suspicion and anger.

"No, nothin' like that," Eric said, but he didn't even believe those words.

"Yeah, uh-huh. Okay, well I best be going. I have an appointment soon," Lucy said and looked him over one more time. "Thanks for last night."

"Yeah, it was a blast," Eric replied. "I'll see you later."

"Yup, sure, see ya around." With that, Lucy was out the door.

"Fuck!" Eric said to the empty room. "You goddamn dummy!"

*****

Eric arrived at work at two o'clock. Rachel was at the customer service desk. She looked tired. Eric smiled at her on his way to clock in. After he clocked in, he went back up front to talk to Rachel.

"Hey, sorry I never called last night," he said. "I hope you didn't wait up for me."

"I did, but it's all good," Rachel said with a little smile. It seemed forced to him. "I watched a couple cool movies and did my nails." She flashed her nails at him.

"They're pretty. I like the color," Eric said and smiled.

"You and the guys get up to no good last night?" Rachel asked.

"Not really. I got way more hammered than I thought I would and passed out early," Eric lied.

"Sounds about right for poker night," Rachel chuckled. Her work phone rang. "This is Rachel." A pause. "Yes, we do, let me transfer you. Hold on." Rachel punched a couple buttons on the phone and hung up. She looked back at Eric, "What are you doin tonight?"

"Nothin', yet. You?"

"Same, no plan yet," she replied.

"Wanna go to a movie?" Eric asked.

"Sure," she replied. "Anything good playing?"

"There's a few I thought looked good, but why don't you pick?"

"Okay, sounds fun," Rachel said and smiled.

"I better get to work before Ken sees me up here."

"Good idea. You two aren't on good terms as it is," Rachel chuckled.

"To say the least," Eric laughed. "Talk to you soon."

"Yeah, bye."

Eric headed over to automotive. He could tell she knew he was lying to her. God, he felt like such a tool. What a dick thing to do. Why was he always doing shit like that? Why didn't he have the guts to be honest with her? If he ever wanted to date her again, she'd be more likely to date him if he had always been honest with her. They were friends, he shouldn't be lying to her. How could she ever trust him going forward if he just kept lying to her? Regardless of any future relationship, he was disrespecting her now. He was being selfish and a bad friend. What was he so scared of? What drove him to be so dishonest with her? And himself?

Rachel watched as Eric walked away. He was lying about something, or, at least omitting something. Same difference, omitting something is lying. Eric was obviously hiding something from her. He was probably seeing someone again. He always acted weird and aloof when he was dating someone. It drove her nuts. She knew that he didn't want to date her again yet, but he could at least respect her enough to be honest with her.

Karissa approached the customer service desk. Rachel let out a sigh and rolled her eyes.

"Hey, girl," Karissa said to Rachel and leaned on the counter.

"Hey," Rachel coldly replied. She wanted to say, *I ain't your girl, bitch.*

"You and Eric get up to some funny stuff last night?" Karissa asked, smacking on a piece of gum and twirling her fried hair.

"None of your business," Rachel said. "I don't talk about my personal life at work."

"Oh, girl! That's a yes!" Karissa sang. "I knew it, cus I heard he got laid last night. I know ya'all left the bar together. Nice work girl!"

"Where'd you hear that?"

"My friend, Kayley, works at the valley store and like, she saw Eric late last night at a bar with some chick. Kayley's my ho, ya know, we tight. She recognized Eric from the picture I posted and thought I should know he has a chick or somethin'. She thinks I should, like, give up on him, but it's like, if you ain't serious then I still wanna chance at that man."

Rachel wanted to grab her by her nasty hair and smash her smug face into the counter. Everyone in that store knew that Eric and Rachel had dated. They all knew the two of them were best friends now. Karissa was no different, she had worked there long enough to know all the store gossip. Rachel knew that little bitch was talking that way to rile her up. Karissa wanted to piss Rachel off.

"You know what, Karissa?" Rachel started, not expecting an answer.

"What?" Karissa asked with a head shake.

Rachel pulled in a deep breath to calm herself and said, "People need to mind their own fuckin' business. If someone 'round here is sleeping with someone it's their goddamn business not the whole fuckin' store's! I'm sick of this high school drama bullshit! It's smarmy little bitches like you that stir the shit pot!"

"Who you callin' a bitch, bitch?!" Karissa said and stood up straight.

"You! I called you a bitch!"

"Ladies, this is not the place for such talk," their supervisor Glorianne said. "Karissa, go back to your register please."

"Okay," Karissa replied and slumped away.

"Rachel, I expect language and behavior like that from Karissa, but not you. What got into you?"

"I've told you before, she rubs me the wrong way," Rachel replied. She had worked for Glorianne for a long time, and they had a good relationship. "She's so intrusive all the time. She pushes my buttons just to get a rise out of me. Usually I don't bite, but today she said some things I couldn't just let go."

"The rumors about you and Eric that are going around today?" Glorianne asked.

"Shit, yeah. How do these things even get started and why?" Rachel slumped over the counter and sighed. She felt like either bursting into tears or screaming.

"It's just the nature of retail," Glorianne said. "Tomorrow it'll be a different rumor. Just watch how you speak up here. I don't want any customers or managers hearing my employees calling each other bitches."

"Okay, sorry, Glorianne."

"It's okay. Why don't you go take your break now and cool off?" With that Glorianne walked over to Karissa.

How did stupid rumors like that get started? Had Karissa made the whole thing up so she could find out if Rachel was sleeping with Eric? Rachel wouldn't put that past her, but the rumor felt deeper than just Karissa being sneaky. Karissa seemed like the type to just come out and ask Rachel if she had slept with Eric. It was all so frustrating and annoying. It was worse than high school. At least in high school you expect that shit because everyone is so young and inexperienced. But grown-ass adults behaving like that was beyond irritating.

Rachel went out front to get away from the store and Karissa. She went around the corner of the building. She was furious, irritated, and confused. She was deep in thought, trying to figure out what Eric was hiding. Had he hooked up with someone the night before? If he had, why didn't he just say so?

Karissa came bounding around the corner and grabbed Rachel by the hair. She was screaming gibberish. Rachel wiggled herself free and punched Karissa in the face. Karissa screeched and stumbled backward. She had a look of pure shock on her now-swelling face.

"You cunt!" Karissa shrieked, rubbing her cheek.

Rachel didn't hesitate; she punched Karissa again. This time she got her square in the nose. Blood gushed out of Karissa's nose, and she ran away crying. Rachel was shaking. She'd probably get in some serious trouble for that, but she didn't care. She hoped they would fire her for it. Then she could move on from the bullshit of that place, and Eric. She was so angry with him! The love that she carried in her heart for him every day had turned to hate. She knew she didn't actually hate him, but at that moment she sure did.

Rachel took a lap around the vast parking lot and went back inside. Glorianne was waiting for her at customer service with the store manager. The operations manager was seated with Karissa in Glorianne's office. Karissa had her head back and a wad of paper towels on her nose. Her right eye was dark and swollen. Rachel couldn't help but smile at the sight of Karissa. If anyone deserved something like that, it was Karissa.

"Rachel, we need you to come back to my office," the store manager, Jim, said.

"Okay," Rachel quietly replied.

By this time most of the employees were hovering around the front end. They were all whispering and pointing. Rachel, although still furious, felt a sense of pride and satisfaction. She followed Jim and Glorianne to the back of the store with a little bounce in her step. Adrenaline was coursing through her veins. They passed the automotive department on their way to Jim's office. Rachel smiled at Eric as they passed him. He looked clueless. The word must not have spread to the back of the store yet.

Eric watched as Rachel followed Jim and Glorianne into Jim's office. There were only two reasons an employee met with their supervisor and Jim in his office. One, they were in some sort of trouble, or two, they were getting a review and possible raise. Eric knew it wasn't time for Rachel to have a review. So, that only meant she was in some sort of trouble.

"Bro!" Deandre said, rushing up to Eric and startling him. "Did you hear what just happened?"

"No, what?" Eric said, setting down a box of windshield wipers.

"Rachel just beat Karissa's ass!" Deandre said as he tried to catch his breath. "She broke Karissa's nose!"

"No shit?! Are you fuckin' with me?"

"No, for reals, bro! That shit went down! Harvey saw it on the camera outside. He's got it queued up in the loss prevention office. Let's go check it out!"

"Is that why she's in Jim's office?" Eric asked, more concerned with what was going to happen to Rachel than with seeing her kick Karissa's ass.

"For sure, bro, but let's watch that shit before Jim comes back out on the floor."

"Fine," Eric agreed. "It would be kinda cool to see Rachel break that annoying bitch's nose!"

"Right, bro?"

Deandre and Eric hurried to Harvey's office. Aaron and Ozzy were already there. Harvey played the footage, and they all gasped and laughed.

"Bro! Rachel's a beast!" Deandre exclaimed.

"Eric, that's why you gotta marry that girl! She's a badass!" Aaron said.

The other guys went on and on about how badass and cool Rachel was. How she was a keeper. It all made Eric feel even worse about what he had done the night before. Had he caused her to do that to Karissa? Was she so angry at him that she took it out on Karissa? Eric knew Rachel knew he was lying, and he had no doubts she was pissed about it. Luckily for Rachel's defense, Karissa had started it.

They watched the minute-and-a-half clip over and over. Harvey paused the clip the moment Rachel's fist connected with Karissa's nose. Everyone, except for Eric who had quit watching, were enjoying every second of that clip. Every one of those guys thought the world of Rachel and not one of them could stand Karissa. They got way more enjoyment out of it than they should have, but none of them cared.

"Eric, walk with me, talk with me, bro," Deandre finally said. "Catch ya boys later."

Eric and Deandre left the office and went out the back door. They lit cigarettes and walked away from the building.

"So, what happened last night, bro? Who was that chick leaving your apartment today?"

"Fuck, Dre, I've told ya, just cus we live in the same complex doesn't mean you can watch my apartment like that."

"Look, I thought you were going out with Rachel last night," Deandre said. "So, yeah, I maybe glanced at your place a few times today to see if I could catch her leaving. Sue me, bro."

"It weirds me out, dude," Eric said.

"It is what it is. Look, it's none of my business, but we are bros. What happened last night?"

"I lied to you guys. I said I was going to call Rachel, but I called this chick Lucy instead," Eric explained. "The truth is, I just wanted to get laid, and I didn't want to muddy things with Rachel. Honestly, man, I really do like Rachel."

"Then why don't you go out with her already? Shit, man, quit fuckin' around with these floosies and grow a pair."

"Dre, you don't understand. None of you do." Eric paused and smoked his cigarette.

"Understand what, bro?"

Eric sighed and looked at Deandre, "I'm scared, man."

"Of what?"

"Hurting her again," Eric said and turned his watering eyes away from Deandre.

"You're already hurting her," Deandre said. "Every time you fuck someone else you hurt her. Every time you lie to her. Every time you keep shit from her, you hurt her. I don't mean to be so blunt, but you're my dog, I gotta be. Hopefully she's still interested in you. I think she is, but, man, you're fuckin' it up!"

"Fuck, Dre, you're right, I know you are. I know I've hurt her so many times." Eric paused again and choked back tears. "Why would she even be interested in me?"

"Maybe she only focuses on the good side of you. She knows the real you. The side of you that only her and I have ever seen. She was there when you saved that kid from drowning in the river, when we were all young. She was there when you kicked that dude's ass at school for calling me the 'N' word. She's seen that protective, loving side of you. She knows you're confused right now. She knows the liquor controls pretty much every decision you make right now. She loves you enough to forgive your mistakes because she knows how loving and caring and protective you can be."

Eric couldn't hold it in anymore and burst into tears. He felt ashamed, but he couldn't help it.

"Let it out, bro," Deandre said and patted his best friend on the shoulder. "Let it all out."

*****

"Rachel, tell us what happened?" Jim asked once they were all seated.

"Karissa put hands on me, so I defended myself," Rachel replied.

"We saw that, but what led up to it? What was with the interaction at customer service?" Glorianne asked.

"We just don't get along," Rachel replied. "We never have and never will. I try to keep things professional, and work related, but she always messes with me. I think she gets a kick out of pissing me off."

"Why you?" Jim asked.

"It's not just me," Rachel said. "She messes with everyone a bit, but more so with me. I think it's because I don't play her games. I don't laugh at her inappropriate jokes. I don't tell her she looks good when she shows up with ten pounds of makeup and one pound of clothes on. She hates me because I don't like her."

"I've been in this business for a long time," Jim began, "so I know people don't always get along, but we do have to keep things professional, regardless. We can't have employees cursing at each other and we especially can't have employees fighting. Dennis is taking Karissa to minor emergency. Now we're down a cashier and that affects our whole store. You understand what I'm saying?"

"Of course, I do," Rachel responded. "I totally understand, and I totally agree. I would never fight someone just because I don't like em, but I will defend myself every time someone lays hands on me."

"That's understandable, but maybe next time walk away. Come inside and get Glorianne or myself." Jim said.

"It all happened so fast. There won't be a next time," Rachel said. "I'm officially putting in my two weeks' notice as of today."

Glorianne gasped and looked shocked. Jim looked up from the legal pad he was writing on.

"Are you sure you want to do that?" Jim asked.

"Yeah, Rachel, you need to take some time to cool off before you make a decision like that. You're one of my best employees; I'd hate to lose you." Glorianne added.

"I'm sure," Rachel said. "I've been contemplating it for some time now."

"Maybe we could work something out to keep you? I could do my best to not schedule you and Karissa for the same shifts." Glorianne pleaded.

"It's not just her," Rachel said. "I've been here four years, and I only make a dollar-twenty-five more than when I started. There are people on the sales floor that have worked here for less than a year and make way more money than I do. I get yelled at, cussed out, and belittled every day. I've even had people throw things at me. I'm burned out on that counter. Karissa was just the last straw for me."

Jim and Glorianne looked at each other. Rachel thought it looked like they were trying to communicate telepathically. That made her grin.

"Would you give us a moment to discuss this?" Jim asked.

"Sure, but I want you guys to know, I have no desire to stay up front. I can't take being yelled at anymore, especially for what I make an hour. I'm really sorry to drop all this on you and for what happened between Karissa and me. This just seemed like the right time to put in my notice."

"Okay, understood. Give us a few moments to discuss some things," Jim said.

"Okay," Rachel replied and left the office.

Rachel paced the back of the store while she waited. Part of her wanted to just clear out her locker and leave for good. She knew what Jim and Glorianne were going to do. They were going to offer her more money. There was no way she'd stay on for any amount of money if she had to stay in customer service. Financially she was in a pretty good spot. She had moved back in with her parents after her brother's accident to help care for him. She had a nice amount of money saved up. She could pay her cell phone bill, car payment, insurance, and other expenses easily for a couple of months while she looked for another job.

The more she pondered it, the more she just wanted out of that store. Out of retail all together. Maybe she could find a job as a delivery driver and have minimal contact with other people. It would be so amazing to work alone. To work somewhere without customers, at least not retail customers.

Rachel stopped pacing when she noticed Eric leaving the breakroom with his backpack. He looked hurried and upset. He had just gotten there, why would he be leaving already? Leaving for the day would be the only reason he would be walking toward the front with his backpack on. What the hell was going on around there today?

We all need a long-ass break, Rachel thought to herself.

Jim popped out of his office and invited her back in.

"I think we came up with a solution that would work for everyone," Jim said with a satisfied smile. "We would like to offer you a position in produce. It's mostly mornings and it's five dollars an hour more than what you make currently. How does that sound?"

Grocery is the best department according to Eric, Rachel thought. *Five bucks an hour more would be amazing. I couldn't find another job for that much. And mostly morning shifts would be badass.*

"When would I start?" she asked.

"A week from Monday. The beginning of the new pay period," Jim answered.

"So, I'd work this upcoming week in customer service?" Rachel asked.

"Yeah, whatever you're already scheduled for," Jim said.

Rachel thought for a moment, she would have the next three days off and then the following Sunday, so that'd only be four days in customer service. Only four more days of getting yelled at every day. Sounded great to her.

"I'll do it!" Rachel exclaimed. "Thank you very much!"

"That's great to hear," Jim said. "We always want to do whatever possible to keep good employees on."

"I'll miss you on the front end, but I am so happy for you, Rachel," Glorianne said.

"Thank you again," Rachel began, "but I didn't think there were any openings in grocery."

"There weren't until this morning," Jim said. "We had someone quit today. It all works out nicely."

"Okay, well I do greatly appreciate this opportunity," Rachel said.

"We all better get back to work," Jim said.

"Okay, thanks again," Rachel said and stood up.

Rachel left Jim's office with a bounce in her step. Not only had she not gotten in any trouble for breaking Karissa's nose, but she also got a promotion and a huge raise. She felt great about work, but she was still on edge regarding Eric. She had seen him leave in a hurry and he looked upset. Deandre would know what's going on. She decided to stop by the lawn and garden department to talk to him, not only about Eric, but she also needed to tell someone about her promotion.

She found him outside watering plants. He looked bummed out but lit up a bit when he saw her approaching.

"I saw what you did to Karissa!" Deandre exclaimed and gave Rachel a hug. "You a bad, bad woman!"

"She started it, and I finished it," Rachel chuckled. "I have some news!"

"Oh yeah, what is it?"

"I just got a promotion to produce!"

"Oh shit! Really?! That's great news. Congrats, girl!"

"Thanks, man," Rachel said with a smile.

"Hey, wait," Deandre started, "let me get this straight, you kicked Karissa's ass, and they gave you a promotion?! Maybe I should break someone's nose too!"

Rachel giggled and said, "well, I got it because I put in my two weeks' notice. They gave me the promotion so I wouldn't quit. They said I'm a good worker and they didn't want to lose me. I told em there's no way I'm sticking around if I'm stuck on the front-end making shit money."

"Nice work! Did you mean it? Were you really going to quit?"

"Yeah, a hundred percent," Rachel said. "I've been contemplating it for a while now. I hate it up there,

Dre. It sucks so bad. The customers are assholes, and Karissa is a fuckin' bitch! I was so over all of it."

"I get that, I worked customer service for about six months. It does suck up there."

"I was just over it," Rachel said. "I really started to think about it and my future here after Myles's accident. My little bro almost died. He had nothing to show for his life. It really made me think about my own life. If something ever happened to me, would I be proud of my life? Would I be satisfied with my life so far? The answer was always no. Now, I feel like I can be proud of my work. People work their entire lives in produce. It's a big deal."

"It really is, I'm proud of you," Deandre said. "Hook a brotha up if they have any more openings."

"You know I will," she said with a smile. "Hey, what happened to Eric? I saw him leaving. He looked upset."

"He's fine," Deandre said. "He's having stomach issues."

"Bullshit, Dre, I know that's probably what he told Ken, but what's really going on?"

"I don't think I can tell you," Deandre said.

"Why not? We're all friends."

"I don't think he'd want me talking about it."

"Oh, I get it," Rachel said, nodding her head. "It's about me and/or whoever he hooked up with last night."

"How'd you know about that?"

"I didn't know for sure until now," she said as anger rushed through her.

"Fuck," Deandre muttered softly.

"No worries, Dre, I know he fucks around like that sometimes. It's honestly all good. I don't give a shit about him hooking up, I just hate that he feels like he has to hide it from me and lie about it."

"Rachel, he's so confused right now. He knows what would ultimately make him happy, but he's scared to pursue it."

"He's an idiot," Rachel said. "I fuckin' love that idiot but he drives me crazy."

"I know, girl, I know, me too. It's frustrating watching someone you care about so much go down a rabbit hole of drinking and bad decisions."

"Is he still doin' coke?" Rachel asked.

"He says no, but I don't believe him. He makes damn good money here, but he's always broke as fuck."

"That fuckin' guy," Rachel said and shook her head.

"He's still in love with you, ya know?"

They heard the intercom come to life and then the following page overhead, "Rachel to customer service please. Rachel to the customer service desk, please."

"Shit, I gotta go," Rachel said. "Talk later, Dre."

"We will. See ya," Deandre replied with a wave as she hurried away.

*****

Eric got back to his apartment and started packing his suitcase. He had told Ken he needed a few days off. Ken agreed and gave him the next three days off. Eric felt relieved and like a small weight had been lifted. He badly needed to sort things out in his head, but he couldn't do that at work. It felt like everything was collapsing in on him. Things had seemed to be going so well until a few weeks ago. Nothing made sense to him anymore. People seemed to be pulling him in a hundred different directions. His life felt like a mess.

Eric knew he turned to vices and sex to distract himself from the real world. He needed to distract himself from getting older. That societal push to be married and have kids. His parents and his friends pushing him to not only date Rachel, but to marry her. He wasn't even ready to date her, and they were telling him to marry her. She *would* make a fantastic wife and life partner. She was already his best friend. She was already the standard he held every other woman to, and none of them came close to being as good as Rachel. Why was he so damn scared to date her? Was it because he was afraid to "give up" his freedoms? Give up those things that were slowly killing him? Was he just scared to give himself totally to someone? Even if it was Rachel?

Eric sat down on his bed with a sigh. He pulled out his phone and sent a group message to Deandre, Aaron, Ozzy, Harvey, Leo, and Rachel. He told them all to somehow get the next three days off and meet him up at his family's lake cabin. He told them they all needed a nice, relaxing, little break from retail and reality. Rachel messaged him and said she already had the next three days off and she'd be there for sure. She added she was going to bring her cousin Gina. Deandre hit back next, saying he'd be there one way or the other. Leo hit back and said he had to work that evening at the pot farm, but he'd be up the next day with enough weed for a week! Aaron responded and said, "you know I'll be there!" Ozzy replied, saying he'd be there. Harvey didn't reply at all.

Eric grabbed his suitcase, his toiletries, and a cooler. He loaded up his truck and left for the grocery store. Normally he'd stock up at work and get his employee discount, but he couldn't go back there after lying about having stomach issues. Eric bought hot dogs, burger patties, buns and a whole lot of beer and Jack Daniels. He knew he'd be drinking a hell of a lot more than he'd be eating over the next several days. He also knew that Aaron and Ozzy would bring a shit-ton of food, they always did.

Chapter Three

Eric sat on the huge porch that surrounded most of the cabin. It was a beautiful, warm day. Not a cloud in the sky. He was drinking his second Jack and Coke since arriving and having a smoke. No one else had shown up yet and he was loving being alone out there. His phone was inside on the kitchen counter so he wouldn't be distracted by it. All of his friends knew how to get to the cabin so there was no need to have his phone handy. It felt great to be alone on that porch looking out over the lake. The cabin sat on over an acre of treed land. His closest neighbors, the Simpsons' cabin was a good hundred yards away, they did share the beach access though. He hadn't seen anyone since he arrived, so it was just him, his drink, his smoke, and the vastness of the water. He watched seagulls fly by squawking. He'd see fish jump every once in a while. It was peaceful, and precisely what he needed.

Eric wanted to take as much advantage of being alone as possible. He knew Deandre would show up that evening for sure, everyone else had said they'd come up the next morning. Just him and Dre for the night would be fine by him. He was excited to have his closest friends up there with him, but at the same time he kind of wished he hadn't invited them. He should have just told Deandre he was going up there for a couple days to decompress. He was enjoying being alone and was starting to regret inviting so many people up. He knew if Harvey did show up, a big if, he'd bring his wife. They all got along fairly well with Casey, but Harvey acted differently around her. He was guarded and didn't let the other guys rib on him as much. Casey was nice, but she wasn't a lot of fun. She belittled Harvey all the time. She made fun of how he dressed and constantly got on him to shave his "douche beard." She thought she was hilarious, but no one else thought picking on Harvey like that was funny. It was as if it made her feel better to rip on her man.

Eric pushed all that out of his mind. He stubbed out his cigarette and went inside to make another drink. He had every intention of getting hammered that night. Falling down, passing out in his chair drunk! He checked his phone and saw there were several messages in the group thread and a personal message from Deandre. He really wished they didn't have cell service up there, but people lived on the lake year-round so there had to be service up there.

The others were chatting back and forth about who was bringing what. Eric read through the group messages, there was nothing important or that required any kind of response from him. They all did confirm amongst themselves that they'd all be up sometime tomorrow. Eric opened Deandre's message and burst out laughing. Deandre had asked if Eric had condoms up there. He was planning to finally make a move on Gina. Eric responded and told him to bring his own rubbers. It made Eric laugh because he had watched Deandre and Gina flirt for years. It was obvious that they had a crush on each other. They had never had the chance to pursue anything. Apparently, for Deandre, this was the weekend to do so.

Eric turned his phone off and went back outside with his fresh drink. He sat down and lit another cigarette. He finally felt peaceful. Things were still swirling around in his head, but he ignored his thoughts. He made himself just focus on the calm water. The lake looked so inviting. Maybe he should change and go for a swim? The more he thought about it, the more that sounded like a great idea. Eric finished his smoke and drink and went inside to change. He grabbed a towel and walked down to the beach.

Eric laid his towel over a chaise lounge chair and walked into the lake. The water was cold but felt amazing. He swam out to the floating dock. He climbed up onto the dock and sat down. There were boats littered about further out on the water. He should have stopped by his parents' place and brought out their boat. Maybe he could text Aaron later and ask him to. It'd be fun to have the boat out there and do some water skiing.

Eric noticed his neighbors, Genesis, Eve, and Mathew Simpson walk onto the beach. Their family had owned their cabin longer than Eric's family had been there. Genesis was a couple years younger than Eric and they had grown up playing on that very beach. He fondly remembered many, many sandcastles being built by them while their parents avoided each other. The Simpsons had always been extremely religious, and Eric's parents were far from religious. The families got along but were by no means close and barely friendly.

Eric didn't believe in God or organized religion, but he never faulted others for being religious. He just didn't like being preached at about God. Everyone has their own beliefs and rituals, but they shouldn't be forced upon others. Genesis's brother, Mathew, had always been the preachy type. His beliefs trumped everyone else's. Mathew acted as if he was better than you if you didn't hold his same beliefs. It drove Eric nuts and caused him to avoid Mathew at any cost. Mathew wasn't good at small talk. He wasn't a pleasantries kind of person. He seemed only capable of talking about God and his faith.

Eric watched as Genesis and Eve waded into the water. Mathew took off back toward their cabin. Eric felt a sense of relief at seeing Mathew leave. Eric knew Genesis would swim out to the dock to talk to him. He was looking forward to catching up with her. He hadn't seen her in a long time. He just didn't make it up to the lake cabin as often anymore. Seeing an old lake buddy was nice.

"Hey Eric!" Genesis exclaimed as she climbed onto the dock. "How are you?"

"Hey Genny, I'm good. How are you?" he asked, noticing that she looked pregnant, but he knew to never ask a woman if she was pregnant.

"I'm good. It's been an interesting year," she chuckled.

"Oh, yeah, how so?"

"Well, I made some mistakes and poor decisions and got pregnant."

"Well, should I say congrats? Are you excited?"

"It's exciting now, but when it happened, not so much," Genesis said and sat down on the dock. "You see, I am not married, and I committed the sin of premarital relations. My family was very upset and ashamed."

Eric internally rolled his eyes. The Simpsons seemed like nice people, but their beliefs were so ancient and foreign to him. His parents had two kids, a house, two vehicles, a dog, and a cat before they even got married. The only reason they eventually did marry was to save money on taxes. It was purely a financial decision, but it never changed how they felt for each other or their family. He felt bad for Genesis; she was such a nice and sweet person. She was naïve and sheltered, but a genuinely nice woman. Eric really felt bad for her when she said things like "sin" and "ashamed." She shouldn't feel bad or ashamed of any of it. She was in her mid-twenties and was pregnant, big deal, nothing to be ashamed of. Giving in to the pleasure of being physical with another person shouldn't be shameful, it should be a beautiful thing.

"Mathew's still very ashamed and upset," Genesis continued, "he won't be seen in public with me anymore. He said I should wear a wedding ring, so people think I'm married. If people see a pregnant woman who doesn't appear to be married, they will look at me like I'm a whore. That's his word, not mine. I don't like words like that. But I guess in a way he is correct. I did do whore-ish things."

"I don't agree with that," Eric said.

Eric felt upset and irritated. Genesis clearly needed someone outside of her family to talk to. It frustrated Eric to think she didn't have anyone on her side. They weren't close friends, but he decided he'd have her side on this. There really wasn't a side to take, in his opinion. She was in the right and her family was clearly in the wrong. They were being controlling and inconsiderate.

"I appreciate you saying that, but it was wrong of me to do what I did," Genesis said, looking over her shoulder to see where Eve was. Eve was floating on an innertube. "Eve knew everything all along. She's been by my side the whole time. She knew about the relations I was having. I told her everything. You probably don't know this, since it's been a while since we've chatted, but Eve has left the church. Can you see her blue hair from here? Mathew and my parents freaked when they saw that. But it's none of their business. She has her own place, a good job, a nice boyfriend- who will be out here tomorrow, you can meet him then. I wouldn't have been able to get through all of this without my sister."

"She sounds like the most down-to-earth one for sure," Eric said. "I don't mean to sound rude or anything, but I don't think it's anyone else's business. You're like what, twenty-four, twenty-five now?"

"Twenty-six next month," Genesis replied.

"Does Mathew or your parents support you?"

"No, I'm a nurse and I completely support myself. I do well, honestly."

"Well, see there, you are a grown woman who fully supports herself. It's your life, your body, and your decision. Nobody should have a say in what you do or who you do."

Genesis giggled and blushed at that. That statement was not something she would ever say but she found it funny for some reason.

"Thank you, Eric," Genesis said and paused. She looked at him, "it took me a while to feel that way, but that is how I mostly feel now. I loved the man I made this baby with. I thought he would be my husband someday. We met at church and dated for about a year. We talked about marriage and children a lot. He always said he wanted to marry me and have kids. He talked me into having relations, saying that we're going to get married anyway, why wait? When I found out I was pregnant, we got in a huge fight. He wasn't at all supportive about it. He tried to even say it couldn't be his. He's the only person I've ever been with. He's never admitted it's his baby. Then I found out some things he had been hiding from me, and we broke up. After we broke up, he took off with his friend Elijah. I was devastated."

"Holy shit! Are you serious?! What a fuckin' asshole! I'd like to knock his teeth down his throat!"

Eric's language made her blush again. She was no stranger to such language; she did work in a hospital, and everyone talked like that but curses still made her blush a little. They still seemed so bad to her.

"It's okay, Eric," Genesis said with a smile. "I have forgiven him. Jesus says to forgive is a divine quality. Holding onto anger and resentment only hurts us."

"I believe in justice," Eric said. "Doesn't God say, 'an eye for an eye?'"

"He does, but that is not for us to dole out. God holds final judgement."

"Well, I stand by what I said. I believe that guy deserves an ass beating for what he did to you. It sounds like he used you."

"Maybe he did," Genesis said with a sigh, "but I was a willing participant. I made the ill-fated decision to have premarital relations. I made the less than wise decision to do so without any form of protection. I have always been taught that relations are to only be done by a husband and wife for the purpose of creating children. I gave into my carnal desires, and I have to live with the consequences of my actions. Not that my baby feels like a punishment or anything. I just mean I have to deal with the scorn and embarrassment I have brought upon my family. I am not even welcome at church anymore. My brother and parents won't allow me to join them anymore, now that I am showing." She patted her pregnant belly.

"It's all bullshit to me," Eric said with an irritated tone. Genesis had always been a childhood buddy, but he still cared for her, she had always been so sweet and nice. Knowing that her family was treating her that way made him angry. "I don't think it's fair for them to treat you like that. You are a grown woman who is more than capable to make her own choices. If you wanna have relations, then do it! If you wanna wait, because *you* want to, then wait. It's no one else's business."

"Do you have relations?" she asked shyly.

"I do, yes," Eric replied. He hoped she wouldn't ask for any details.

"Are you married yet?" she asked, but knew he wasn't.

"Nope, still as single as I was last time we chatted," Eric replied. What was she getting at here?

"Do you ever feel bad for having relations and not being married?"

"No, never, and can we call it sex or hooking up? 'Relations' sounds so cold and clinical to me. That term takes away the beauty of the act."

"I don't like the term, 'hooking up,'" she said with a tone of distain. "Calling it 'sex' is fine with me. I'm just used to it being called relations around my house and church. Kind of a habit I guess."

"I get that. I just don't like that term for it." He paused and studied her for a moment. "Did you enjoy it?" Eric asked, hoping not to embarrass her too much or offend her.

"Relations, er, I mean sex?" Genesis asked, surprised by the question.

"Yeah, was it fun?"

"Oh, my, that's a personal question," she blushed.

"You don't have to answer it if you don't want to, but I am going somewhere with it."

"Okay, it's embarrassing, but I did enjoy it. I enjoyed it a lot, to be honest." She was beet-red.

"It shouldn't be embarrassing," Eric said. "You should enjoy it. Did you enjoy church and all the rules of your religion?"

"I did enjoy church a whole lot," Genesis said, and the redness began to fall out of her cheeks. "I love worshiping the Lord with my family and friends. We have a wonderful community of people."

"It all seems so stifling to me," Eric said. "You are so ashamed of being a woman and enjoying yourself with a man because of that church. You shouldn't be ashamed of it. You talk about these things like a shy teenager, no offense. Embrace your womanhood and don't worry so much about what others think."

"What I did with him is a sin, Eric, I should be ashamed."

"No, you shouldn't!" Eric exclaimed. "You were twenty-five at the time. Everybody your age is doing that and doing it a lot if they can. It's normal, it should never be shameful unless you're doing some sick shit."

"Like what?" she asked.

"No need to get into any of that, I'm just saying having sex at your age shouldn't be shameful."

"I don't feel ashamed of having sex anymore, I feel ashamed that I sinned and brought embarrassment to my family. I am ashamed that I lied about it to all of them for so long. I am ashamed that I wasn't honest with them, Toby, or myself. I didn't really want to have sex yet, but I felt pressured, so I did. Once we did it a few times, it was fun, and I wanted more. That made me feel good and guilty at the same time. I knew I shouldn't be doing it or even wanting to yet, but I really did. So, I kept doing it. I thought Toby and I would be together forever. I thought we'd have three or four kids together. Get a nice house and a dog, you know all of that family life stuff. But he bailed on me and now I'm here alone. Mathew wants little to do with me or Eve now. My parents have refused to provide any sort of help with the pregnancy or baby. Except for Eve, I'm completely on my own now."

"They'll all come around once the little guy or girl is born," Eric said reassuringly. "They'll see their grandbaby and fall in love. They will want to be a part of both of your lives, trust me."

"Genesis! Eve!" Mathew yelled from the beach. "Dinner!"

"I gotta go," Genesis said. "Thanks for the talk and thank you so much for your opinion and advice. It helped a lot. You're a good friend, Eric. I'm glad to have you in my life, even if it is for brief moments here and there."

"You're welcome," Eric replied, slightly floored by what she had just said. "I'll be up here for a few days. Don't be a stranger."

"Thanks," Genesis said and dove into the water.

Eric watched as she swam back to shore. His heart broke for her. She did not deserve to be treated like that by anyone, especially her family. Eric jumped into the water and swam back to shore. He needed another drink and smoke as soon as possible. Genesis's story had pissed him off, bummed him out, and flustered him. It'd be an interesting story to tell Deandre later. Dre knew Genesis fairly well too, at least as well as Eric did.

*****

Eric was outside grilling a couple of hotdogs when he heard soft footfalls on the front porch. He walked around the corner and saw Genesis walking toward the front of his cabin. She had a backpack with her. She looked as if she had been crying. Genesis noticed Eric walk around the corner and burst into tears.

"Are you okay?" Eric asked and instinctively went to her and hugged her.

She dropped her backpack on the porch and melted into his embrace. She bawled on his shoulder for several minutes. Her entire body shook as she cried.

"No," Genesis sobbed after a few minutes. "I got into another fight with Mathew and my dad. I think my mom is mostly okay with everything, but she would never say so in front of my dad or Mathew."

"Why don't we sit down in the chairs over here," Eric said, releasing her and leading her to patio chairs. He went to the barbeque and pulled off his hot dogs, setting them aside and turning off the grill.

Genesis sat down and looked up at Eric, "I'm sorry to interrupt your dinner."

"It's okay, it's just a couple cheap wieners," Eric said with a chuckle. "I'll be right back. Would you like some water or tea? A soda maybe?"

"Some water would be great, thank you," Genesis said, sniffling. The tears had stopped.

Eric went inside and made a tall, strong Jack and Coke. He grabbed a bottle of water out of the fridge for Genesis. Eric set his drink down on the table between their chairs and handed her the water, she thanked him. He stepped back inside and brought out a box of tissues for her. She looked so defeated and deflated. How could someone's own family treat them that way? How could her parents see how upset she was and not feel an ounce of sympathy for their own daughter? Strict religious practices and beliefs sure did turn some people into uncaring monsters in his opinion, which was extremely ironic to him. The bible preaches love and acceptance. Jesus said love all my people as I love you, or something to that effect. Eric had never read much of the bible. He had flipped through it and read a handful of verses. He did know some of the more "critical" passages just from being around people and watching TV and movies.

"So, what happened?" Eric asked her. "I mean, if you wanna talk about it."

"I do want to," she said, looking over at him with sad eyes. She rolled the unopened water bottle in her hands as she spoke, looking at it instead of Eric. "What you said really hit home with me. You made me feel less ashamed of everything. I'm still mad at myself for lying, but the rest of it really is only my business. I know why I lied. I lied because I knew how they'd react. I knew they'd be like this, and I still did what I did. I knew when Toby and I started having relations that if Mathew and my parents knew about it, they'd be horrified and potentially disown me, but I did it anyway." She paused and shook her head, still focusing on the water bottle.

"There's a lot of things I have never and will never tell my parents about. I've done some things in my life that would embarrass them, but it's my life and my business," Eric said and then took a long sip off his drink.

"What would your parents do if you got a woman pregnant out of wedlock?"

"They'd be fuckin' thrilled!" Eric exclaimed. "Are you kidding me? They've been asking for grandbabies for years now."

"It wouldn't bother them if you had kids before you were married?" Genesis asked, still fidgeting with the water bottle.

"Oh, hell no! They had kids before they got married. They only got married to save money on taxes. Once we were all grown up and on our own, they divorced on paper, once again to save money on taxes and health insurance. My parents have been together for thirty-five years and no matter what they have always been best friends and madly in love with each other. They are tremendous people, and they love us kids unconditionally."

"My parents love us," Genesis said softly.

"Do they?" Eric asked and wished he hadn't. It was a cold thing to say.

"Yes, of course they do," she replied, a bit offended and looking at Eric again for the first time since she sat down.

"I'm sorry, that wasn't a nice thing to say," Eric said. "But I gotta be honest and I'm not trying to hurt your feelings."

"It's okay, Eric," Genesis said, shifting her attention back to the water bottle. She stared at the bottle as she rolled it back and forth between her hands. She looked back at Eric and asked, "do you really think they don't love us? They've always provided for us. They've always been there to teach us to be good Christians and live a life in honor of Christ."

"That's what I'm getting at, Genny," Eric started, "I feel like your parents and brother love the church and their religion more than they love you and your sister. They put their rules and beliefs before your wellbeing and happiness. Their own too, I'm sure. I bet your brother has feelings and desires that he hides. I bet he punishes himself in some way because of those normal, human feelings. It all saddens me and pisses me off."

"I see what you mean," she said with a small sigh and messing with the bottle again. "My faith has been waning for a while now, but more so in the last few months. When I first stopped going to church, I thought I'd miss it terribly. And I did, for a couple of weeks. After a while I began to realize I didn't miss church itself, and especially the strict rules, I only missed some of the friends I had made there. Then I slowly started to realize they were not real friends. They all looked down on me. They all abandoned me, 'the sinner.' I don't have any friends, Eric. Except for Eve, I don't have any family either. I'm so lonely."

"I'm sorry, Genny, I truly am," Eric said. He wanted to take her hand to comfort her, but he didn't know how she'd take that. She was vulnerable and lonely. He certainly didn't want to risk giving her the wrong impression. "What about at work? Don't you have any friends at work?"

"Sort of," she said, thinking about it. "There are other nurses I get along with well, but we never hang out or chat outside of work. I've always thought they were cool and nice, but none of them seemed appropriate to hang out with, you know?"

"No, I don't know," Eris replied. "How would someone be inappropriate to hang out with?"

"Well, they aren't church going types."

"Neither are you now."

"True," she replied and pondered that.

"Look, people can be good people without being religious or church goers. People can be fun and loving without answering to a God. I've never been to church in my life, and I feel like I'm a good person. Most of the time, anyway."

"You are a good person, Eric," Genesis said and smiled at him. It was nice to see her starting to relax and smile again.

"Most of the time I feel like I am," Eric said and sipped his drink. "I make a lot of mistakes and poor decisions. A lot."

"Like what? What do you consider mistakes and poor decisions?" Genesis opened the water bottle and took a sip. She was starting to relax a bit.

"Oh, jeez, I don't know if you even wanna know. You think pretty highly of me as is, I may ruin that image if I tell you," Eric said and chuckled nervously.

"Try me," she said. "I've become a lot less rigid over the past year."

"Okay, well one that gets me in trouble a lot is this," Eric said raising his drink and shaking the ice. "When I drink too much, I do dumb things."

"Like what?"

"I sleep around. I sleep with the wrong women. I hurt people's feelings."

"From what I've seen on TV that seems pretty normal."

"Unfortunately, it is."

"What else?" Genesis asked.

"I do drugs sometimes," Eric replied.

"What? Like pot?"

"Yeah, but I ain't ashamed of that. It's legal here now. I do cocaine sometimes," he said and trailed off. "Well, more than sometimes lately. I've been doing it daily for a few weeks now."

"Oh, no, Eric, that's not good. Are you addicted?"

"No, I don't feel I am," he replied. "I could easily quit. I've just been dealing with a lot of mixed emotions lately. The combination of booze and coke numbs my brain to a point where I don't dwell on shit anymore."

"You should quit then," Genesis said with genuine concern in her voice. "It's not helping you at all, it's just prolonging your pain." She paused and looked at him. "There's something bigger than all of that, isn't there?"

"Well," Eric began, "I, um, I…" he trailed off. He didn't want to say it, but he knew Genesis was the perfect person to talk to about it. She was totally removed from it all.

"What is it? Or who is it?"

That surprised him. How did she know it was a who?

"Excuse me for another moment," Eric said and stood up.

Eric went inside and made a fresh drink. He paced the kitchen for a moment wondering if he should get into everything with Genesis. She seemed genuine and he felt like he could trust her. He had known her, although not tremendously well, his entire life. Did he want to dump all of his problems on her? She was dealing with so many problems of her own. Would getting into the saga of his life bring her down more? Would it stress her out or worry her? Would she even care, considering the depth of her problems? Was being in love with someone but too chicken to ask them out really such a big problem?

"Eric," Genesis said, walking in the front door. She startled him. "I didn't mean to scare you. Could I use your bathroom? You pee a lot when you're pregnant."

"Of course, it's just down the hall," Eric replied.

"Before I go, I just wanted to say that no matter how big or small what you're dealing with seems, it still matters. You will not overwhelm me or burden me by confiding in me if you wish to do so."

Genesis went into the bathroom. Eric stood there in shock. Was this woman in his head somehow? He sipped his fresh drink, which settled his nerves and brought him back down to earth a little. It slowly began to dawn on him that she probably *wanted* to hear his story. She probably welcomed the distraction from her situation. Here she was, staying with family that were embarrassed and ashamed of her. Family who clearly let her know about it regularly. Genesis was probably dying to talk about anything besides herself for a bit. She was an intelligent woman and Eric assumed she just figured out he was struggling with telling her because he was afraid to burden her. She probably knew he was hesitant because he was a bit embarrassed himself.

Genesis returned from bathroom with a little more bounce in her step. Eric had watched her go from almost inconsolable to relaxed and cool. It made him happy to see her settle down with him. He was glad he could make her feel better and make her feel more comfortable in her own skin. He could tell without a doubt that she didn't feel comfortable at all around her family anymore. She said she and Eve were still quite close, but Eric could tell from Genesis's body language when she talked about Eve, that Eve's new lifestyle made Genesis uncomfortable.

"I don't mean to impose, and you can say no, but do you have anything to eat? I didn't make it through dinner before Mathew and my parents laid in to me. I just grabbed my things and came over here."

"I can que up some hotdogs, or burgers," Eric replied. "I have stuff to make sandwiches too."

"A sandwich sounds wonderful, but pregnant women aren't supposed eat deli meat, so a burger would be great. If's it's no trouble. I hate to be kind of picky," Genesis said sweetly.

"No trouble at all. You're not being picky. I understand pregnancy comes with a lot of life changes," Eric responded.

"I really appreciate it, Eric. You're too kind," Eric smiled at her and nodded as he grabbed patties from the freezer. "You wanna tell me about her while we make burgers?" Genesis asked.

Eric sighed and said, "I do, yes. I've gone back and forth on it, and I think getting your perspective would be extremely helpful. All of my friends love to give me advice and they seem to have my best interests in mind," Eric paused and sighed. "But they don't really listen to me. They don't seem to recognize that I am pretty torn up about all of it. I guess that's partially my fault. I'm not very good at vocalizing my emotions. I tend to drink, snort, and smoke my emotions away."

"That's not a healthy way to handle feelings, Eric."

"I know that but it's all I've ever known. People in my family and my life don't openly talk about their feelings or emotions. We say we love each other, we're always there for each other, but we almost never confide in one another."

"That's sad," Genesis said with a sigh. "I know from personal experience it is very relieving to talk about feelings and emotions. I also know that's there's a point where there is too much sharing. That's how my family is. They're always in everyone's business. They're all so intrusive."

"Why'd you come up here to stay with them?"

"It's my dad's birthday weekend. Spending his birthday at the cabin has been family tradition our whole lives," Genesis replied. "I felt obligated even though not an ounce of me wanted to come. And there's a whole lot more ounces of me now!"

Eric laughed at her joke and said, "I get that! Sometimes we do things we don't want to because it's just what we've always done, or we feel like we have to. That's weddings for me, I fuckin' hate weddings, but I go because I feel like I have to."

"Weddings are the worst!" Genesis exclaimed with a chuckle. "It's all about the bride and groom parading themselves in front of everyone they have ever met in their lives!"

"So brutal!" Eric laughed.

There was a pause in conversation. It wasn't at all awkward. Eric seasoned the patties and asked Genesis to follow him out to the barbeque.

"Tell me about her," Genesis said, sitting down in a lawn chair as Eric relit the grill.

Eric flopped the patties onto the grill and sighed. He took a sip of his drink and then grabbed a cigarette from the pack on the table. He stepped away from Genesis and lit his cigarette. He took a long drag and exhaled a plume of smoke. Genesis never minded smoking, a lot of people at her church smoked. A surprisingly large number of people in fact.

"Well," he began, "she's freaking amazing. I've known her since middle school. I think you may have even met her; she's been out here a million times. Her name is Rachel."

"That sounds familiar," Genesis said. "I can't picture her though."

"Well, she'll be out here tomorrow. I'll reintroduce you to her." Eric said and continued, "we dated for some time a while back. It was great. She was a perfect girlfriend, everything you'd ever want in a partner. She loved me, supported me, she learned my passions and pursued them with me, and she made me feel like a million bucks."

"What happened?" Genesis asked. "That sounds amazing."

"She said, 'I love you' and I freaked out," Eric replied.

"That's it? That ended it?"

"Well, yeah, I got scared and I just sorta bailed on her."

"Eric, that was so selfish of you," Genesis said with a heavy tone of disapproval.

"I know," he replied quietly. "Total dick move on my part, but I didn't know what else to do."

"Did you love her at the time?"

"Now, I can say yes, but back then I didn't know what love was. I was a party boy. My number one focus was getting wasted. Like every day, just shit-faced, falling down, fucked up. I thought that was the life. I thought that shit made me cool. My buddies used to think it was cool, but not Rachel. She dealt with it because she loved me. She partied with me because that was the only way she got to be with me. I basically used her, in a way. She doted on me, shit, she almost worshiped me and that made me feel like superman. I treated her like shit most of the time, especially when we were at parties. When it was just us, things were awesome. We have always gotten along so well, and we desire each other like nothing either one of us has ever experienced. But" Eric sighed, "I fucked it up. I was, well, still am, very selfish. You know, I could have been happier than ever the last several years if I had only pulled my head outta my ass and loved her the way she deserved to be loved. I'm a fuckin' idiot."

"No, you're not," Genesis said. "You're human. No offense, but I think you have a substance abuse problem. Seems like maybe you need to get that in check before you do anything else."

"No doubt I do," Eric agreed. "I've known it for a while, but I'm too scared to quit."

"Why?"

"It's been a huge part of my life for as long as I can remember. I'm not sure how to function without it. Like, what do I do after work if I'm not drinking? How do I unwind without it? I'm not sure who I'd be without it."

"There are a lot of things to do without out it. Things that'll make you happier and healthier. That stuff is so bad for you," Genesis said.

"I'm sure there is," Eric agreed. "Rachel doesn't drink the way I do, maybe if we spend more time together I can at least, maybe, cut down on it."

"Cutting down could be a start, but you should strongly consider quitting." Genesis looked at Eric and could tell he didn't want to talk about his substance abuse anymore so she asked, "what's the situation with Rachel now?"

"We're the best of friends," Eric said, clearly relieved to get off the topic of his vices. "We love each other, and I think she wants to date me again."

"You don't want to date her?"

"I do, sorta. I mean she's perfect and would be a tremendous partner but I'm still scared. I don't wanna hurt her again. I devastated her last time."

"I know I'm not the best person to be giving out advice on dating, but if you still love her and she's so great, why not take a chance on love? Why string both of you along? So, what if it doesn't work out, at least you would have all that time together. I was so mad at Toby for so long until I realized for a while we had a great time together. I loved him in the beginning. He was my first everything and I know that's a big deal. Thinking back on everything now, I wouldn't change a thing."

"Do you have any regrets?" Eric asked, flipping the burgers.

"Oh, yeah, of course. Many, but who doesn't?"

"Could I ask you a question that may sound a little rude?"

"Sure," Genesis replied.

"How are you so happy and grounded despite everything that has happened to you? And I mean no offense by that, I'm genuinely curious."

"I think it's partially from growing up with faith in Jesus to always take care of me and guide me. Also, I think it's just my nature. I don't like being mad, or sad, or frustrated, so I take things as they come and roll with it."

"I wish I could just roll with things," Eric said. "Things get under my skin so easily."

"Well, no offense friend, but I think your vices play a big part in that."

"Have you ever partied?" Eric asked, he was getting a little annoyed with her saying those things about his vices.

"No, never. It's not allowed. Good Christians do not part take in such things. But since I'm no longer a 'good' Christian I'd like to try it. After I have my baby, of course," Genesis said.

"If you don't do it already, there is no reason to start now," Eric said. "Speaking of vices, I need a refill. Would you excuse me?"

"Of course," Genesis said with a smile. "I'm not trying to harp on you about your vices, I feel it is normal and acceptable to have a few. It's just when they take over your life that problems arise."

"That is true," Eric said. "I'll be right back."

"Okay, Eric."

Eric went inside and Genesis went to the railing of the porch to look at the lake. Eric was glad to see Genesis feeling so comfortable. He was also glad that she wasn't getting berated by her family for a bit. That had to be torture. People you grew up loving and caring about treating you like that? It had to be awful. He felt so bad for her. He decided he'd invite her to stay the night. They had enough room and enough beds for her to stay. It was just going to be him and Deandre that night anyhow.

Where was Deandre? He should have been there by then. Maybe Dre had sent him a message or tried to call. He had better turn on his phone and check. Deandre had messaged him several times. Deandre said he had gotten a flat and had to wait on a tow truck because his spare was also flat. He explained that he'd get his truck towed home and then head out in his car. Deandre told Eric he was pissed about it all but what could he do? He ended with, "I'm sure you're half tanked already and have your phone turned off. You probably won't see any of these, but I'll message you when I'm on my way up there. Love ya, bro." The last message had been sent over an ago. Deandre should be on his way shortly.

Eric replied to him, "Sorry about the tire, that sucks bro. I'm not half tanked yet lol. I'll leave my phone on. Keep me posted."

Deandre sent back, "In the tow truck now, headed home. I'll keep you posted bro."

Eric replied, "Cool, man. We might have a guest tonight, the neighbor girl, Genesis.

"Sounds good, bro. Keep your hands to yourself lol."

"Haha, you're hilarious, Dre."

"Lol. Later bro."

"My friend Deandre is coming up tonight," Eric told Genesis as he came back outside with his fresh drink. "You're welcome to stay the night if you don't wanna go back to your family."

"Oh, my, Eric, that would be lovely," Genesis said. "Are you sure though?"

"Yes, of course," Eric replied.

"I don't want to impose," Genesis said.

"You aren't. I'm inviting you. Honestly, I'd sleep better knowing you're here and not getting hassled by your family," Eric said with a smile.

"Thank you so much. You're a good friend."

"My pleasure," Eric said. He checked on the burgers and they were ready. "Let's eat!" He exclaimed pulling the patties off the grill.

They went inside and dressed up their burgers. They sat at the table and chatted while they ate. Nothing heavy or emotional, just basic banter. He asked her what was like being a nurse in a hospital and she told him many stories. Some good and happy stories and a few sad and heartbreaking stories. She told him she never knew what the day had in store for her and she loved it that way. He laughed and told her his job was the opposite. He knew exactly what he was in for everyday and it was almost always soul crushing.

After they had finished dinner and relaxed for a bit, Eric asked, "do you feel up to a walk? I kinda wanna get out of the cabin for a bit."

"Sure!" Genesis exclaimed and stood up. "That sounds great."

They headed outside. There was a paved pathway that went around the entire lake. They set off on a walk. They didn't talk at first, they just enjoyed the quietness of the evening. As they passed the Simpson's cabin, Eric noticed Matthew on the front porch, glaring at them as they walked by. Eric didn't dwell on it too much; he knew Matthew was a weird guy. Genesis kept nervously looking at Eric.

"Eric?" Genesis said after a bit.

"Yeah?"

"Um, well, this is a little awkward." She paused and looked at the sky. Not a cloud insight and the stars were dancing in the dark sky. "I, uh, well, jeez, this is harder than I thought," Genesis nervously said with a little chuckle.

"Just say it," Eric said. "I ain't gonna judge you in any way."

"Okay, well, I wanna talk about sex," she said and blushed.

Even in the dark Eric could see how red she was.

"Oh, okay," Eric replied. "What about it?"

She sighed heavily and said, "I wanna talk about *us* and sex."

Uh oh, where was she going with this? He had never thought of her in that way. She had always just been his summer buddy. The thought of fooling around with her in any way hadn't ever crossed his mind.

Eric nodded at her and nervously said, "um, okay, go ahead."

"I don't think we should do it," Genesis said. "I feel like we should remain friends and only friends. I would like to become better friends and maybe talk more than just the random times we're up here. I think sex would muddy things."

Eric didn't reply right away. He was extremely relieved she had just said all of that. Was he a bad guy? Had he been considering it? Had she picked up on some vibe he hadn't intended? Genesis was the one woman he had never thought of that way. What had changed that it even had to be brought up? Was it just a proximity thing? Was it her vulnerability? Was she *even* vulnerable? Had he just put that on her in his mind? Did he seem vulnerable? Fuck! He needed to quit doing coke! It messed with his mind and made him question everything.

"I couldn't agree more," Eric finally replied. "Was it even ever a possibility? What made you bring it up?"

Genesis sighed again and said, "Look, I mean no offense by this, but you made yourself sound like you like to sleep around. I know you invited me to stay the night to get me away from my family. I don't think you had the intention of trying to sleep with me, but I just wanted to say something about it anyway. I hope that doesn't offend or upset you."

"Oh, God, no, it doesn't," Eric replied. "I did only invite you so you had a safe place to stay. I wasn't sure if you had planned on going back to their cabin or maybe driving home tonight. I just wanted to offer you somewhere else to stay if you wanted to. And I would love to talk more regularly. I feel like you are already a close friend. You bring a completely different perspective to everything. I love your outlook on life and your positivity. I need that in my life."

"Thank you so much, Eric!" Genesis exclaimed. She felt a wave a relief as well. "Can I maybe someday help you with your addictions? I did some substance abuse counseling for the church."

"I'd like that, Genny, thank you."

"I'm not saying you necessarily need it, but I wanna be there for you however I can."

"I feel like I'm getting to a place where I may need help," Eric said with a big sigh. "I've made excuses long enough about all of it. Shit like, 'oh, it's no big deal, I have control over it now.' Sometimes I feel like I have control of it, but sometimes I don't. Those are the times that scare the hell out of me."

"You're a good man, Eric. It's normal to be scared sometimes. I get it," Genesis said and stopped walking. She looked at Eric once he stopped walking. "I wish I had vices to carry me through my many struggles in life. I used to turn to the bible a lot. I spent more time at church, just to distract me from my feelings. I didn't always have a strong faith or belief. I had to make myself believe in God. I've never felt His presence like most people say they have. I wish I could have experienced drugs and alcohol at some point. Maybe it would have led me away from the church sooner. Maybe I could have enjoyed my early twenties more. Do you believe in God?"

"No, never have," Eric replied. "It's too far-fetched for me, especially nowadays with all we know about the world and life itself. And believe me, drugs and alcohol would've derailed your life. They have mine, at least. We all unwind and relax in our own ways, Genny, but I get what you mean. You just wish you had different experiences that could have shaped who you are now. I wish I had done things differently in my life. I still have time to change. I'm still young enough to learn from my many, many mistakes and turn my regrets into a new life. Do you regret how you've lived so far?"

"Not really anymore, it was my life. It shaped who I am today," Genesis replied. "I just wish I hadn't put so much stock into religion, and I wish I hadn't saddled myself with the rules."

"You still can. You're still young too. You can still live a more carefree life. A baby ain't gonna hold you back that much."

"I know, but it will be so different. Dating will be different. There's a lot of guys out there who probably don't want to date a girl with a baby."

"For sure, but there's just any many that will," Eric said. "There's just as many men our age who have kids too. It does take two to make a baby after all."

"You really think so?" Genesis asked, feeling a swell of emotion. She so desperately wanted a "normal" life.

"I really do," he replied. "There are far more people who think like me than there are who believe what your family does. Once you get out of that community, you'll see how accepting most of the world can be. Honestly, most people just don't give a fuck what others do or have done. There will be plenty of men out there who don't give a damn that you have a kid. If they like you then that's all that'll matter to them. If they respect you, they'll be fine sharing your time and attention with your child. If they aren't then get rid of them immediately. Don't ever let anyone else control you again, Genny. You're better than that."

Genesis burst into tears again. No one had ever told her she mattered. No one had ever told her she deserved respect. She searched for a way to respond to that but had nothing at that moment. She was consumed by the idea that she had value. That she mattered, not someone else's idea of how she mattered.

Genesis was about to thank Eric when a loud roar pierced through the silent night. Eric and Genesis both jumped. They frantically looked around. Then, another loud roar. Those yells were close, remarkably close.

"What in the fuck?" Eric stammered. His buzz was fading, and his head was hurting.

"Probably just people screwing around," Genesis offered.

"Oh, shit, you're probably right," Eric said and settled down a bit. "Let's get back to the cabin any way. I need to check my phone to see if Dre messaged."

"Okay, sounds good," Genesis replied. "My feet are starting to kill me. It's brutal carrying around this kind of weight. Did you know women's feet flatten out when they're pregnant? I have no more arches on my feet. It's hurts like hell."

"No, I didn't know that," Eric said as they started walking back to the cabin. "That does sound brutal."

"It is," Genesis said. "But being pregnant is pretty brutal most of the time. You'd think our bodies would be more adaptable to it since they're designed to carry babies."

"You'd think so," Eric agreed. "It's a good thing men aren't the ones to get pregnant. The species would've died out after two generations!"

Genesis laughed way harder than the joke was funny. She was enjoying the randomness of their conversations. It felt tremendous to just chat with someone about anything and everything. She was so relieved to be able to be herself around him. She didn't have to act in a certain way or be prim and proper. Despite the heaviness of some of the conversation,

Genesis felt relaxed and relieved. She hadn't ever fully let her guard down around anyone else. Not even Toby or her sister. Especially not Toby. He would never let her be herself. She had to be what he expected her to be. Genesis appreciated Eric being so kind and welcoming. She appreciated him being himself as well. There was no fakeness or awkwardness between them, and it felt fantastic!

They walked back in silence. Genesis was letting herself enjoy the evening air and enjoy not being so anxious and scared for the first time. Eric looked around as they made their way back. He hoped those screams were people screwing around but he had a bad feeling they were not made by people. He didn't know what could have made those roars, but it didn't sound like people to him. He didn't want to say anything to Genesis, she had clearly convinced herself it was people. She had finally relaxed and was smiling. He didn't want to bring her down on an unexplainable hunch.

They got back to the cabin and Eric grabbed his phone. He stepped back outside to smoke while he checked his phone. Genesis had to use the bathroom again.

Deandre had sent Eric another message. It read, "hey, bro, it's pretty late already. I'm gonna crash out here and head out first thing in the morning."

Eric replied, "no worries, bro. See ya tomorrow."

Eric looked up at the stars as he finished his smoke. Everything was so calm and quiet. As his dad used to say, "it's so quiet out tonight you could hear a mouse fart." That had always cracked Eric up. It made him chuckle again just thinking about it. The lake looked like a sheet of dark glass. It looked like he could walk on that water.

Eric heard movement to his right. Someone was walking up the road. Mathew rounded the bend in the road and Eric's heart jumped in his chest. There was only one reason Mathew would be walking his way. Eric felt his nerves tingle. He had no desire to get into it with that guy and he had no intention of letting him talk Genesis into returning to their cabin.

"Hello, Eric," Mathew smugly said from the road.

"S'up, Matt," Eric replied. He knew Mathew hated being called Matt.

"Where's my sister?"

"Which one?" Eric asked with a tone of contention. He and Mathew had never gotten along well.

"You know which one," Mathew replied irritated.

"She's inside."

"Would you tell her it's time to come home. It's past curfew."

Eric busted out laughing, "past curfew?! Are you kidding me?! She's twenty-five!"

"We still have rules in our household," Mathew replied, flipping his bangs out of his eyes.

"Well, she ain't a part of your household anymore," Eric replied.

"She surely is," Mathew replied.

"The fuck she is!" Eric exclaimed. He knew using coarse language would ruffle Mathew's feathers even more. He just wanted to pummel the guy. "Look, I have invited her to stay the night here and she has accepted that invitation. You may return to your cabin now."

"That is not a possibility," Mathew replied and stepped toward the porch. "Genesis will not stay alone with another man. She has already given into the sins of the flesh once; we cannot allow that to happen again."

Rage bubbled up inside Eric. He was fuming. Eric took a big, deep breath and slowly exhaled. If he didn't at least try to calm himself down, he was going to kill Mathew.

"Get the fuck out of here!" Eric growled at Mathew. "*You* can't allow it?! Allow what? Huh? What can't you allow? For her to make her own decisions in life? For her to be her own person? What is it, Matt? Huh, tell me?"

Eric was yelling at Mathew and Genesis could hear it from inside. She peeked out the front window and saw Eric leaning over the porch railing. Mathew was standing just off the road on the front lawn of the cabin.

Mathew looked scared and Genesis loved that. She laughed to herself. God, she loved Eric! No one in her life had ever stood up for her before. No one had ever talked to her brother like that.

"Genny is twenty-five-fuckin'-years-old," Eric yelled at Mathew, "she has an excellent job, her own place, and she's about to be a mother! She is more than capable of making her own choices in life now. She doesn't need you or your fuckin' family meddling in her life anymore! I can't control how you all conduct your family business, but I can control what happens on my fuckin' property! Now, go away!"

Mathew stood there in shock, just staring at Eric. No one had ever talked to him that way before. He didn't know how to act or respond.

"Matt, leave," Eric said quietly but with a tone of hatred.

Mathew noticed Genesis in the front window and with a nervous tone he said, "I need to speak with my sister."

Eric stared at Mathew for a few moments. He noticed Mathew's eyes kept going to the front window. Eric straightened up and turned to the window. He saw Genesis standing there, smiling. Eric walked into the cabin and closed the door. He came right back out and went to the railing.

"She doesn't want to talk to you," Eric said. "And neither do I, so, please leave."

Mathew didn't respond or leave. He just stood there shaking and staring at Eric. Eric took his hoodie off and rushed down the front steps toward Mathew. As soon as Mathew saw Eric coming after him, he took off running. Eric stood on the road and watched Mathew run back to his parents' cabin. As soon as Mathew disappeared Eric burst into laughter again. He doubled over in the middle of the road and howled with laughter.

"He'll probably go get my dad and they'll come back shortly," Genesis said from the porch.

"I don't give a fuck," Eric said as he walked back to the porch.

"Maybe I should just go back. They're not going to drop it."

"Hell no, not a chance," Eric said. "I will not give in to them and I won't let you do it either. They don't control your life, Genny. Remember that, okay?"

"They'll just keep coming over and harassing you. I don't want that," Genesis said, starting to tear up.

"I do," Eric said confidently. "Someone needs to put those guys in their place, and I am more than happy to be that someone! I can't let them treat you like that. You know what your brother said?"

"I can imagine, but what?"

"He said you needed to return home because it was past curfew! You're twenty-five why would you have a goddamn curfew?!"

"It's a family rule, if you're staying at the cabin, everyone must be in and settled by nine," Genesis replied.

"That's stupid!" Eric exclaimed. "Come on, let's go inside."

They went back inside, and Eric locked the front door, something he never did when he stayed up there. There had never been a reason too.

"I like and respect you a lot, Genny, I cannot stand by and let them treat you like a child. Or a piece of property. I just cannot let that go on."

"Eric, I appreciate you, but you don't need to get involved. I can handle their bullshit."

Hearing her say 'bullshit' floored him. He had never once in all of their life heard her swear. It made him laugh out loud.

"What?" Genesis asked with a smile.

"You just said bullshit!" Eric laughed. "I've never heard you cuss before."

"I don't think I ever have," Genesis said, pondering it for a moment. "Maybe you're a bad influence on me."

"Maybe," Eric chuckled. "It's good for ya, though."

"I think so," Genesis laughed.

They stood in the living room laughing for a moment. Eric went into the kitchen and made another drink. He motioned for Genesis to sit at the table with him.

"Do you really think they'll be back?" Eric asked.

"Maybe not tonight," Genesis replied. "I think they would've been here by now if that were the case."

"Dang-it, I was looking forward to yelling at Mathew again," Eric said and laughed.

"My dad will be more intimidating than Mathew," Genesis said.

"I ain't worried about either of them."

"Thank you, Eric. Thank you for standing up for me."

"My pleasure," Eric said and smiled at her. "No one should be treated like that! You're a special person and it pisses me off how they treat you. You should walk away from them. I know that's your family, but you don't deserve to be controlled like that or spoken to in that way. You are a grown woman. You are not their property."

"I know that, but I feel bad for my mom," Genesis said. "I know from spending time alone with her that she is a lot more liberal than she lets people know. She is so afraid of my dad and how he'd treat her if she voiced an opinion that she just keeps quiet about everything. In their house, my dad has final say on everything. Even on what she wears. I stick around for her. I feel if I can be the one my dad and brother are harping on all the time, they'll leave my mom alone."

"That's so sad," Eric said shaking his head. "You're a good daughter, but at some point, you will have to move on. Your mom is a grown woman too, you know. If she decides to stick around and take the abuse from your dad, I'm sorry to say, but that's on her."

"She doesn't know any other way to live," Genesis said. "They got married when she was only nineteen. My dad has controlled everything from day one. That's how it works in their church. Women don't get a say. My dad has busted dishes onto the floor because someone put them away in the wrong spot. One time, he was so angry with my mom because she missed a spot vacuuming that he went outside, got a shovel full of dirt and threw it onto the carpet. Then he stood over her while she vacuumed it up and got the spot she missed. Lots of stuff like that."

"Jesus Christ, are you serious?! That's abuse! No one should ever be treated like that. Your dad is a dick! How can you treat people like that? Especially your wife and kids. It's all so sad and frustrating," Eric said shaking a little bit from anger. "It's almost unimaginable, especially compared to how I was raised. My parents loved and respected each other. My mom's opinions and ideas were just as valued as my dad's. They discussed every pertinent thing and always made decisions as a team. You know how many times I remember hearing them arguing or fighting? Never, not one time. I'm sure they did, every couple no matter how great they are together will fight, but they made sure us kids never heard it. I'm sure they wanted to make sure we didn't worry about it."

"That all sounds so lovely and far-fetched to me," Genesis said. "I know couples like your parents exist, and hopefully they way outnumber the ones like my parents, but hell, I have never seen it."

"If your baby's father had stuck around and you two had married, would he have expected you to act like your mother?"

"Oh yes, for sure," Genesis replied. "That's how marriage works in our church."

"Would you have been like that?" Eric asked with a concerned look.

"No, not to the extent of my mom and Toby knew that. I think that's partially why he left. Elijah had a hand in him taking off too, I'm quite sure of that. I also think he wanted someone like my mom. A woman who would stay home and take care of everything the exact way he dictated while he worked. I told him up front that wasn't me. I wasn't going to quit my job, ever. I said I would be a dutiful wife, but I would work outside of the house, which would mean he would have to help with the kids and whatnot."

"I'm glad he left," Eric said. "I can't imagine someone treating you like they own you and your opinions. You gotta get further away from that church and people who are a part of it. Even if that includes your family. They're toxic and backward."

"I know you're right," Genesis sighed. "But they are my family. They should be a part of my baby's life."

"Why? They treat you like shit. Why would you want people like that around your kid? Why would you want your kid to see the way they talk to you?"

"I never thought about it like that," Genesis replied. "I think you're right. I don't want my baby growing up like I did. Especially if I have a girl."

"My advice would be this, keep your child away from them the best you can, unless, for some reason they drastically change their ways. I would also suggest you don't go too far in the opposite direction, by which I mean, don't be too liberal. I think you and I were raised in two very different, but equally extreme environments. Your parents were too strict. Too conservative and way too controlling. It made you timid and a bit naïve, but it also made you too giving of yourself. I, on the other hand, was raised in such a liberal household that it made me very selfish and somewhat aloof. In the same way you struggle to do things for yourself because you're so used to doing what is demanded of you, I struggle to do things for others. I struggle to give myself to others. There has to be a nice medium. Someway to raise your kid with a little of both."

"Wow, yeah, Eric, I think you are spot on," Genesis said. "The same way I need to learn to be a little more selfish, you need to learn to be less selfish. I think we can help each other with that. Don't you?"

"We sure could," Eric replied with a smile. "I'm not completely selfish, I'm always there for my friends to help them with whatever they need. Be it moving or projects, but I'm rarely there for anyone emotionally. I don't think you are completely selfless. Clearly you have done things for your own pleasure." Eric pointed to her pregnant belly and chuckled. "So, we're kinda on the right path already."

They heard an ear-piercing scream from outside, followed by several gun shots. The sounds were quite a distance away from Eric's cabin, but quite loud, nonetheless. Eric jumped out of his chair and ran to his bedroom. He returned with a 9mm pistol.

"Stay here," he said to Genesis. He grabbed his keys off the kitchen counter. "Lock the doors behind me and hide in the bathroom."

Genesis looked terrified and did what Eric said. He ran out the front door and into the road. Off in the distance, just past the Simpson place he could see several people milling about with flashlights. Eric rushed back to the cabin. Genesis saw him coming and opened the door for him.

"I need a flashlight. There are other people up the road. I'm going to go up there and see if they know anything. Stay put, please."

"I will, Eric, I will," Genesis said. "I'm not going anywhere."

"No matter what, stay here," Eric said again. "Even if your dad or brother come for you, don't go."

"Okay," she replied. "Be safe, Eric and come back."

"I will," he replied and was out the door again.

Eric clicked on the flashlight in his left and held the pistol to his side with his right hand. He slowly approached the other people. Eric made sure to wave his light around, so they'd see him coming. They did see him coming and started toward him. There were two men, probably in their forties and a woman of roughly the same age. He could never tell for sure with women.

"What happened?" Eric asked the group.

"No idea," the dark-haired man replied. "We heard a scream and gunshots, same as you I assume."

"We did hear it too," Eric replied. "Any idea where it came from?"

"Sounded like it was out on the water just over there," the same man replied, pointing across the road to the lake.

"This is our place," the other, balding man said, pointing to a nice little cabin behind them. "We were inside drinking and playing cards when we heard that scream. Sounded like it was literally across the road. There's nothin' out there but beach and water."

Eric flashed his light onto the beach. There was nothing on that beach at all. Not even chairs or floaties.

The lake was calm and still looked like a sheet of glass. The night was dead quiet. There wasn't a single sound to be heard except for the four of them breathing.

"Earlier, my friend and I were on a walk, and we heard two loud roars, sounded almost like a monkey screaming. We figured it was other people fuckin' around. Think this could be just people messin' around?" Eric asked the others.

"I would hope people weren't out here screaming and firing a weapon," the balding man said.

"Yeah, I would hope not. There are so many families out here at any given time. That would be extremely careless of them," the dark-haired man said.

"What else could it be?" Eric asked.

"No idea," the balding man said, "but we're hoping to find that out."

The dark-haired man glanced down at Eric's gun and said, "what's that for?"

"Protection," Eric replied. "I heard gun shots. I wasn't about to go investigate gun shots without my own gun."

"Why would you even have a gun up here?" the dark-haired man asked. "Nothin' ever happens up here. We don't have bears 'round here or anything like that."

"Well, seems like tonight it may come in handy," Eric replied, becoming annoyed with the man.

"Leave him alone about it, Vince," the woman said. "He's got a right to have it."

"Thank you," Eric said to the woman.

"You're welcome. I'm Nina, this is my husband, Josh, and that's his brother Vince."

"Nice to meet you all, I'm Eric." He shook hands with everyone. "What was your plan?"

"We haven't really thought of anything yet," Vince replied. "You have any ideas?"

"From the cabin we couldn't tell where that scream came from. We knew it was down this way somewhere. The gun shots freaked me out more because they sounded closer than the scream. I hadn't thought of a plan yet, I just wanted to investigate to make sure my friend and I are safe for the night."

"We had all our windows and doors open to let in the cool, clean night air," Josh said. "That scream was damn close to us, like we said, seemed to come from the middle of the lake."

"The gun shots sounded like they came from across the lake to us," Vince added.

"That's weird, cus the gun shots sounded very close to me and that scream seemed so far away," Eric said.

"Probably just the way the sounded bounced of the hills," Vince offered.

"We're being rude," Nina said. "We should offer our friend here a drink while we figure out what to do. Would you like a drink?"

"I sure would," Eric replied. "I just made a fresh one at my place. Let me run back there and get it so I can tell my friend what is going on."

"Okay, sounds good, just come on by our cabin," Nina said with a smile. "We'll be in there figuring out what to do next."

"Hey, you got a boat?" Josh asked.

"No, I didn't bring one up, but my friend's bringing one up tomorrow," Eric replied. "I'll be right back."

"Bring your friend back too," Nina said to Eric as he turned to leave. "Safety in numbers if some shit is going down 'round here."

"Okay," Eric shouted as he jogged back to his place.

Eric went into the cabin and hollered for Genesis. She came out of the bathroom. He went to the table and drank what was left of his previous drink.

"There are some people a few cabins down that wanna investigate that scream and those gun shots," Eric told her as he made a fresh drink. "There's two men and woman. They want me to bring you back when I go back over there."

"Okay," Genesis replied. "Will I even be of any help?"

"I think so. Besides, I'd rather have you close than worry about you here alone. I have a little .22 pistol in my room if you want that."

"Oh, no, I don't know anything about guns. I don't think that's a good idea," Genesis replied as she put on her shoes.

"Okay, I'm grabbing it anyway," Eric said and went to his room.

He came back out with both guns tucked into his pants and another flashlight. Eric handed Genesis a flashlight and they left the cabin. Eric locked the front door and walked around the entire house making sure every point of entry was locked.

"What's going on?" Genesis asked with fear in her voice.

"No idea," Eric replied, "but I'm hoping we can figure it out. I suggested it was people fuckin' around like those screams we heard earlier. Those other people said there's no way people would be up here screaming and shooting."

"I wouldn't put anything past anyone these days," Genesis said.

"Neither would I," Eric agreed.

They arrived at the other cabin and Eric introduced Genesis to Nina, Josh, and Vince. They invited Eric and Genesis to sit at the dining room table with them.

"Hey, thought you were grabbing a drink," Vince said to Eric.

"Shit, I made a fresh one and then totally forgot it," Eric replied.

"No worries, friend, we have plenty. Whatcha drinking?" Josh said and stood up.

"Jack and coke, if ya got it," Eric replied. "Heavy on the Jack and light on the coke. Thank you."

"You got it, man, no worries. And what about you, young lady?" Josh asked Genesis.

"Just water for me, please," Genesis replied. "Thank you."

"You bet," Josh said and walked to the booze counter. They had one entire kitchen counter full of every liquor imaginable. Their very own bar.

"Okay, so, we were thinking about scouting out the entire beach," Vince said. "That scream was awfully close to us."

"Sounds good," Eric said. "Can you handle that, Genny?"

"Yeah, I feel fine," she replied. "I want to be a part of it."

Josh handed Eric and Genesis their drinks. He had a fresh one for himself as well.

"Should we split up and cover more ground?" Nina asked.

"No, way! That's how people die in horror movies," Josh laughed.

"I think we should split up," Eric said. "Genesis and I can go one way and you three can scout out the other direction." In reality, Eric just didn't want to be saddled down with those people. If there were sinister things going on out there, those three felt like they'd be liabilities, not helpful. He had to protect his property and Genesis above all else.

"I agree," Vince said.

Everyone agreed and they all set off for the beach. Eric and Genesis went to the left, toward their chunk of beach, while the others went right. The beach was empty and quiet.

"What'd you think of those people?" Eric asked as they walked.

"They seemed nice enough," Genesis replied.

"They seemed nice, but dumb to be honest," Eric said as he scanned the beach with his flashlight.

"That's not very nice, Eric," Genesis chuckled.

"I know, but it's true," Eric replied. "That Vince guy was giving me shit for having a gun up here. I know we ain't exactly in the middle of nowhere, but emergency response time up here could take up to an hour. Some fool tries to break into my place while I'm there, I'm blasting him then waiting on the cops."

Genesis laughed and said, "You're so tough!"

"Knock it off, Genny," Eric laughed. "You know what I mean, though."

"Yeah, I do. It's always better to have something like a gun and never need it than to not have one and need it."

"Exactly!" Eric stopped walking. They had reached their part of the beach. "Should we just go back to the cabin and get some sleep? Doesn't seem like there's shit going on out here."

"I'd like to," Genesis said. "I'm awfully tired."

"Me too," Eric agreed, and they started for the cabin. "Ya, know, now that I've thought about it more, those gun shots could've actually been fireworks. The fourth was last weekend."

"Oh, I bet you're right!" Genesis exclaimed. "We've probably got some teenagers up here being fools."

"Most likely," Eric agreed.

Eric unlocked the front door and let Genesis inside. He closed and locked the door on his way back in. The drink he had made and left on the counter was on the floor in the middle of the kitchen. The glass was shattered. Even if he had left it too close to the edge, it would have fallen straight down, and it would've done it before they even left. There was no way that glass could have broken where it had unless someone dropped it there. Or something.

Eric rushed around the cabin looking for anything else out of place. Everything else was in its place.

"Eric," Genesis said from the kitchen. Eric came back into the kitchen, "The window over that counter is open. I bet the wind blew your drink off the counter."

"Maybe? I'm pretty sure I checked that window though. I swear it was closed and locked."

"We were in a hurry and preoccupied, I bet you just missed that one," Genesis said reassuringly. She wasn't sure how the hell that glass got there, but she wanted to keep with rational explanations.

"Shit, you're right," Eric said. He grabbed a towel and started to clean up the mess. "Let's get this cleaned up and go get some sleep."

"Sounds good."

"You're sleeping in my room," Eric said. "There's another bed in there, we don't have to sleep in the same bed."

"Okay, I'd like that. I know we're fine, but I'm still a little scared."

"Me too. I'll sleep better knowing you're in the same room as me."

"Thank you," Genesis said with a smile. "You've been so good to me today."

"You deserve it, Genny, you're an awesome girl," Eric said and smiled at her. "Ready for sleep?"

"Yes, very."

Chapter Four

Genesis sat in her car outside of the doctor's office, bawling. Her doctor had just confirmed that she was indeed pregnant. Genesis already knew, she had taken six home pregnancy tests and they all came back positive. Part of her had hoped she had done the test wrong, but how do you mess up peeing on a stick? She had tried three different brands and had hoped that she somehow contaminated the tests. There was no way she could be pregnant. Toby had told her that the pullout method was bulletproof. She would later find out that method had a higher fail rate than anything else. How could she have been so naïve?

How was she going to tell her parents? They knew her and Toby were dating, the whole family wanted them to marry. How was she going to tell Toby?! He was going to flip out. Maybe they could quickly get married and then the pregnancy would seem planned. That most likely wouldn't work, she was already eight weeks along. By the time they planned a big wedding, she'd be showing. Genesis screamed into her windshield. Part of her thought about just driving west and not stopping until she found a nice, quiet, liberal seaside town. Somewhere people wouldn't look down on a single mother. Somewhere far, far away from the church and its archaic rules. Somewhere she could maybe, just maybe, finally be her true self. She didn't want to fake it anymore. She didn't want to be someone's property. Her fear slowly turned to anger. The guilty feeling she had been living with for weeks was turning into murderous rage. This was all Toby's fault.

Genesis was starving, she had been hungrier the last few weeks than she could ever remember being. She threw up a lot of her meals, but that hunger was always there. She decided she was going out to eat. She wanted a huge, greasy bacon cheeseburger, a bucket of fries, and like, ten Pepsis. Genesis wiped her eyes dry, backed the car out of its spot, and headed to the local diner. She knew she could get a good burger at Tom's Diner.

Genesis found a stool at the counter and ordered her food as soon as the server checked on her. No need for a menu, she knew exactly what she wanted.

"Is a cute, petite thing like you gonna be able to eat all that?" the middle-aged server asked. She seemed like a sweet lady and that question wasn't at all offensive. More of a little joke.

"Oh, yes, ma'am," Genesis replied with an eager smile. "I'm pregnant, so I'm eating for two now."

"Congratulations!" the server exclaimed. "That's wonderful news, dear. And call me Ruth, please. No need for that ma'am stuff 'round here."

"Okay, Ruth, thank you," Genesis smiled. Ruth was the first person to say 'congratulations.'

"You are welcome, dear," Ruth said with a smile. "I'm going to get this order in so you and your baby can eat!"

"Thanks again," Genesis said and watched as Ruth scampered off to place the order.

Her and her baby. That statement had sent chills down Genesis's spine. Her and her baby. It couldn't be true. It had to be some long, never-ending nightmare. The back pain *felt* real. The morning sickness sure as hell felt real. Toby, her parents, and Mathew freaking out on her was going to feel all too real.

It was no dream, and she obviously knew that. Genesis surely wished it was all just a nightmare. She wished she had never given in to the temptation of being with a man. She wished she had never sinned like that. *Why* had she given in to those temptations? She had never done it before, why was Toby so different? Was it because she thought they'd marry eventually so why did it matter? That's what Toby had said. That's how he had convinced her it would be okay.

That rage was back. Toby had said they could have relations before marriage. It would be okay because they had plans to marry. Then he also told her that using protection was a sin. Premarital sex was okay because they had discussed marriage, but putting on a damn condom was a sin? Genesis could feel her face flushing as the anger and contentment grew inside of her. Growing inside of her much the same as a tiny human being was, except the rage was growing faster and it actually felt great! It felt wonderful to feel anger. It felt normal. She was experiencing normal emotions and that was all okay. She should feel that way. Toby had lied to her. He had convinced her to do things that she hadn't wanted to. Once they started doing it, she grew to really enjoy it and wanted it regularly but look where that got her. Sitting on a stool alone waiting on a bacon cheeseburger with a baby inside her.

Fuckin' Toby! she thought. That word would never leave her lips, but it felt good to at least say inside her head. *Fuck! Fuck! Fuck!* she screamed inside of her racing mind. That made her smile. The smile widened and she began to chuckle. Before she knew it, she was laughing out loud. *Oh my, people must think I'm a loon!* Genesis quickly pulled out her phone and pretended to be looking at something hilarious on it, because she couldn't stop laughing.

"Somethin' pretty funny on that phone, huh, dear?" Ruth asked as she placed a Pepsi in front of Genesis.

"Yeah, it caught me by surprise," Genesis said and laid her phone on the counter face down.

Ruth smiled at her and walked away. Genesis could tell Ruth didn't believe her. Ruth had probably seen her burst out laughing before she even picked up her phone. Oh well, who cared? Let these people think she was a loon. That's exactly what she felt like. Genesis was losing her mind. Her world was crumbling around her and all she wanted was a damn bacon cheeseburger! Were they slaughtering the cow back there? What was taking so freaking long? Genesis felt like she was about to spit fire. Or fall off her stool laughing.

"Here you go, dear, enjoy," Ruth said, sliding a plate in front of her with the most beautiful bacon cheeseburger and fries she had ever seen.

"Thank you, Ruth!" Genesis exclaimed. "Oh, my gosh, it looks delicious!"

"It will be, we cook up the best burgers in town," Ruth said. "Those chain restaurants ain't got nothin' on us!"

"Thank you again," Genesis said.

"You're welcome. Holler if you need anything else."

"I will, thank you."

Ruth walked away and Genesis dove into the burger like she hadn't eaten in weeks. She didn't care what she looked like. She had no reason to be ladylike or prim and proper. Every bite of that burger was like heaven on her tongue. She devoured it in no time. Ruth brought her another Pepsi. Genesis drowned her fries in ketchup and ate every last one of them. Wow, that was amazing! Ruth came back to check on her.

"Anything else, hun?"

"No thanks, Ruth," Genesis replied with a satisfied smile on her face. "I'll pay up and be on my way."

"Okay, dear, it'll be 14.58," Ruth said.

Genesis dug a twenty out of her purse and handed it to Ruth. "No change. Have a good day," Genesis said and stood up.

"Thank you. Please come see us again," Ruth said with a smile and jammed the twenty into her apron pocket.

"Oh, I will!" Genesis exclaimed. "Maybe every day 'til I have this baby!"

Ruth chuckled at that and went on her way.

Genesis turned for the front door and bumped into a man.

"Oh, so sorry," Genesis said.

"No problem," the man said. "I should have announced myself. I'm Drew."

"Uh, hi, I'm Genesis."

"That's a beautiful name," Drew said with a smile.

"I'll let my mom know you think so, she picked it out," Genesis chuckled.

Drew threw his head back and laughed. It was a major overreaction to her silly little joke. Genesis stiffened a bit. This guy was coming on way too strongly already.

"Could I buy you a coffee?" Drew asked.

"No thank you, I just ate and had some Pepsi. I need to be on my way."

"Can I have your number? Maybe we can get a coffee another time? Or a drink?"

"No, I have a boyfriend," Genesis said coldly.

"Oh, sorry," Drew said and his whole demeanor changed. "Have a good one."

Genesis walked around him and left the restaurant. Right when she was kind of feeling better that guy swoops in and pisses her off again. She should've raged on him. No one would hold it against her for screaming at a man who was hitting on her and checking her body out like that. Her whole body was shaking. Would she ever feel normal again? Had she ever felt normal? What was normal? Was it the way her and her family lived? Or was it how people like that Drew guy lived? Trying to pick up a girl at a roadside diner. A girl that had just wolfed down an entire bacon cheeseburger and a pile of fries. Dude had to have seen that. Genesis was certain she had noticed him checking her out as she walked in.

Genesis got into her car and started it up. Time to bite the bullet and go tell Toby. That Drew guy was a distant memory by the time she pulled into traffic. She wasn't really mad at him. If she was honest with herself, she'd even say she had been flattered.

Genesis pulled up at Toby's place and, of course, he wasn't home. He was never around when she actually wanted him to be. She called him and he answered after serval rings. He seemed distracted.

"What's up?" he asked.

"I have something very important I need to tell you," Genesis said.

"Can it wait? I'm at Elijah's."

"No, it really can't," she replied.

"Well, I'm busy. I'll call you back later."

"Goddammit Toby!" Genesis yelled and instantly regretted taking the Lord's name in vain like that. It sure got Toby's attention though. "We need to talk, and we need to do it now!"

"Okay, okay, what is it?" he asked, stunned by her tone and language.

"I'm not saying it over the phone," Genesis said, a little calmer.

"Is it bad? Are you in trouble?"

"Toby, I'm at your place, just get over here already."

"No, just tell me on the phone. I said I'm busy."

"Busy with what?" she growled. "You guys playing video games again? What's so important you can't come talk to me?"

"Elijah is having a rough time. That girl from prayer circle he likes turned him down when he asked her out. He just needs his best friend right now."

"Toby!" Genesis yelled. "I can hear you mashing the buttons on the controller! Get home, now!"

"Don't you talk to me like that woman!" Toby yelled. "A woman is to never disrespect a man in that way. You will never raise your voice to me or use such coarse language."

"Oh, you wanna hear coarse language?" Genesis asked, fuming. Her entire body was moving up and down with every angry breath she took.

"Stop it, Genesis," Toby said. "You do not want to go there with me."

Genesis screamed. Despite having her phone in her hand, she banged her fists onto the steering wheel. She hit the wheel so hard she cracked her phone. She put the phone back to her ear, but Toby was gone. Genesis screamed again. Off to Elijah's. Guess he'll get to know the news first too.

Genesis arrived at Elijah's and approached the front door. She could see them on the couch through the front window. It looked like Toby was touching Elijah's crotch. No, that couldn't be. That's a mortal sin, neither one of them would do anything like that. It must have just been the angle she was at. Genesis climbed the three steps to Elijah's front door and pounded on it. She heard Elijah nervously yell, "just a minute!" It took a while for him to answer the door.

Genesis didn't wait for an invitation to come in, she just pushed her way past Elijah. Toby was standing in front of the couch, looking guilty.

"What are you doing here?" Toby asked irritated.

"I came here to tell you I'm pregnant!" Genesis shouted.

A look of shock, disbelief, and sheer panic filled both young men's faces.

"No way!" Toby exclaimed. "I pulled out every time! No way you're pregnant."

"Well, I am!" Genesis said, her eyes full of rage and hatred.

"Well, it can't be mine!" Toby said defensively. "I pulled out."

"That doesn't work, and you damn well know it," she growled at him.

"Are you, uh, sure?" Elijah asked, almost trembling.

"Shut up, Elijah! This doesn't concern you!" Genesis snapped at him.

"Yeah, well are you sure?" Toby asked, fear still all over his face.

"Oh, yeah, one hundred percent. Six at home tests and a doctor's test today. No doubt, totally, very, very pregnant!"

"Shit," Toby muttered and dropped to the couch.

"What was that?!" Genesis asked. "Giving me a hard time about my language!"

"I'm sorry," Toby muttered. "This can't be happening."

"Well, it is, and we need to deal with it."

"Have you told anyone else yet?" Toby asked.

"No, I thought you should know first," Genesis said. "And I guess Elijah."

"I need time to process this," Toby said. "You should go tell your folks."

"That's it?!" Genesis yelled. "You need time to process it, and I should just go? We did this! This isn't me just trying to stress you out! You got me pregnant!"

"Hey!" Toby yelled and jumped to his feet. "You were a more than willing participant! We shoulda never had sex!"

"Too late now, Toby! Way too late now!"

"Okay, okay, you should both calm down a bit," Elijah interjected. "Things are getting too heated. Things are being said that shouldn't be."

"I told you to be quiet, Elijah," Genesis said to him. "This doesn't concern you. I didn't want you involved in this, but Toby wouldn't go home. So, here we are."

"He's right," Toby said. "It's getting too heated. We both need time to cool off."

"Cool off? This isn't some misunderstanding where a little time will help us calm down. We're pregnant Toby! It's not going to just go away!"

"Alright, enough!" Toby yelled at her. "You are way out of place right now! You do not talk to me that way! I am the man, and I am telling you we are done talking about this! Now, please go so we can both calm down a bit. I was trying to be supportive of my best friend and you come in yelling and carrying on like this? We're done."

"Carrying on?" Genesis said each word dripping in anger. She lowered her voice and continued, "Toby, we are pregnant. It's not just me. It took us both to do this. Look, this is what we were planning anyhow, it just happened a lot sooner than we wanted it to. I am sorry I spoke to you that way and I am sorry for raising my voice. That was disrespectful and not at all helpful. Toby, I can't do this alone. I need you. Our baby needs you."

"Genesis, I would like to be alone with this news," Toby said almost too calmly. "I will call you later and we will plan out a time to discuss this rationally. I would suggest you go home for a bit, cool off, take a nap or whatever. You're right about one thing; this isn't going to just go away and that means we have time. It's not something that I am willing to discuss any further at this time and that's final."

Genesis didn't say another word. She knew she would not be able to talk to him without yelling at him. She wanted to wrap her fingers around his scrawny little neck and squeeze the life out of him. Genesis had known he would freak out about it, but she hadn't expected him to freak out *on* her like that. Blaming her for it, as if she had made it all up. Accusing her of sleeping around by asking if she was sure, it was his. Genesis was livid. She was seeing red.

Genesis left Elijah's, but she didn't go home. She didn't go to her parents' house either. She went over to Eve's apartment. Genesis had told Eve she was pregnant. Eve was being very supportive already.

As she pulled up to Eve's apartment building, Genesis could see Eve on her patio smoking a cigarette, a nasty habit she picked up after moving out of their parents' house. Eve hid it from their parents and Mathew. She didn't care if Genesis knew. Eve saw Genesis get out of her car and waved to her big sister.

Eve stubbed out her cigarette and met Genesis at the front door.

"Hey pregnant sis!" Eve exclaimed and hugged Genesis.

"I told you to stop calling me that," Genesis said with a laugh.

"You okay?" Eve asked. She could tell Genesis was upset and had been crying.

"No, I really am not," Genesis replied. Her and Eve sat down in the living room. "I told Toby today and he completely freaked out. Blamed me for it all and then told me to leave. Said he needed time to process it. Process what? I'm pregnant whether he wants to believe it or not."

"Fuck him," Eve said. That word still sounded so weird coming out of Eve's mouth. Genesis still didn't like that word. "He's a fool, always has been. I warned you about dating him in the first place. He's just like dad and Mathew."

"We had a decent relationship," Genesis said.

Eve laughed and said, "decent? Is that what you're looking for in a relationship? Don't you want fun, passionate, amazing, wonderful, comforting to be words used to describe a relationship? Decent isn't good, Genny."

"You know what I mean," Genesis said. "We had a good relationship. We had fun together."

"Did you?" Eve asked, studying her sister. "Think about it, did *you,* Genesis, have fun in that relationship? Besides the fuckin', did you enjoy spending time with him? Seemed to me like he spent more time with Elijah than he ever did with you."

"Well, I mean, yeah, I guess I did, sometimes," Genesis stammered. "And would you not use the 'F' word so much, please?"

"Sorry, I forget that it still bothers you for some reason. You know it's a hellava stress reliever. You should try it sometimes."

"I'll pass, I don't care to be seen as crass like that, no offense. I just don't think words like that add anything of value to language."

"The hell they don't!" Eve exclaimed. "If I got in an argument with someone and I yelled 'screw you!' that would carry a little weight. It'd tell the other person I was mad, but if I yell, 'fuck you!' that's way more powerful. That person would definitely know I was pissed off and fed up."

"Or they'd think you were poorly educated," Genesis replied.

"Whatever, sis, I'll try to limit my shits and fucks when I'm around you, but I think you should loosen up about it. Most people talk like that."

"I know men do and I'm okay with that. I don't think a lady should."

"I could go on and on about this. We could go back and forth, but let's just drop it and get back to Toby and the baby," Eve said. She respected Genesis enough to watch her language. She didn't agree with Genesis about it, but that didn't matter.

"Oh, yeah, about that, Elijah knows now too," Genesis said.

"Oh, I'm sure he does. Toby probably called him right away," Eve replied.

"No, I told Toby at Elijah's place because Toby wouldn't go home to talk to me alone."

"That doesn't surprise me at all. Those two spend a lot of time together," Eve said. "You know what I heard and I'm beginning to think may be true?"

"No, what now?" Genesis asked, rolling her eyes. Eve loved her gossip.

"I heard those two fool around together," Eve said quietly for some reason, even though they were alone.

"What?! Eve, you should never repeat such nonsense," Genesis said.

"I don't know if it is nonsense," Eve countered.

"Who told you that?"

"Benjamin."

"What?! How would he know anything like that? He hasn't hung out with Toby and Elijah in over six months!"

"Exactly!" Eve said, smiling ear-to-ear. "He told me he quit hanging with those guys cus they wanted to fool around with him. Some sort of circle jerk thing."

"Eve Mary! Now you're just being nasty!" Genesis said with disgust in her voice. "Why would you repeat something so disgusting?! Benjamin probably made it up because he is angry with them."

"I dunno, I tend to believe him," Eve said and sat back in her chair. "Benjamin seemed very genuine about it. He seemed really upset by it, you know, like disturbed. I did not get the feeling he was making it up out of spite or anything. What he told me seemed far too detailed to be made up."

"What did he tell you?" Genesis hesitantly asked. She was pretty sure she didn't want to hear it.

"You sure you wanna hear it? You may be marrying Toby."

"Why would you even bring it up then?" Genesis asked, growing annoyed with her little sister. Ever since she left the church, Eve had become a gossip hound and a shit-stirrer.

"Well, I thought you should know," Eve said. "Honestly I have been wanting to say something for a while."

"I changed my mind," Genesis said. "I don't believe any of it, so you can spare me the details."

"Suit yourself, but I believe Benjamin," Eve said. "Dudes do that kinda shit, ya know?"

"Not my Toby," Genesis said. "He is a God-fearing man that has dedicated his life to the Lord and Jesus. He would never commit such a sin."

"He committed many sins with you, just sayin'."

"Are you trying to make me angrier than I already am?" Genesis asked. "What is this, pile on Genesis Day? Let's see how frustrated and pissed off we can all make Genesis today! I cannot take much more!"

"I'm sorry, I wasn't trying to upset you," Eve said softly. She got up and sat on the couch next to Genesis, taking her hand. "I think you are going to find out a lot about the type of person he is going forward. He already showed you he cares more about himself than you or the baby. A real man would be there for you and with you. Don't marry him."

"I have to, we're having a baby together. I wish we could marry tomorrow so our baby will be blessed by a holy union."

"Stop it, please, Genny, quit thinking with your church brain and think with your heart. Do you really want to be married to him? He's totally dad. He'll treat you the same way dad treats mom. Can you live like that for sixty plus years?"

Genesis pondered that for a moment. She didn't need to; she knew she certainly could not live like that. Part of her knew that Toby would be very controlling, but she also knew it wouldn't be as bad as her parents' marriage. Toby would be at least a little *less* controlling.

"Let me ask you this," Eve said, interrupting Genesis's thought process. "If you weren't pregnant, knowing what you now know, would you still want to marry him?"

"You can stop asking such things," Genesis said and put her hand up. "We both know I wouldn't. We both know I don't want to marry him now."

"Then it's a done deal. Break up with him and move on."

"I can't do any of that," Genesis said. "We're having a baby together. A child should be raised by both parents in the same house."

"No, a child should be raised by devoted, happy parents and if that means their parents aren't together, then so be it," Eve said and stood up. "I'm getting a beer. You want anything?"

"Do you have any Pepsi?"

"I do. Be right back."

Eve walked across the room and into the kitchen. Genesis didn't like to see her sister drinking, but she was a twenty-three-old woman who could drink whatever she wanted to. Just because Genesis didn't partake in drinking, didn't mean Eve couldn't. It wasn't Genesis's place to say anything about it either.

"Here ya go," Eve said handing Genesis a can of Pepsi.

"Thanks," Genesis said. "I changed my mind again, tell me what Benjamin said."

"Okay, but fair warning, it's graphic," Eve replied.

"That's what makes me want to know," Genesis said with a nervous sigh.

"Well, Benjamin said that he was hanging out with Toby and Elijah playing video games. Toby paused the game and looked at Benjamin. He asked Benjamin if he had ever gotten a hand-job. Benjamin said no, never. Toby then asked him if he masturbated, and Benjamin told me he didn't answer that question-but I think he told me that so that I wouldn't find out if he did or not. He does, they all do, and if they say they don't, they're lying. All guys jerk off, they can't help it. Their little dicks are right there in reach, so of course they're gonna play with it, like all the time."

"Eve, get back to the point, please," Genesis interrupted. She didn't want to hear her sister ranting and raving about such things.

"Sorry, I just get so frustrated with men and their lies," Eve sighed. "I think I'm gonna start dating girls."

"Eve! Enough already, please get to the point."

"Sorry, big sis!" Eve said over exaggerating each word. "Anyhoo, Benjamin *claimed* he refused to answer Toby, but that don't matter anyway. He then said that Toby asked him if he wanted a hand-job. Benjamin said from who? And Toby said he'd give him one, while Benjamin gave Elijah one, and Elijah would give Toby one. You know, like at the same time."

"You cannot be serious," Genesis said with doubt, disgust, and rage inside her.

"Hey, I'm just telling you what Benjamin told me. I believe him."

"Okay, say it is true, what did Benjamin say happened next?"

"He said he started laughing because he thought they were messing with him," Eve continued. "But then Toby said they were serious. He told Benjamin that he and Elijah do it all the time and it feels amazing. He said they've been doing it for years. They thought Benjamin would like it too."

"Years?!" Genesis exclaimed and sat up. "Are you telling me the entire time Toby and I have been together he was doing that with Elijah?! That, that, oh…"

"Just say it, you won't go to hell for calling him an asshole, or piece of shit."

"That asshole!" Genesis shouted. It did feel good to call him that.

"Good girl!" Eve said and smiled. "He is an asshole."

"What should I do? You really think Benjamin is being honest about that?"

"Hundred percent," Eve said. "Why make something like that up? Especially about those two. They seem like proper and perfect Christian men. No one except for people like me would believe it and they'd all think Benjamin is a liar. Why make something up that will make you look worse than the people you are saying it about?"

"That's a good point. If Benjamin said that to anyone else, they'd call him crazy, and he'd be demonized. Toby and Elijah would persecute him to no end." Genesis looked at her little sister, "damnit, I believe it now."

"Good, cus I do too. Benjamin and I are tight, and we go way back. He wouldn't lie to me or make shit up."

"Okay, so if we agree it's true, what should I do?"

"Dump his cheating ass!" Eve said.

"Should I confront him about what he and Elijah do?"

"Only if you want to but do it in a way where you leave Benjamin out of it. Maybe tell Toby you suspect it. You've noticed things. Somethin' like that where he will feel like you already figured it out and he may confess it to you. I doubt he will, but you never know."

Genesis let out a big, angry sigh, "you know, what those two do is the behavior that lets the devil in. Satan feeds off of sins like that!"

"Oh, my God, really?" Eve said and rolled her eyes. "That is more common than you think and honestly quite normal. Besides him doing it while you guys were together, I don't see what's so wrong with people experimenting. He cheated on you, that's the real issue, not how he did it or who he did it with.

"Okay, fine! All of those sins then!" Genesis snapped. "The bible says adultery is a sin and so is homosexuality."

"It also says that wearing different fabric at the same time is a sin. What is your top made of? Cotton and polyester? Look, there are so many things the bible says is a sin and so many other things it says is okay. It says it's okay to beat a slave to death as long as they do in fact die. But then it says you can't eat meat on Fridays. It was written to control a population. I don't think for a hot minute it's the literal word of God. Jesus had a lot of positive teachings and ideas. It's too bad people aren't good at living by them. They're damn good at telling us to live that way while they lie, cheat, and steal. Like your soon-to-be ex-boyfriend."

"Eve, you have stumbled far from the church," Genesis said and shook her head a little.

"You should too, sister," Eve replied. "Life is a lot better without their stifling rules and mind-fucks. You don't have to stop loving Jesus and the Lord. I still love and worship them, I just do it on my terms without a patriarchal church telling me *how* I should love them. Or how I should behave simply because I was born a girl instead of a boy. That's why I left."

"I'm so confused by all of it," Genesis said and began to cry. "Dad will ban me from going to church once he finds out I'm pregnant."

"He certainly will," Eve agreed. "There's no way he will let the church know his eldest daughter is with child out of wedlock. It would bring shame and judgement upon him and the family. It's all so ridiculous."

"I agree, to a degree," Genesis said. "They chose that church and that life. It's their right to believe how they do."

"True, and that would be all good, *if* they kept it to themselves. *If* they didn't force it on the rest of us."

"Okay, bottom line, without all the rhetoric and opinions, what would you do in my shoes?"

"I'd leave Toby and the church," Eve responded. "I promise you can have a relationship with God without going to that church."

"I don't think I've ever even had a relationship with God," Genesis replied. "I've never felt his presence."

"Neither have I, but I still believe in God," Eve said.

"Well, shouldn't we though? Why does he 'touch' some and not all?"

"Honesty, I think those people are making shit up," Eve said. "I think they want to believe so badly that they manufacture some kind of interaction with God, so to speak. They say they felt Him, some way and somehow. I don't buy it."

"You don't? How can you believe and not know for sure?"

"Same as every other believer, it's just that- a belief. I don't need to believe in the sun because I know it exists. I believe in God because I want to. I want to believe He's real. I want to believe there is a heaven."

"So, that means you would believe in hell also?"

"Well, yeah, to a degree," Eve replied. "I don't think heaven or hell is how the church describes it. Do you believe in ghosts?"

130

"Of course not," Genesis replied. "The church says ghosts are not real. Demons are what people claim to be ghosts."

"Okay, so same difference," Eve said. "My point was going to be, I believe hell is a soul being trapped here and once you make your amends, you can go to heaven, which is not like what the bible says it is."

"Eve, I appreciate your opinions and whatnot, but we are getting off track again."

"You brought up hell, remember?"

"I did, yes, I wanted to know if you feared going to hell. Does your current lifestyle make you afraid you will go to hell? Or, as you believe, stay trapped here?"

"No, not all," Eve said. "What's wrong with my lifestyle?"

"Well, you drink, you smoke, you have relations with God only knows who. Those three alone will get you banished to hell."

"Drinking and smoking will? Everyone in the bible drank and smoked. Jesus turned water into wine!" Eve said with a snort. "And, as far as me clearly being a whore in your eyes, that's hurtful sis. I do have sex, but only in a committed relationship. I don't sleep around."

"I'm sorry, Evie, I'm just so messed up right now," Genesis said and began to cry yet again. "That was uncalled for and very unfair. I love you and I am proud of the person you are. I'm even jealous of you."

"You are?!"

"Yeah, look at you, you have it all figured out and you're so happy."

"It all started with me leaving the church and thinking for myself," Eve explained. "You can't keep pouring from an empty cup. You have to do you. You have to stop thinking how your decisions and actions will make mom, dad, and Mathew feel. Mathew is our little brother, why do you let him have so much control over your life and your feelings?"

"I don't know, it's just how it's always been," Genesis sobbed.

"Change it now, sis," Eve said and took her big sister into her arms.

"How?"

"Start by being honest with them. Tell them you're pregnant and you're not going to marry Toby. You're not going to hide anything anymore."

"I'm going to start by breaking up with Toby," Genesis said and pulled away from Eve. "I'm going to tell him he can do whatever he wants with Elijah, but we're done. Then I'll tell mom and dad."

"How long ago did you tell him about the baby?" Eve asked.

"Right before I came over here. Why?"

"Well, mom and dad may already know," Eve said. "Elijah is tight with Mathew, I bet he probably called him already."

"They would've called by now," Genesis replied. "Hey, you don't think Elijah and Mathew are close the way he and Toby are, do you?"

"What?! Ew, God I hope not!" Eve exclaimed. "I don't even wanna think about that."

"Neither do I, sorry I even mentioned it," Genesis said.

She looked at Eve and began to laugh. Eve joined her and they laughed for a few minutes. The laughter felt amazing. Genesis felt as if she was going insane. One minute she's bawling, another minute she's seeing red with anger, and the next, she's dying of laughter. Genesis knew all of those emotions were normal and healthy. At least she was processing everything that was going on. So many life choices to be made now. Everything she had ever known was about to change in a big way. In every way possible, in fact.

Genesis made up her mind that she would start her new journey by talking to Toby in depth about everything, if he'd even be willing to. It was time for her to take control of her life. She needed to stop worrying so much about disappointing others. If *she* felt like she was doing the right thing and she wasn't hurting others, then that was all that mattered. She had a little baby to think about now. Genesis was no longer making decisions just for herself. Her life choices would affect her child, and she did not want to raise her kid the way she had been raised.

Eve stood up and went to the kitchen. She grabbed another beer and went out to the balcony, where she lit up a cigarette. Genesis waited inside, going over what she would say to Toby. She wanted to confront him about what Eve had just told her, but at the same time she didn't even want to know the truth. Genesis couldn't imagine that going on and certainly didn't want it confirmed. Then again, she kind of did. Was not knowing worse than knowing? Was wondering about it forever going to drive her nuts? If they were going to break up, did it even matter? He would be a single guy; he could do whatever sick stuff he wanted to.

"Hey," Eve said as she came back inside, "do me a favor, take some you time before you tell mom and dad. Don't feel like you need to tell them anything right away. They're not going to be supportive no matter when you tell them."

"I kinda did that today," Genesis said. "I went out to eat by myself and ordered a huge bacon burger with fries. It was so good!"

Eve chuckled and said, "that's a start. I meant like take a trip or go up to the cabin by yourself. Something. Get away from here for a while. In fact, do it before you talk to Toby again. Let him stew on it for a bit."

"Really? I don't want to go to the cabin, everything up there will remind me of them and what I need to tell them. Where else would I go?"

"Go west. Go to the beach and rent a little bungalow and just relax. No offense, but you've always been wound pretty tight. I know you have always felt pressure to be what everyone wanted you to be but throw that all away. Go on a shopping spree. Buy some cute summer clothes to enjoy before you're showing. Just do something that is selfish and all about you!"

Genesis smiled and shook her head, "you sure have embraced this new lifestyle. You really think I should do that? How would that make any of this any better?"

"It won't make a difference in what's going on. It's not like it'll suddenly make everything better. But it might make you *feel* better to spoil yourself a little. Just a suggestion."

Genesis pondered it for a moment. A smile crept across her face. She was falling in love with the idea. It would feel good to spoil herself. A vacation would also be amazing. Genesis whipped out her phone and searched for beachside bungalows or hotels. She found a nice one and booked it for the following two nights.

"Wanna go shopping with me?" Genesis asked with a big grin.

"Hell yeah!" Eve exclaimed.

Chapter Five

Eric and Genesis were awoken by a loud *thud* on the backside of the cabin. It sounded like a tree had fallen on the cabin. Eric flew out of bed and grabbed his 9mm. Genesis slowly stood up and looked at him.

"Come with me," Eric said quietly. "Stay close."

Genesis nodded and followed Eric out of the bedroom. Eric grabbed flashlights out of a kitchen drawer. They slinked toward the back door. As Eric slowly unlocked the back door, he looked over his shoulder at Genesis and made the *shhh* sign. He opened the door slowly, hoping it wouldn't make a noise. It didn't. They slipped out the door.

Eric and Genesis clicked on their flashlights. They walked around the backside of the cabin and stopped, staring at the back of the cabin. How was there not a tree laying on top of the cabin? That thud was so loud it had to have been a tree. They walked to the other end of the cabin where that noise had come from. Right next to the bedroom window was an indentation. It looked as if a boulder had been thrown at the side of the cabin. Eric got close to it and really inspected it. There were no boulders anywhere around. How was that damage even possible? What could have caused that perfectly round, basketball-sized indentation?

"What's going on around here?" Genesis whispered. "I'm so scared."

"Me too and I have no idea," Eric replied looking at the ground underneath the dent.

"What's that smell?" Genesis asked, gagging a little.

"Oh my God what is that?" Eric said and coughed. "Shit, it smells like something died back here."

"It does, but like it died a while ago."

"There's no way," Eric said and scratched his head. "This is like ten feet from where I was cooking earlier, we woulda noticed this smell sooner. What in the fuck?"

"Eric," Genesis said in a whisper he almost didn't even hear her. "Do you see that?"

"What?" he whispered back, looking around.

"A dark shadow in the woods over there," she said and pointed to her left. "It's darker than the night."

"I don't see anything," Eric replied and shined his flashlight in the direction she was pointing.

Neither one of them saw anything. The wind picked up and blew the smell of death away. Clouds rolled in and rain dumped down on them. They rushed back into the cabin.

"Somebody's fuckin' with us," Eric said, after they got back inside.

"Maybe," Genesis said as she flipped on the lights. "But what was that smell?"

"The woods," Eric replied. "Woods smell like death sometimes."

"That was a strong stench, Eric, like you said we should've smelled it earlier."

"Maybe the wind shifted or something," he said, trying to convince himself just as much as her. "I'm more concerned with what, or who, hit the cabin. I'm getting pissed off about all of this. The screaming, the gun shots- or fireworks, whatever that was- and now my cabin!"

"Maybe we should call 911," Genesis suggested.

"It'd take almost an hour for anyone to get out here," Eric said. "I got this bad-boy," Eric patted the 9mm tucked into his waistband, "if this shit continues, I'll scare the holy hell outta whoever is doing this."

"You still think it's a someone?" Genesis nervously asked.

"Yeah, what else could it be?"

"A some*thing*," Genesis said, looking around the room. She felt like they weren't alone. Like something was in that cabin with them.

"What?! What kinda something?" he asked, looking around the room because she was. He was getting creeped out by her behavior.

"I don't know, but it's sinister," Genesis replied and locked eyes with him. "I'm scared, Eric, like a level of scared I've never been before."

"I'm becoming angrier than anything else. Not at you, for the record, just at whoever is doing this. I know in my guts it's some punk-ass teenagers fuckin' around. They probably came up here to hang out at one of their parents' cabins for the weekend. Now they're all drunk and doing stupid shit. They probably think it's all just so fuckin' hilarious."

"What if it's not kids screwing around?" Genesis asked, looking around the room again. Something was in there with them, she could feel it and it had ill intentions.

"It can't be anything else," Eric replied. "They probably saw us walking earlier and screamed to scare us. Then later they thought it would be hilarious to scream again and set off fireworks so they could watch the 'old' people freak out about it. Ima kill em if I catch em!"

"Eric, you will do no such thing!" Genesis said and looked over at him. He was pacing the kitchen. She went to him and hugged him. "If you're right, and I hope you are, then we call the police and let them handle those kids."

Genesis's hug calmed him down a bit and he said, "you know I was just venting. I'd never actually kill anyone."

"I know, Eric, I know," Genesis said.

Eric gave Genesis's shoulders a reassuring squeeze and he released her. He looked at her. Her eyes were worried, and her cheeks were flush. In that moment she looked stunning to him. She had a vulnerability to her that was endearing to him. He knew she didn't need him to protect her, she was a tough woman, but he felt like he wanted to. With everything that had gone down that day and night, from the very personal conversations to all of this weird activity, he and Genesis had gotten so much closer. He looked at her now as one of his closest friends. They had always been somewhat close, he had always felt like he could trust her, but that day had cemented their relationship.

They wouldn't be heading back to bed for a bit, so he made a drink. Eric stepped out onto the porch for a cigarette. The rain was loud on the covered porch. It sounded, and smelled, amazing. There was no other sound out there except for the rain beating down on the cabin. Raindrops danced on the once glass-like surface of the lake.

"Eric?" Genesis said from the doorway.

"Yeah?" he replied, turning to face her.

"Would you be willing to take me home tomorrow? I don't like it up here anymore. Something evil is going on, I can feel it."

"I could, if that's what you want," Eric replied with a smile. "But I really don't think we have anything to worry about. Plus, all my friends will be up here tomorrow. We'll have strength in numbers."

"Okay, I'll just see how I feel tomorrow then. Thank you," she said and closed the front door.

Genesis stepped in front of the big window and stared out at Eric. Backlit from the kitchen light, she looked creepy and almost sinister. He quickly looked away from her. It gave Eric the chills. Eric knew it was the combination of the rain, the weird events, and the lighting that made her seem sinister. Genesis was as sweet as they came, there wasn't a sinister bone in her body.

As he looked out at the rain hitting the lake, his mind wandered. What if he was up there with any other woman besides Genesis? Would he be making his move? Would he be in bed with her already, despite the weird activity? Why did any other woman matter in that way? He knew he loved Rachel. No matter what he'd always love her. He needed to pull his head out of his ass and figure out why anyone else was worth his attention. Even Genesis. Rachel wouldn't be happy when she found out Genesis spent the night, even though nothing happened. He needed to start thinking with his heart instead of his libido. That wasn't even accurate, only Rachel had ever got his libido going one hundred percent. He needed to quit being a scared little boy and become a man Rachel would want to be with. She loved him, but he was not good enough for her yet.

Thunder boomed off in the distance and startled Eric back to reality. He was exhausted and frustrated. They needed more sleep. Could they even get back to sleep? His heart was still racing, and he could tell Genesis was deeply concerned about everything. She was also worried about something evil going on. That confused him, he hadn't had any strange feelings. Okay, that was a lie, and he knew it, but he hadn't felt any presence like she seemed to. The way she had looked around the room was as if she saw someone else pacing around in there.

Sleep, they must get some sleep.

"Genny," Eric said as he walked back inside, "we should go get some more sleep."

"I'm not sure if I can sleep anymore," Genesis said. "We're not alone in here."

"Yes, we are," Eric said. "I know the feeling you have. It's just stress and exhaustion. They both play tricks on your mind, kinda like you when you do 'shrooms. You feel things that aren't there."

"Maybe it's always been here and we're just now feeling it because we are so tired?"

"Maybe," Eric said to humor her. "I think our best bet is to get more sleep."

They headed to the bedroom. If either of them had turned around, they would have seen to two red eyes that had come to life when Eric killed the lights. Those eyes stayed focused on the bedroom. There was a slight gleam to those eyes.

*****

Eric and Genesis did fall asleep and slept soundly. They were awoken by Deandre coming into the cabin the next morning. He hollered out to Eric as he dropped his things on the kitchen counter. Eric and Genesis came out to the kitchen rubbing the sleep from their eyes. Deandre shot Eric a 'what did you do?' look as he watched Eric and Genesis come out of the same bedroom.

"Dre!" Eric said and gave his oldest friend a hug. "Do you remember Genesis?"

"Oh, yes, of course I do," Deandre said. "How are you, Genesis?"

"I'm good," she replied. "I'm pregnant, just wanna get that out the way right off the bat."

"Congratulations!" Deandre said.

"Thank you," Genesis said.

"Man, did you guys get dumped on last night? It rained like hell in town," Deandre asked as he began to load his food and drinks into the large fridge. He kept giving Eric a look. He needed to get his friend alone.

"It rained hard out here too," Eric replied. "Luckily, we have this cabin and we weren't tent camping!"

"No, shit, bro," Deandre agreed.

Genesis excused herself to the bathroom. She said she wanted a shower. She mostly did it so the guys could chat in private.

"Wanna smoke?" Eric asked.

"Yeah," Deandre replied and followed Eric out to the porch. "So, what happened between you two last night? Did you sleep with her?"

"No, I didn't," Eric replied, lighting a cigarette.

"That's good, but why were you two in the same room?"

"She was scared, and I wanted her close. It got creepy last night."

"Like what?" Deandre asked surprised.

"I think there's kids up here pranking people, setting off fireworks and shit like that. No biggie, honestly, but it really freaked Genesis out. I just wanted her to be able to sleep so I let her have the spare bed in my room."

"Dude, you gotta stop with that kinda shit. Even if nothin' happened, it still *looks* like somethin' happened. You need to focus on Rachel. She's your one."

"I know, I know," Eric said, shaking his head. "Everyone keeps saying that. I hear those words in my dreams."

"We ain't trying to be annoying about it," Deandre said with an exhale of smoke. "We just lookin' out, ya know?"

"Yeah, I know," Eric said. "But I gotta be honest, I'm all sorts of confused now. I've known Genesis my whole life, you know, we grew up together out here, sharing that beach and these woods every summer. Even in the puberty and horny teenage years I never thought of her as anything but my lake buddy. Never once did I even think about her in a sexual way. She was always the proper little church girl. So polite and naïve. But now she's a changed woman. I saw her as a woman for the first time yesterday. I even thought for a moment I might be attracted to her for the first time ever."

"Oh, Jesus Christ, dude!" Deandre exclaimed. "You gotta stop doing this shit. Quit distracting yourself from Rachel."

"Seriously, Dre, if Rachel were truly my one, I wouldn't be distracted. Other women wouldn't tempt me. I'd be all about Rachel."

"You're not tempted by these other chicks cus she ain't your one. You're tempted and distracted because you let yourself be. You do it, not the other women. You put yourself out there. Rachel's your unicorn, quit being so scared to be happy."

"You really think so?" Eric asked, he had never thought about it that way.

"Yeah, bro, I know so. I did that shit when I was with Melonie. She was so perfect for me, but I was too chicken-shit to realize it. I fought every feeling and emotion. I thought I was way too young to be quote, end quote, tied down. But that's the thing, when someone is your one, it ain't tied down. It's a partnership, a partnership that should be based on love and respect, admiration and a guttural desire you've never felt before. That's what I could've had with Mel, but I blew it and you're so damn close to blowing it with your one."

"Genesis seems good for me too," Eric replied.

"Seems and good are not unicorn, the one shit," Deandre said as he stubbed out his cigarette. "It's like you're trying to convince yourself that Rachel isn't your one even though you know she is. Listen to you, talking about Genesis as if she's something more than just a friend. Come on, man! Lemme ask you this, when you're alone with Rachel, you know just chilling, not fooling around, how does she make you feel? How do you feel being with her?"

"Fuck, dude, you know," Eric said. "She makes me float. She makes me hum. Like, I'm so happy around her. She's a smartass like me, she's funny, she's brilliant, gorgeous, sexy, and she's real."

"Now, how did you feel hanging with Genesis?"

"Comfortable, easy-going, kinda laid back, even though we were talking about a lot of heavy shit. Genny brings a calm to me that no one else has."

"Those are two very different feelings," Deandre said. "One gets you going in every way possible, the other is comfortable."

Eric looked over at Dre and didn't say a word. Deandre, and everyone else, had been right. He was wasting his life being scared to be happy with Rachel. He had wasted her life too. Genesis was cool and beautiful, but she wasn't *Rachel* cool and beautiful. Where Genesis was pretty, Rachel was stunning. Genesis was funny, but Rachel was hilarious. Genesis made him feel comfortable, Rachel made him feel *alive*.

The feelings he thought he was getting for Genesis vanished in that moment. It had been the stress of the activity from the night before. It hadn't been anything except for the fact that they had shared those scary moments. His instinct to protect her had kicked in and made him feel something for her that wasn't truly there. No matter what he had done, or who for that matter, nothing changed the way he felt for Rachel. That fire and nervous feeling for her was always in his guts. Everything he did, said, or thought was with Rachel in mind. He'd been a fool for too long. He was asking her out that day, as soon as she got there.

"You got it now, huh?" Deandre said with a smile after he watched it all finally dawn on Eric.

"Yeah! I do!" Eric replied with a huge smile. "I've been a fool for too long. I've been distracted too long. I did have a moment last night, when I looked at Genny, she just looked so vulnerable and scared. I had this thought that she meant more to me than just a good friend. It scared me, but as I thought about it more, I realized I was confused. Then you asked about her and, fuck, I don't know."

"I think you are so used to anything with tits being an option that even Churchie Genny caught your eye for a split second. But now you've realized that about yourself, we all knew it, but you needed to figure it out. I'm proud of you, brother." Dre put his arm around Eric and gave him a loving pat on the shoulder.

"Thanks," Eric said and returned the bro-hug. "I appreciate you guiding me to this conclusion."

"I always got ya."

They heard the front door open and saw Genesis standing there with wet hair. She looked at the two bald men and giggled, "For some reason, I was going to ask if either of you have a hair dryer, but I'm guessing the answer would be no."

Eric laughed and said, "no, would be the correct answer."

"No worries," Genesis said and went back inside.

"She is a cool chick," Deandre said.

"Yeah, she has become one of my closest friends, after you of course," Eric replied with a smirk.

"Better be," Deandre laughed.

"I'm gonna go start some breakfast, I'm starving," Eric said and turned for the front door.

"Me too, bro," Deandre said.

"Genny," Eric called to the bedroom, "you want some breakfast?"

"Oh, yes, that would be lovely," she replied walking out of the bedroom. "Could I be of any help with it?"

"No, I got it," Eric smiled. "I wanna make my special egg scramble. You'll love it!"

"Sounds good, if you need help let me know," Genesis said with a smile and sat down on the couch.

The cabin had a wide-open design. The living room, kitchen, and dining room were all one big room, with the bedrooms and a bathroom all on the west side of the cabin.

Just as Eric began prepping the ingredients, there was a knock at the front door. He knew it wasn't any of their friends, they never knocked. Everyone knew the cabin had an open-door policy.

"My dad," Genesis sighed. "It's gotta be."

Eric went to the door and opened it. Genesis's dad and Mathew were standing on the porch. Eric sighed and rolled his eyes.

"Eric," her dad began, "is Genesis still here?"

"Maybe?" Eric answered.

"I would love for you to send her home, please. She has been out all night and that is worrying, considering."

"Genny?" Eric asked, turning toward her. "You wanna go back?" Genesis shook her head, 'no.' "She's good here. Thanks for dropping by."

"It's not up to you," her dad said.

"You're right, it's up to her and she does not want to go. I'm not trying to be rude, but we are in the middle of making breakfast, so I'll have to be going now," Eric said and began to close the door.

"What are your intentions with my daughter?"

Eric wanted to punch him. That was none of his business!

"To treat her with love and respect for the first time in her life," Eric replied, seething.

"Eric, she does not belong here," Mathew said from behind his dad.

"She sure does!" Eric said with a smile. "Genny is a grown woman, if she wants to stay here, she can. Now, for the last time, I am asking you to leave my property. You two are not invited, therefore you are trespassing. Have a blessed day." Eric closed the door in their faces.

Eric chuckled and went back to prepping for his egg scramble. He had barely gotten the bacon chopped and into the pan when there was another knock on the door. Eric let out a frustrated sigh and went to the door again.

"Better not be your dad or brother again," Eric said to Genesis as he crossed the living room to the front door.

Eric opened the door, and Eve was standing there with her backpack. He motioned for her to come inside.

"Can I hang here for a bit? It would just be 'til my boyfriend picks me up this evening." Eve asked. "I cannot stand my dad and brother anymore. They're driving me nuts with their shit-talk!"

"Of course," Eric said. "You have good timing. I'm cooking up some breakfast."

"Cool, thank you so much!" Eve exclaimed and took a seat next to Genesis on the couch.

"You're welcome," Eric said and returned to the kitchen area. "Do you remember Dre?"

"Oh, yeah, I do," Eve said. "Hey, how's it going?"

"It's all good," Deandre replied. "What's going on with your family?"

"They've lost their fuckin minds since they found out Genesis is pregnant," Eve replied. "I mean they've always been super conservative and mostly crazy, but it's gotten so much worse."

"Why even come up here with them?" Deandre asked.

"One, it's tradition we spend our dad's birthday weekend up here. Two, Genny and I hoped spending some time with them away from their church life would help settle things. Maybe if we could all be alone with minimal distractions, we could discuss things further. But no, that didn't happen at all. It was even worse up here. Mathew and our dad have lost their minds over it and our poor mom is stuck in the middle," Eve replied.

"Jesus," Deandre said and shook his head. "I'm sorry to hear that."

"Thanks, but it's always been this way," Eve said, looking at Genesis. "We should all be so excited to have a little niece or nephew. I should be planning my sister's baby shower. You know all that fun, new baby stuff, but we're not doing any of it. Mathew and my dad are either ignoring Genny and I or they're yelling at us, calling us tramps and hussies- whatever the fuck a hussy is!"

"That's so fucked up," Deandre said. "You two don't deserve any of that."

Eve took her sister's hand. She could tell this was upsetting Genesis. "Well, it is what is, but now we're somewhere safe and open-minded. I really appreciate you letting Genesis crash here last night, Eric."

"My pleasure," Eric replied from the stove. "I'm so glad she was here! I'm glad I had someone with me last night when all that weird shit was going on."

"I know!" Eve exclaimed. "What was all of that?! Something hit our cabin hard in the middle of the night. I went out to see what happened because Mathew is a giant pussy, and my dad was passed out drunk. There was a hole in the siding the size of my head!"

"Something hit my cabin too," Eric replied, pouring eggs into the pan.

"Probably just some rambunctious teenagers," Genesis said, happy that conversation had shifted from her dad and brother.

"Most likely. That's what I was guessing," Eve said.

"Whoa, shit, I missed a lot yesterday," Deandre said.

"Yeah, you did, bro, hopefully those kids are leaving today," Eric said as he seasoned the eggs. His scramble was almost ready.

"Or hopefully with all of us here tonight, they'll leave us alone. We'll run em off if they try any shit today," Deandre said.

"Nothin' happened 'til it got dark," Eric said. "Oh, hey, is Aaron bringing the boat?"

"Yup, he messaged me and said he was on his way to pick it up about eight this morning, so he should be here shortly," Deandre said. "Well, shit, I hear someone pulling into the driveway, maybe that's him!"

Deandre went to the back door and opened it. Rachel and her cousin had just pulled up. Deandre went to them and helped unload their stuff and carry it inside.

"Damn! It smells good in here!" Gina exclaimed.

"Yeah, it does," Rachel agreed. "Hey, Eric."

Rachel dropped her arm load behind the door and hugged Eric. Eric pulled back a bit and kissed her. He kissed her passionately and she returned the passion. He wanted that kiss to say, "I want you."

"Get a room," Deandre said as he skirted past them with Rachel and Gina's kitchen stuff.

"We got one!" Eric laughed. "We're sharing a room with you!"

"The hell you are!" Deandre replied laughing.

"Gina, I want you guys to meet our neighbors, Genesis and Eve." Eric said.

"It's very nice to meet you," Genesis said to Gina. "I think we've met, Rachel. I've seen you up here a million times with Eric."

"Yeah, we've definitely met before," Rachel replied wondering what these two women were doing in the cabin so early in the day.

"So, I'm getting this out of the way first thing," Genesis began, "I am pregnant. I just don't want people to feel awkward about my appearance."

"Why would anyone feel awkward? Congratulations!" Gina said.

"Thank you," Genesis replied and patted her belly. It still felt weird having a big belly. "My dad and brother say an unwed pregnant woman is awkward for others."

"That's BS," Gina said. "Well, anyway, welcome to our impromptu camping trip!"

"Thank you so much," Genesis said.

"You too, Eve, welcome," Gina said. "I love your hair!"

"Thanks!" Eve said.

"Breakfast is ready!" Eric exclaimed.

They all dished up and sat around the big dining room table. Eric and Genesis told Deandre, Rachel, and

Gina what had gone down around there the night before. It worried Rachel and Gina quite a bit. Eve assured them everything would be okay; it had to be kids fooling around.

They heard a truck pull into the large driveway. Moments later Aaron and Ozzy came in the back door.

"The boat's in the water!" Aaron exclaimed as he set some things down on the counter. "I think we should do some water skiing!"

"No Harvey," Ozzy said. "His ol' lady said 'no'."

"Figured," Eric said. "What about Leo?"

"As far as I know he'll be here," Ozzy said. "You know if he worked late last night he went home and got really high. He's probably still sleeping."

"Probably," Deandre said.

"So, who are these lovely ladies?" Aaron asked with a grin.

"Oh, shit, sorry," Eric said. "These are our neighbors, Genesis and Eve. This is Aaron and Oswald."

"I go by Ozzy, no one but my mom calls me Oswald," Ozzy said and shot a giggling Eric a dirty look.

"Nice to meet you both," Genesis said with a sweet smile.

"Yeah, nice to meet you guys," Eve said. "We've seen ya'all up here a lot."

"Yeah, I thought you guys looked familiar too," Aaron said. "You guys wanna do some boating?"

"I'm in!" Eve exclaimed.

"I'll go on the boat, but I can't do any skiing or anything," Genesis replied.

"Why not?" Aaron asked.

"I'm pregnant," Genesis replied.

"Hey! Congrats!" Aaron said.

The alarm on Ozzy's phone went off. He looked at it and smiled.

"Time to start day drinkin!" Ozzy exclaimed and grabbed a Coors light from his cooler.

"Breakfast of champions!" Aaron said and grabbed his own Coors light. "Anyone else?"

"I'll have one," Eve said with an eager smile. Aaron handed her an ice-cold Coors light. "Thanks!"

"You bet!" Aaron replied. "Should we wait for Leo or go hit the water?"

"Leo ain't gonna be up here for hours," Deandre said. "Let's get on that water!"

Everyone agreed they should get the boat out on the lake. They all went off into separate rooms and changed. Genesis and Eve went into the bathroom to change.

"You gonna wear a bikini?" Eve asked with a smile.

"No way!" Genesis replied. "I'm wearing my one-piece."

"Why? We're all adults here."

"If dad or Mathew saw they'd have a fit," Genesis replied.

"So what?! I'm wearing mine," Eve said.

"If you really don't care, then why didn't you wear that one yesterday?"

"You know dad would've forbidden me to even leave the cabin," Eve replied. "Somethings aren't worth the trouble in the moment. I hate one-pieces, but I hate dealing with dad more. Today, no dad or Mathew, so I'm wearing what I feel most comfortable wearing and what makes me feel good."

"What about all the guys?" Genesis asked in a whisper.

"What about them?"

"Aren't you worried about them checking out your body?"

"If they're gonna check me out they're gonna do it whether I'm in a one-piece or a bikini. I feel good in a bikini, so that's what I'm wearing!"

Genesis put on her one-piece and Eve shook her head. Eve put a cover on over her swimsuit. Genesis looked in the mirror. The one-piece was slightly too small for her pregnant body. She had parts hanging out where she didn't want them hanging out. She quickly changed into her bikini, which fit her a lot better, and then put on shorts and a tank-top over it.

"I'm not skiing anyway," Genesis said to Eve.

"Lookin' good, sis," Eve said with a smile.

"Thanks," Genesis said and took one last look at herself in the mirror.

They left the bathroom and found everyone else in the kitchen, filling coolers with water bottles and drinks.

"Ya'all ready?" Aaron asked.

"Hell, yeah, let's do this!" Ozzy exclaimed.

The group headed out and walked down to the beach. Mathew stood on the porch of his parents' cabin and watched as his whore sisters wandered down to the beach with the degenerates. His sisters were flaunting their bodies and giggling as they made their way to that boat. Mathew shook his head in disgust. Those sisters of his had become dirty, filthy whores. He was glad his dad wasn't outside to see them that way. Eve, in her bikini, and Genesis wearing short shorts and a tight tank top. It was disgusting and beyond immoral. They'd rot in hell for those decisions. Mathew watched as everyone climbed onto the boat. As he watched the boat speed away, Mathew descended the front steps to the gravel road.

*****

    Leo finally pulled up to the cabin. He could tell by the rigs in the driveway that everyone else was already there. He knew Harvey had to bail, which meant he was the last one to show up. As Leo pulled into the driveway, he noticed the back door was open. That must mean everyone was still inside. They hadn't hit the water yet.

    Leo grabbed an armload of stuff and walked into the open back door. No one was there. The place was a wreck. It looked like someone had ransacked the place, except, it was only women's clothing thrown about. Tops, pants, shorts, undergarments were tossed everywhere. As he took in the scene, it looked to him as if nothing else had been touched. Who would've dumped out someone else's clothing like that? Was this some weird prank the others had pulled on him? Maybe they were messing with him to freak him out? He could see Rachel tossing her things about to mess with him. But they would've done more if they were messing with him. If his friends were going to go through the trouble of messing up the cabin to prank him, they would've made it look like someone got murdered in there.

    The whole thing freaked him out. He set his gear down. Leo walked through the rest of the cabin. Everything else did seem to be where it was supposed to be. In one of the bedrooms, he saw Rachel's backpack, she had a Marvel backpack, so he knew it was hers. The backpack was obviously full, and it was zipped up. There was another backpack next to it that was also closed and full. So, who's clothes and underwear were strewn about? It was clearly not Rachel's.

Leo found the cabin keys on the kitchen counter and grabbed them. He left the cabin, locking it up, and headed for the beach. He was hoping he could get the others' attention somehow. He walked out to the end of the dock and waited for the boat to make a loop close to him. Leo could see them all out there, but they were too far away to get their attention. So, he just waited.

Aaron was pulling Rachel and Gina on an innertube when he noticed someone standing back on the dock. He couldn't tell for sure, but he assumed it had to be Leo. Aaron turned the boat and headed for the dock. It was indeed Leo standing there.

"You made it!" Aaron exclaimed as he pulled up.

"I did," Leo said, adding, "did you guys pull a prank on me back at the cabin?"

"What do you mean?" Aaron asked. Leo's question had gotten Eric's attention.

"There's women's clothes and undies thrown all over the cabin. The back door was wide open when I got there," Leo explained.

"What?!" Eric exclaimed. "Someone was in the cabin!"

Eric quickly climbed out of the boat. Eve and Genesis followed him. Rachel and Gina were still on the innertube. Leo looked at Eve and Genesis, they looked vaguely familiar, but he didn't know who they were.

"I locked up the cabin," Leo said to Eric, handing him the keys.

"Run up there," Aaron said. "We'll get Rachel and Gina on board then we'll meet you back at the cabin."

"Sounds good," Eric said.

Eric, Eve, and Genesis rushed back up to the cabin. Aaron started tying the boat to the dock as Ozzy pulled Rachel and Gina in.

Eric opened the cabin and the three of them ran inside.

"This is our stuff!" Eve exclaimed.

"What the hell?" Genesis said, looking around frantically.

"You don't think your friend did this and is lying that he found it this way?" Eve asked Eric.

"What?! No way! Not a chance. Leo would never do something like this," Eric replied, slightly offended by the accusation.

"I'm not trying to offend you," Eve said. "It just crossed my mind, is all."

"No worries," Eric said. "Leo ain't like that and if he was, he woulda went through one of the guy's things. Leo is gay."

"Oh, shit, sorry, man," Eve said. "I'm just so pissed and confused right now."

"Mathew!" Genesis shouted out of nowhere.

Eric and Eve looked around expecting to see Mathew standing in the doorway or something. No sign of him anywhere.

"Mathew probably did this!" Genesis growled.

"Why would he do this?" Eric asked.

"Shit, sis, I bet you're right," Eve said.

"He'd do it to teach us some sort of lesson," Genesis said. "In his twisted brain he probably thinks this'll make us want to go back to them."

"I bet she's right!" Eve exclaimed. "He probably thinks we will blame one of you and run back to him and dad. That's it! I'm so done with him!"

"We can't know for sure it was him," Eric began, "but from what you've said I wouldn't put it past him either. Shit, I miss the days when we could leave our doors unlocked around here."

"Me too," Eve said. "Come on, sis, let's gather our things."

"It grosses me out to think Mathew may have touched my panties!" Genesis said, seething with anger.

"What if it was those kids that have been messing around up here?" Eric offered.

"Don't you think they woulda messed with everyone's stuff?" Genesis asked.

"Yeah, and they probably woulda stolen our booze," Eve added.

"Good points," Eric said. "Want me to go confront Mathew about it?"

"Yes!" Eve shouted and startled both Eric and Genesis.

"No, Eric, stay out of it," Genesis said and shot Eve a look. "We don't need to drag you into our family drama."

"You aren't," Eric replied. "I wanna go give that fucker a piece of my mind. And maybe a taste of my fist!"

"Yes!" Eve shouted again. "I wanna see that!"

"Both of you knock it off!" Genesis said sternly. "We are not stooping to his level. There will be no punching going on. We'll ride this out 'til they're gone tomorrow morning. They'll be out of here by seven am in order to make it to church. And, Eve, you're leaving in a few hours anyway."

"The hell I am! I wanna stay here with you, if that's cool with Eric," Eve said and looked at Eric.

"Hey, I'm cool with that," Eric said. "Your boyfriend too?"

"No, I'll call him and ask him to pick me and Genny up tomorrow," Eve said. "He gets super anxious around a lot of people and the last thing we need with everything going on is an anxious guy."

"Whatever you want. Just so you know, he's welcome too," Eric said.

"Thank you so much, Eric," Eve said with a smile.

Everyone else showed up at the cabin. As Eve and Genesis gathered their things, Eric told the others what they believed had happened.

"Jesus," Aaron said shaking his head. "We should go mess that guy up!"

"I want to go confront him," Eric said, "but Genny asked me to stay out of it. She just wants to ride it out 'til tomorrow."

"If he comes back around here, we'll do somethin' about him," Aaron said.

"That family is messed up," Deandre said. "I remember watching them on the beach when we came out here as teenagers. Those two girls looked so scared, and they clearly were not having fun."

"I remember their dad yelling a lot," Eric said. "He'd always be yelling that whatever those girls were doing wasn't ladylike."

"What if we just say we need, like, sugar, or somethin'," Ozzy said. "You know an excuse to go over there so the girls won't know we're confronting that guy."

"All four of us dudes gotta go next door for sugar?" Eric asked. "Genny and Eve would know we weren't going over for sugar."

"I say if they want us to stay out of it, we do," Deandre said. "They know how to handle their family. We'd just end up making things worse for them."

"Even though I wanna mess that guy up, I agree with Dre," Eric said. "I suggest we barbeque up some lunch and start drinkin'!"

"Damn good idea!" Deandre agreed.

"Then maybe lock the cabin up and get back out on the water!" Aaron exclaimed.

Genesis and Eve returned from gathering and putting away their clothes. Everyone agreed lunch sounded great and more boat time- with lots of booze- sounded even better! Eric, Ozzy, and Deandre queued up some cheeseburgers, while everyone else milled about the kitchen prepping fixings and tidying up.

Rachel watched Eric cooking with his friends. He looked so happy and at peace. He had a Jack and Coke in one hand and a smoke in the other. The guys were laughing and joking about who made the better burger. She was so in love with that man. Rachel was still upset with him and wanted to get more information about the Genesis situation. It seemed like there was always another woman situation. The kiss had made her feel a lot better, though. The way he had kissed her felt different, more love and hunger to it. He had always been a good kisser, but that one was different. The passion in it made her float. It was just a kiss though and he had a lot of explaining to do. She didn't like being lied to, but she knew Eric was a confused guy. He had been through a lot in his life. A lot of things no one else there, except for Dre, knew about. Like watching his fifteen-year-old cousin die of cancer when he was only twelve. Or his older brother beating on him so much that he ended up with broken bones. His parents would always talk to Eric's brother about it, but that was the end of it. Donnie just kept beating Eric up.

He was able to defend himself now. As he got older and bigger, he got sick of Donnie pummeling him and started to fight back. After Eric knocked Donnie's two front teeth out, Donnie stopped starting shit with Eric. Rachel had seen Eric get into a few bar fights too. It took a lot to get Eric to that level, but once he was there, he was almost unstoppable. It made Rachel feel very safe with Eric, but it also scared her. Rachel knew Eric had an angry side to him. Not that he would ever, in a million years, lay a hand on her, but one day he may grapple with the wrong guy and end up badly hurt, or worse. She hoped if they became a couple again, her love and support would help calm him down. She wanted to help him realize he didn't have to fight things out anymore. They were in their late twenties, he twenty-seven and she twenty-six, he was getting too old to solve problems by knocking guys' teeth out. Rachel chuckled at that thought because she had just broken Karissa's nose the day before. Maybe they both needed to learn violence isn't always the answer. When pushed hard enough, yes it was, but for the most part, just walk away.

"Burgers are ready!" Eric said with a smile as he walked into the cabin.

"Finally," Aaron said sarcastically.

"Let's eat!" Deandre said, setting down the plate full of burgers.

They all lined up at the kitchen counter and one-by-one built their burgers. Everyone made their way out to the huge porch and found somewhere to sit and eat. People chatted and laughed. Everyone was relaxed and happy, almost giddy. They had all really needed this little getaway. Genesis and Eve were accepted into the group as if they had always been a part of it. They felt like they fit in well too. Maybe Eve fit in a bit more easily because she drank and smoked like the rest of them, but no one made Genesis feel like an outsider because she didn't smoke or drink.

"Genesis! Eve!" their dad shouted from the road. "You two will return home immediately!"

"Goddammit!" Eric shouted and bolted to his feet, knocking over his drink. "I've had enough of you coming onto my property and harassing these two!"

Eric walked toward Mr. Simpson. Deandre, Aaron, Ozzy, and Leo all got up and followed Eric.

"They are grown women who can decide who they hang out with! You are insulting me and my friends with the accusations you and Matt are throwing around!" Eric stopped ten feet in front of Mr. Simpson. Eric could see he was intimidating the man. "Now," Eric continued with a calmer tone, "please leave and do not return. My friends and I are only going to ask nicely this one last time. And tell Matt if he comes by again and goes through any of our shit in *my* cabin, he will get an ass-kicking!"

"I will not be spoken to in this way!" Mr. Simpson snapped. "Those are my daughters! I have the right to make them return to *my* cabin!"

"Sir," Eric began with a heavy sigh. He was fighting the urge to hit the man. "I am doing my best to stay calm, but it gets increasingly more difficult every time you or Matt come around demanding that two grown women come 'home' as you put it. They both have their own homes! Your cabin isn't their home. It's time to let go and allow them to be themselves. They're terrific people, you really should get to know them."

Mathew timidly walked up behind his dad. Mathew had probably heard Eric yelling and somehow thought he may be some sort of backup for his old man. Mathew looked horrible. He looked tired, haggard, and as if he had spent the previous night drinking heavily and doing hard drugs. Eric knew that was not the case, but Mathew was a wreck. He certainly wasn't in any condition to be of any threat. Even on his best day, Mathew was no threat.

"Eric, this is a family matter, and it does not concern you or your friends. You and your friends are heathens. Sinners of many sins," Mr. Simpson said with a shaky voice. Mathew whispered an 'amen' and nodded. "I have forbidden my daughters to hang out with people like you. They are disobeying me, and I have come to retrieve them and set them straight."

Eric lunged at Mr. Simpson and Deandre grabbed him around the waist. Dre whispered something into Eric's ear and Eric wandered back to the porch, seething and staring at Mr. Simpson.

"Sir," Deandre began, "you have no right to come onto our property and insult us. We are not asking anymore. We are telling you to leave and not to return. If this is a family matter, you can sort it out when Genny and Eve are ready. Take your son and leave now! Next time you spout out some vile shit like that I will not restrain my friend over there. Go!"

"We will..." Mr. Simpson started but Deandre interrupted him.

"Go!" Dre shouted. He, Aaron, and Ozzy stepped towards Mr. Simpson and Mathew.

Mr. Simpson looked at Mathew then back to Deandre and the others. Mathew turned around first and bolted back to the Simpson cabin. Mr. Simpson glanced up to the porch at his daughters one more time before he too turned and high-tailed it out of there. Eve burst out laughing and everyone turned to look at her.

Eric was fuming. He was pacing the edge of the porch, power smoking a cigarette.

"Those motherfuckers!" Eric shouted, startling everyone else. "I cannot take their shit anymore! Why didn't you let me beat the shit out of them, Dre?!"

"Look, bro, this is supposed to be a relaxing weekend. We're supposed to be chilling up here, drinkin' and boating. We can't control them being dicks, but we can control how we react to it. Let's just let it go and get on with the party!"

"I'm so sorry about them," Genesis said with tears in her eyes.

"Don't be!" Eric said. "It's not your fault and they need to learn they don't control you guys anymore."

"It is okay," Deandre added. "You guys are a part of this family now."

That last statement made Genesis cry. She had never felt so welcomed anywhere. She had always felt like a piece of the background, an afterthought. Unless, of course, she was "sinning," then all attention was on her.

"You guys are all so fuckin' cool!" Eve said with excitement in her voice and tears in her eyes. "Thank you for letting us crash your party and having our backs. My sister and I came to the decision to leave that life in very different ways, but we are both in much better places now. It's funny how we have good jobs, nice apartments, and now, good friends, and Mathew is still just a leach on my dad's ass." Eve chuckled at herself as tears slowly rolled down her cheeks.

"We appreciate that, Eve," Rachel said with a warm smile.

"Your family is fucked, no offense," Gina said. "Me and Rachel grew up in a religious family, but no one ever treated us like that. I feel for you two, I really do."

"We're getting through it," Genesis said, her cries were beginning to turn into soft sobs. "We just gotta cut them out completely."

"I'm fuckin' ready too!" Eve exclaimed. "Especially after this weekend! What the hell has gotten into them?"

"Old me would've said Satan," Genesis replied. "New me knows it's booze for dad, pills for mom, and spinelessness for Mathew."

"Do they ever scare you guys?" Leo asked. "If it was your brother that dumped your stuff all over the cabin, that shit is scary and fucked up."

"Oh, yeah, for sure they're scary," Genesis replied. "That's why it's taken so long for us to do things like this. We, or at least me, have always been worried they'd do the shit they've been doing this weekend."

Hearing her sister say 'shit' made Eve laugh. She agreed with Genesis and added, "that's one reason we even agreed to come up here this weekend, it's like the last hurrah, you know? Like 'this is it, I'm fuckin' done after this one last weekend'. Me personally, this was always going to be the last weekend spent with them. Hopefully, besides their funerals, the last time I'll ever be in the same room as them."

"That's sad to think, but I get it," Deandre said. "Eric and Rachel know this, but most don't, my dad was an abusive sonavabitch. Beat the tar outta me more times than I can count. Roughed up my mom all the time too. Left my sister alone for some reason, maybe cus she was older and not his biological kid. But the point is, I still had this weird admiration for him. It was like, he's my dad, I *have* to love him. Finally, several years ago, I stood up to him and told him I never wanted to see him again. That gave my mom the courage to leave him too. Never talked to him since and I don't miss the asshole."

"Jeez, that's even scarier than what we go through," Genesis said.

"Yeah, fuckin'-a, man, sorry," Eve said. She was finally with people she could swear around and she was loving it.

"Naw, it's all good, ladies," Dre replied. "The abuse you've been through is just a bad, if not worse. Me, I just got beat on when I fucked up. He never tortured us like your dad does. That shit, I think, would be even worse. Besides getting whoopin's I had a pretty normal childhood. Playin' ball and fuckin' off up here with this guy. You guys were put through the wringer from birth. So, I'm sorry ladies."

"We're all sorry. We all feel bad about the shit we've been through. Let's celebrate where we are now, this time in our lives," Aaron said. "We all been through some shit, no doubt and it sucks, but look what we've all accomplished despite all that! We ain't out there being abusive or any shit like that. I think we should spend the rest of our time up here celebrating that our shit didn't make us shitty people!"

Everyone else cheered and hollered. Aaron always had a way of pumping people up. A lot of that talent had to do with the fact that he hated when things got heavy. He was extremely uncomfortable around big feelings. Aaron buried his big feelings deep inside of himself, under his upbeat attitude. It's what worked for him.

"Then it's decided," Aaron said, "we're partying hard today! Sorry you can't fully partake, Genesis, but you can still party with us without getting fucked up!"

"I sure can! And I fully intend to!" Genesis exclaimed.

"Let's get on that boat!" Leo said.

They gathered what they all needed to spend a few hours on the boat. Eric grabbed a floating key chain and hooked the cabin keys on it. After everyone had piled out of the cabin, Eric locked it up tight. He walked the entire perimeter and made sure there was absolutely no way anyone could get into the cabin. When he was certain the place was locked up tight enough, he caught up with the group. Eric found Rachel and took her hand. They walked down to the water hand-in-hand, smiling at each other.

Chapter Six

Mathew paced his tiny bedroom. There was just enough space in that room for a twin bed, a small dresser and about six feet of walking space. He hated sleeping on that little twin, but it was only for a couple of nights when they stayed in the cabin. He looked awful. You could see the stress and angst all over him.

"I will," he whispered to the room. "Gotta wait for mother to swallow her pills. Gotta wait for father to pass out drunk." He paused but kept pacing. "I know they're sinners too. Pills and getting drunk are sins, I know that. Father always says it is not, he says people drank in the bible. Jesus okayed alcohol by turning water into wine. I know, his sin isn't drinking, it's getting drunk. Ephesians says, 'do not get drunk on wine, which leads to debauchery.' Father is a drunk. Mother is a pill popper."

Mathew sat down on his little kid's bed and shook his head. God was telling him he must spite the sinners. Bring their attention to their sins. He must make them feel the wrath of the Lord! He had wanted to save his dad, and his mom, if God would've let him. Those nasty, rotten sisters of his could burn in hell for all he cared. They were gross and dirty from all sorts of sin, but the worst of all was the sin of relations. Filthy, unwed relations! His sisters were whores! God would punish those whores mightily. God had wanted him to give his sisters a chance to repent, they were still young, but that Eric character wouldn't even let him or his father near the girls. So, be it, then. It was their grave to lie in. Their hell awaited them.

"I know!" Mathew whispered loudly and bit his tongue. He did not want his parents to hear him. "But they do not deserve another chance." He paused again, as if listening to the other end of a conversation. "That vile man will not let me speak to them. Besides, Eve is too far gone. She belongs to Satan already. I am afraid Genesis is too far gone too. Eve has filled her head with lies. The lies have blinded Genesis to her true path." He paused again. He had a pained look on his face. "But..." Another pause. "But they are whores!" He flopped dramatically backwards onto his bed. "Let them burn." It was barely audible. "Please just release them from this world. I do not want to watch them continue their sinful ways." Yet another pause. "You will, Lord? You will release them unto their rightful place in hell? All of them?"

Mathew stood and looked around his room. He cocked his head as if he had heard something to his right.

"I must do it?" he whispered. "I am the instrument of the Lord? How will I know which ones to send to hell?" Mathew paused and looked around the room. "You have marked the cabins? Thy will shall be done, My Lord."

Mathew had first heard the voice of God when he had given into temptation and looked at porn. The videos, and what he did to himself while he watched them, made him feel good, but in a terrible way. He had instantly felt guilty. Mathew knew all along that what he was doing was a sin, but sinners got redemption, so he did it anyway. No matter what one did, if they ask God for forgiveness, all will be forgiven. The Lord knows humans are sinners and he expected them to sin. God wants righteous followers who know their place. Followers that realize they will sin, its human nature, but are righteous enough to admit their sins and repent.

    God told Mathew back then that he was a Chosen One. God explained that he had plans for Mathew, that one day he would call upon Mathew to hold the greatest sinners accountable. Mathew was honored to have been chosen. God spoke to him often. God told him to bide his time, the rapture was on its way. If Mathew followed orders, he would be saved and live-in eternal bliss with God and Jesus.

    The time had finally come. This was the night it was going to happen. Mathew would finally get to release the sinners from this world. He'd get to send their souls to hell! It was a tall order, and it wouldn't be easy. The sinners would fight back. Mathew knew he had to plan it out just perfectly. He had to be sneaky about it. He'd start with his parents, but he had to wait for nightfall. He had to wait for them to pass out. God told him not to talk them into repenting. God said they would never change their ways. They would always be a drunk and a pill popper. There was no saving them. They had already secured their place in hell.

    It had saddened Mathew to know that. He had grown up admiring his parents, especially his father, for their dedication to the Lord and their church. He had always assumed they were saved and would ascend to Heaven upon their demise. The thought of his parents spending eternity in Heaven with God had made the thought that they would someday die a lot easier to handle. But not only were they damned; he was the one who had to send them there. He would take no pleasure in that.

He would, however, take great pleasure in releasing Eric and his heathen friends. He couldn't wait to see the look on Eric's face as he stabbed him over and over. That visual made Mathew smile. Mathew had always hated Eric and his family. It had infuriated him ever since he could remember watching Genesis hang around Eric. He and his entire family were sinners and heathens. Those nonbelievers and their party life. They all deserved to go to hell, and he was damn glad to be the one to do it.

The most difficult part of his mission would be his sisters. He loved them dearly even though he despised them. Mathew knew well enough that he could love his sisters and hate their decisions and their sins. If only his entire family had repented their sins and changed those sinful ways before it was too late. If they had, would God still have tapped him to release the others? Mathew was really looking forward to that part. If having to release his family meant he got to release the others, then so be it.

Mathew's mother called to him that lunch was ready. Good, just a few more hours before he could carry out his mission. God was going to be so proud of him.

"Now?" Mathew whispered to the empty room. "But I thought I'd wait until they are both passed out." He paused and tilted his head. Mathew had always assumed the voice of God would be more angelic, more song-like. It was far from it. God's voice was deep and gravelly. His voice had a hiss to it that Mathew hadn't expected. He knew it was God. The Lord had told him so. He had said he can see everything Mathew does. He knew what Mathew was thinking even before he thought it. "I should wait. It'll be easier."

"NOW!" God's voice filled the entire cabin. It shook the floor.

"Yes, My Lord," Mathew whispered. "Thy will shall be done."

Mathew slinked out to the kitchen. His parents were sitting next to each other at the dining room table. They were both reading their own copy of the bible. His parents paid him no attention, as usual. Mr. and Mrs. Simpson paid little attention to any of their adult children. They hadn't paid much attention to them as kids, either. Mathew stood in the doorway of the kitchen and watched as his parents slowly ate. Their full focus was on their bibles.

Mathew pulled a large chef's knife from the butcher block. He turned it over, fascinated by the glint of light that reflected on the blade as he moved it. He could almost see how sharp that knife was. A smile crept across his face. Mathew looked up from the shiny blade to his absent-minded parents. He should kill his father first. His father may try to fight him off his mother if he started with her. She would be easy. He could tell by her posture that she had already taken several of her pills. Nasty pill popper! His father had that sway he got when he was half drunk.

If he snuck up on his father and buried that beautiful blade into his neck, he'd hopefully die immediately. Mathew tip-toed through the kitchen, staying close to the wall and out of sight. He made a loop into the dining room so that he could sneak up behind his father. Mathew did just that and raised the knife. He hesitated for a moment. His parents were so out of it they didn't even know he was standing right behind them. God had been right, there was no reason to wait until they passed out.

Mathew plunged the blade into the side of his father's neck. The blade punctured through to his throat. His father gurgled and sat up straight. His mother shrieked and jumped to her feet.

"Sit, mother," Mathew growled at her. He looked possessed to her.

His mother did not sit down, she ran. Mathew pulled the knife out of his father's neck. His dad fell forward onto the table. Blood poured out of his neck, turning the white, lacey tablecloth red. Mathew chased his mother into the living room. She was running for the front door. He grabbed her by the hair and threw her to the ground. She shrieked again as her head bounced off the carpeted living room floor. Mathew climbed on top of his mother. He raised the knife above her chest with both hands.

"Why Mathew?" she cried.

"You are sinners, mother," Mathew replied and buried the knife between her breasts.

He quickly yanked out the knife and watched as blood poured out of the wound. She was crying. He watched with great fascination as the blood soaked her blouse. So much blood for only one stab. Her breasts were now covered in blood. Her bosom had sustained his and his sisters' lives when they were infants. It was the only motherly thing she had ever done for them. Dirty pill popper!

Mathew stabbed her again, and again. Over and over, he drove that blade into her chest. She had died over ten stab wounds ago, but he didn't stop. He just kept stabbing her until he couldn't physically do it anymore.

His dad made a noise and Mathew jumped to his feet. Mr. Simpson was still slumped over on the dining room table. Mathew saw his father's head move slightly and rushed to him. Mathew kept the knife out as he reached his father.

"Why, Mathew?" his father gurgled. "Why would you?"

"You are a sinner, father," Mathew said softly, leaning down to be close to his father's ear. "God has tapped me to rid this lake of sinners! After this lake, I will move onto towns, then cities, and then the world!" Mathew let out a laugh.

His father never said another word. Mathew stood over his father and watched him die. He turned and looked at his mother on the living room floor. He had really done a number on her. He was proud of his work and went to the kitchen. Lunch was still warm on the stove, so he dished up and sat at the far end of the dining room table, the only spot of the table his father's blood hadn't saturated yet. Mathew ate his lunch and then went to his room for a nap.

He needed to rest up before he finished his mission that night.

*****

Eric sat at the back of the boat watching Rachel water ski. Everything about her was radiant. Why had she put up with his shit for so long? She was incredible in almost every way. No one is perfect and everyone has their quirks that can be annoying. Rachel chewed her fingernails while they watched tv and for some reason that annoyed Eric a little. Not enough to bring it up or to even matter, just enough to be noticed. Eric knew his bad habits and quirks were a hell of a lot more annoying. That brought him back to his previous question. Why *had* she put up with so much? It was all too much to think about right then. He pushed those thoughts aside and watched his girlfriend ski and enjoy herself.

That's right, girlfriend! They hadn't even made it official yet, but he wanted it to be. Eric knew she was pissed about Genesis staying over. He hoped she knew enough about his relationship with Genesis to know nothing happened. But he still needed to explain the situation, he was well aware of how it looked by the look Deandre had given him. He did want to talk to her about it. Eric did want to tell her he had an epiphany talking to Deandre. He wanted to tell her he had behaved the way he did for so long because he was scared. He was immature and selfish. Eric really wanted her to know that he understood what had led him to all those poor choices. Now he knows it will never happen again. It was her and him forever now.

    Rachel waved at him, and he realized he was staring at her. He waved back, slightly embarrassed. She would later tell him not to be embarrassed, it had been flattering to have him stare at her like that. She joked with him and said, "I'm hot! I'd stare at me like that too, if I could!" And that was why he loved her so much! Rachel was real and down to earth. She'd get angry, or frustrated, but she never held on to feelings like that. That's why she was his unicorn.

    They all heard a scream. The same screams Eric and Genesis had heard the night before. Eric whipped around to look at the line of cabins. He saw a bunch of teenagers down the road running away from something. Soon, a loud bang rang out. It had been goddamn teenagers! It pissed Eric off but sent a wave of relief through him. Nothing but stupid kids doing stupid kid things. Eric remembered setting off fireworks up there with Dre when they were teenagers too. They never went around beating on people's cabins or screaming like someone was being murdered. That shit was too much.

Rachel fell and Aaron slowed the boat to loop around to get her. She'd been out there for a while; her arms were probably jello. Eric watched as the people he had met the night before ran after the teenagers. He laughed a little because Nina, Josh, and Vince were not fit people, and it didn't take long for the kids to outrun them. Eric kept his eyes on the kids and saw which cabin they ran to. He and the guys would be going down there for a chat with those teenagers later.

"I know where those punk kids live!" Eric said to Deandre. "Later we gotta go have a chat with them. Hopefully they have parents we can chat with too."

"Sounds good, bro," Deandre replied. "I sure as shit don't wanna listen to them screaming and blowing shit up all night."

"Fuck, no, me neither!" Eric said.

Aaron scooped up Rachel and pulled in the tow rope. They had all been out there for hours and were ready to head in. They were all a little sunburned and getting hungry. Buzzes were wearing off and it felt like time to kick this party into high gear. This group of people weren't the 'turn the music up and dance' type of partiers. They were the 'sit around a table playing cards while they got hammered' types. And that was exactly their plan for the night.

Back at the cabin they all changed and settled into chairs to relax for a bit. Rachel asked Eric if he'd like to take a little walk, just the two of them. He agreed and they set off.

"I'm having such a good time already," Rachel said as they started walking. "But we need to have a talk."

"Me too and I know we do," Eric agreed.

"I love you, Eric, but you piss me off sometimes. It seems like there's always a distraction with you. You're all over the fuckin' place sometimes. The other night we were hanging out having a great time before Poker Night and you seemed so into me. Then you went and fucked another chick! Now I show up here and you have another woman staying here." Eric started to say something, and Rachel cut him off. "Before you say it was only Genesis, I know it was only Genesis, but that don't mean shit to me, Eric. She's still just another chick in your life, just another goddamn distraction. And I know weird shit went down last night, you guys told us all about it, but you need to understand how certain things look. You have to understand that I see things without knowing the whole story yet and given our history, I assume the worst. And I have the fuckin' right too, Goddammit! You arranged this whole weekend to get away from distractions, to 'get your mind right' as you put it. Then you just let yet another distraction in. You gotta think past yourself."

He stopped walking and looked at her. She turned to face him.

"I love you too and I've learned that and I'm sorry."

"Hopefully you're more than just sorry," Rachel said.

"I am," he replied. "I'm done being dumb. Dre and I chatted about everything again this morning. You know they always call you my one or my unicorn?" Rachel nodded. They started walking again. "Well, to be honest, I have always believed that deep down, but I have struggled with it too." She shot him a confused look. In her mind you either believed it or you didn't. "It's like, um, well, like what Dre said this morning. I, well, I don't know how much you wanna hear of this."

"I want to hear it all, Eric. Look, at this stage of the game, there is next to nothing that will change my feelings for you. In fact, you being one hundred percent open and honest will only make my feelings for you stronger. I don't wanna be lied to or misled anymore. I don't want information withheld from me because you think it'll upset me. If it's upsetting information, then I have every right to be upset. Just talk to me and tell me everything."

"Okay, sorry I ever lied to you. I was scared and a chicken-shit. So, Dre helped me to figure out that I was leaving myself open to other women. I made myself think that if I was interested in other women then maybe you weren't my unicorn. But I realized that I was putting myself out there to be tempted. I was scared of commitment. I was scared to be happy. My life has always been somewhat turbulent and mostly because I made it that way. I constantly made poor choices and put myself into ridiculous situations. By doing so, I was able to excuse my drug use and heavy drinking. I don't want to quit drinking and enjoying nights out with you and friends, but I do want to stop getting hammered every damn night. I do wanna stop doing coke. I'd like to wake up in the morning and feel human. Now it takes me hours, and weed, to feel even a tiny bit normal. I'm rambling, but my point is, I see things a lot more clearly now. Being up here, talking to Genesis yesterday, talking to Dre this morning, made me see my life in a new way. It made me realize my life felt shitty because I was missing you in it. You've always been a part of my life, but I need you. I need us."

"Answer me a question and be totally honest," Rachel began, she could tell by his expression that he already knew what she was going to ask. "Did you and Genesis sleep together last night?"

"We did sleep in the same room, separate beds, so, no, we did not fool around in any way at all whatsoever. To be honest, for a split second I thought I found her attractive for the first time ever in my life. You know we grew up together. I've known her longer than anyone else."

"I also know you guys have never had feelings for each other. Never a crush or anything."

"That's right, so I realized pretty quick that I wasn't actually attracted to her, I was just in a protective mode yesterday. All the shit going on around here made me feel like I had to protect us somehow. That endeared me to her in a new way. I had an epiphany today. I finally saw what you and everyone else have been telling me. I am a selfish prick, and I hurt you over and over for self-preservation. I did the things I did because I was a scared little boy. Too damn self-centered and afraid to open myself up. Afraid to be vulnerable. Scared that'd I lose part of myself in a committed relationship and that's fuckin' stupid. A good, strong, loving, trusting partnership would only make me a better person and a better man. I want you and only you, Rachel."

"Those are beautiful words and sentiments," Rachel said and looked at him. "But right now, that's all they are, words. I need action, Eric. I need to *see* these changes you're talking about. I need to *see* that you see the world differently. I need to see with my own eyes and my heart that I am your unicorn."

"You will," Eric said.

"I'm willing to give this another chance if I see this new you," Rachel said. "Don't fuck me over again."

"I won't," Eric said softly. They were silent for a moment before Eric added, "Lemme ask you a question," Rachel nodded, "after all of the stress and pain I've caused you and all of the back-and-forth bullshit, why do you wanna be with me? Why are you willing to give me another chance?"

"Because I love you," Rachel said without hesitation. "Also, and probably most importantly, because I know you're *my* unicorn. I know this is right, the same as you do now. The only difference is I knew way before you did." She paused, stopped walking, and looked at Eric. "Remember Tommy?"

"Yeah, how I could I forget a douche like that," Eric said and rolled his eyes.

"He turned out to be a douche, but at first, I really liked that guy. I thought maybe I even loved him." Eric looked uncomfortable. "I know you don't like hearing about my exes any more than I like hearing about yours, but they're part of our history as people and a couple. My point is this, when he abruptly dumped me, I felt devasted. At first, I was sad, I cried. Then I was mad, like pissed off spitting mad. I punched my pillows. I threw shit around my room. I felt like I had lost something so special, and I didn't even know why. I felt like I'd never have that relationship feeling again. You know that calmness and that peace that comes with being in a relationship. Like you don't worry about anything except you and your partner. It's a good feeling even if it isn't with the right person."

Rachel paused and chuckled to herself. She knew she was rambling, and Eric was getting more and more confused. She could see it all over his face.

"Now look who's rambling," she chuckled. "What I'm trying to say is, I never had that feeling with you. When we broke up the first time, I was sad, but I never got mad or any other emotion over it. Partly because we stayed such good friends but mostly because I knew that wasn't the end. It was just a break. I've always known you and I would be together forever. We weren't ready for life-long commitment at that time. We both played the field a bit during the break. No biggie, we were young. I think if we hadn't broken up when we did, we wouldn't be where we are now. If we had forced it back then, we woulda ended up possibly hating each other. And I've hated you many times, Eric, but never to the point where I don't want to see you." She paused and looked past Eric to the lake. "Let me rephrase that, I hated the things you did, I never actually hated you. I love you Eric Palmer and I want to be Rachel Palmer someday, but only if I see those changes. Only if we can move on and learn from what we've put each other through. I haven't been perfect either, but the things you've done will take a while for me to come to terms with. I am willing to do that though, because I believe in us. I know that was a long answer to your question. Do you get what I'm trying to say?"

"I think so," Eric replied. "You're saying despite all of our ups and downs, despite my behavior, you always knew we'd be together. Are you saying that we needed to grow up before we could grow together?"

"Yes, exactly. You remember why we even started dating back then right?"

"Yeah, we were having sex, so it just seemed like the next logical step."

"Precisely and it was a mistake," Rachel said. "We shoulda just fucked and called it good at that. It was, and still is, mind blowing. Dating put pressure on us that we were too young to handle. Then I dropped the 'L' word and that was that. But you know why it was too much to handle? Why no other relationship felt like it had that kind of pressure? Or why neither of us have ever dated someone for more than six months- and even the six-month ones were rare?"

"Um, no, why?" Eric asked, somewhat confused but suddenly very relieved.

"Because we are meant to be together," Rachel replied. "We are each other's one. Even back when we were young, we knew that to be true. That's why there was all of that pressure. That's why we never felt it with anyone else. They weren't our one, so if we lost them, it was no big deal. Sure, it sucked at first, but we quickly got over it. Now that we're pushing thirty and have had life experience, we're finally ready to be together forever. You would've never had your epiphany if you weren't ready. I still wanna see the changes but I know you're all in."

"I never thought of it that way," Eric said and looked deep into her eyes. "That makes a lot of sense. And for the record, I don't hate hearing about your exes, I hate how those fuckers treated you."

"I know, it's different for us than others. We were around when we were dating other people. Most of the time you get into a relationship and tell your new person about your past. You and I lived it all together and I wouldn't change any of it. In fact, I feel so relieved, so happy and elated now, today, in this moment with you, that I wouldn't change a fuckin' thing! Every action, every decision, every emotion, led us to this precise moment. I strongly believe that."

Eric watched as tears streamed down her face. Tears welled up in his eyes as well. He let them escape and roll down his cheeks. Rachel was the most beautiful woman in the world. All the way around, inside and out. Head to toe dynamite. Perfection wrapped up in a beautiful 5'7" frame. Rachel was right about everything. Eric had blamed himself for being a fuck up, and he certainly had been exactly that, but he now understood that he needed to be that fuck up. He needed to make those mistakes and poor decisions. It seemed weird to think like that, but they did kind of need to hurt each other. They needed to see how much they meant to each other. Eric would spend the rest of his days showing Rachel she was his world.

"I believe it too," Eric said. "There is nowhere in the world I'd rather be right now. I don't know what life has in store for us, but I'm not worried about a damn thing anymore. Together we will kick life's ass and take names! We are a rockstar couple!"

Rachel smiled and laughed at that. He was right, together they would conquer the world.

"I love you, you dork!" Rachel giggled.

"I love you."

Eric kissed her. They kissed for a while before setting off on the path again. They walked in silence, both with huge smiles on their faces. Eric knew there was no chance he'd fuck it up again. He was all in until the day he died. He felt new. Like a brand-new man. Rachel relieved every stress he had. Rachel knew he wouldn't fuck it up again. She saw and heard a difference in the way he spoke about it. He was calm and confident. The way he looked at her had changed too, like she was the only thing that existed. The way his eyes danced over her entire body and face was new too. The way he held eye-contact had intensified. He looked into her not just at her. She had butterflies about it all, but they were the good kind.

She did have a nagging feeling she couldn't explain. It was a feeling of doom, like something bad was going to happen. It didn't feel like it had anything to do with their relationship, but it did include them both.

She pushed it aside, telling herself it was a nervous anxiousness about recommitting to each other. It wasn't, but that's what she told herself.

*****

Mathew woke up from his nap and stretched. He could smell the sweet, metallic smell of blood as he walked down the hall to the kitchen. He felt dehydrated and went to the fridge. Mathew grabbed a Gatorade and chugged the whole bottle. It hit the spot. He stood in the entryway to the kitchen and dining room. He looked at his dad and then at his mom in the living room. They didn't look real anymore. They looked more like movie props. The blood on and around their bodies had started to dry already. There was something fascinating, and sickly satisfying, about how their blood pooled around them.

It dawned on Mathew that he had wanted to do that for a long time. He loved his parents, especially his father, but he hated them too. He hated how hypocritical they were, again, especially his father. His mother acted like a doting, loving mother around others, but behind closed doors she was distant, aloof, and stoned out of her mind on pain pills. How did she even keep a supply of those damned pills? Oh, well, that was of no concern anymore. His father acted like a loving, firm, devoted father around the church crowd. He'd brag about his kids and their many accomplishments in school and the church, most of which were greatly exaggerated to make him look better. At home, though, when no one else could see, he was an abusive alcoholic. Mostly verbal abuse, but he had laid hands on each one of them more than once. Mr. Simpson never hit any of them where the bruises couldn't be covered by clothing. The one time he smacked their mother across the face, he made her tell people she had walked into a cupboard door she had left open. Who knows if anyone actually believed that or not? Mr. Simpson didn't care, that was the story in his mind.

Mathew smiled to himself and grabbed the knife off the kitchen counter. The blood on the knife had already dried. Mathew went to the sink and cleaned the blade. He got out the knife sharpener and gave the blade a sharper edge. He wiped it clean with the kitchen towel and smiled. Next were the loud, drunk neighbors down the road.

They would be difficult to dispatch. The two men were quite a bit larger than him, but they were old, fat, and drunk. He'd have to figure out a way to separate the men and kill them individually. But how could he do that? Those three seemed like they were always together. They probably did some sick three-some shit like he'd seen on the videos he used to watch. Disgusting, sexual deviants. Mathew was looking forward to eliminating them from his world. He'd get great pleasure out of this mission.

Mathew had an idea. Maybe if he stepped outside and let out one of those blood-curdling screams again, those drunks would investigate. Then he could sneak into their cabin and hide, biding his time until he could catch one of them alone. A quick slice of the throat and they'd go down quietly, without alerting the other to his presence.

He stepped out onto the porch and let out a long, high-pitched scream. Mathew stood on the porch with the knife held behind his back and waited. He saw some teenagers light a cherry bomb down the road and then run. The bomb went off and got the attention of everyone nearby. The three drunks ran after the kids. Perfect! Mathew rushed to their cabin and snuck in. He looked out the window and saw the three drunks standing in the middle of the road, bent over panting. Mathew laughed at the sorry sight of them and went to the bedroom. One room was obviously occupied by a couple and the other by just one man. Mathew hid in the closet of the single man's room. If he could kill that man, the woman and other man should be easy enough to handle.

Mathew didn't have to wait as long as he thought he would. He heard the three come back in, cussing and carrying on about those "goddamn fuckin' punk kids!" One man said his shirt got too sweaty and he was going to change real quick. The nice thing about those cabins were, they were small enough you could hear everything from anywhere inside.

Mathew peered around from the back of the closet. The closet was empty, Mathew knew the man would not be fetching a clean shirt from the closet. Mathew highly doubted that man even owned a truly clean shirt. What a disgusting looking man. He was pudgy, hairy, unkempt, and Mathew thought he could even smell the guy as he walked in. The man was still wheezing and muttering cuss words under his breath.

The man turned away from the closet door and opened a backpack on the bed. As he rummaged through the backpack, Mathew slipped out of the closet. He slowly and quietly snuck behind the man. Mathew froze as the man stood up straight. The dark-haired man grabbed the bottom of his stinky, sweaty shirt with both fat hands and tugged it up. As soon as the shirt covered the man's head, Mathew stabbed him between the ribs. The man gasped and let go of his shirt. He put both hands to his side where Mathew had just stabbed him. Mathew grabbed the man's greasy black hair and pulled his head back. In one, quick, sweeping motion, Mathew slit his throat and let go of him. The dark-haired man slumped over onto the bed and bled out.

Mathew smiled at his handy work and wiped the blade clean on the sheets of the bed. He had to act quickly, the other two would be looking for this guy soon. Mathew walked to the open door and stood there, listening for the others. He could hear them clanking around in the kitchen, probably making more alcohol drinks. Fuckin' drunks! Dirty, nasty people.

The man on the bed loudly coughed and gurgled his last breaths. The clanking in the kitchen abruptly stopped. They had heard that too. Mathew ducked down the hall quickly and into the bathroom. He stepped behind the door and peered through the back of the door and doorframe. The others did come to check out the noise. The woman shrieked as soon as she walked into the bedroom. The balding man took one look into the room, turned away from the doorway, and emptied his stomach onto the hallway carpet.

That made Mathew giggle. He dashed out of the bathroom and buried the knife into the balding man's belly. Mathew pulled it out quickly and drove it into that fat belly again. The man swatted at Mathew but had no strength. He fell to the floor in a heap. The woman shrieked again but didn't move. She stood there in the doorway staring at Mathew. Mathew smiled at her and walked toward her. She still didn't move. Strange, but made Mathew's job a lot easier.

Mathew looked her in the eyes and slit her throat. Her eyes widened as she fell to the floor. Mathew wiped the blade off on her shirt. He went to the kitchen. Mathew was looking through cupboards and drawers. He could hear the balding man whimpering on the hall floor. He went to the man and slit his throat. That was an extremely efficient was of dispatching the sinners. Mathew went back to the kitchen. He searched the cupboards and drawers again until he found a box of wood matches. He lit the tablecloth on fire. He walked to each window and set every curtain ablaze. Mathew let himself out the back door. He wandered off toward his cabin.

"That was stupid," God said in his head.

"I know," Mathew said, dropping his head.

"I thought I had tapped the right instrument for the job."

"I'll put it out!" Mathew shouted and ran back to the cabin.

The flames hadn't spread much, but they were hot. Mathew pulled all the burning curtains down and stomped them out. He grabbed a large pot, filled it with water from the sink and started dousing the rest of the flames. After several pots of water, he finally got all the flames out.

"No more flashy stuff," the Lord said.

"Sorry, My Father, I don't know what I was thinking. That would have gotten fire up here quick."

"Right. Carry on, My Son."

"Thank you," Mathew said and bowed. "I will be smarter."

"You better or I'll banish you and tap another."

"Yes, My Lord."

With that the gravely, hissing voice of God was gone again. What a dumb thing to do! Why did I do that?! Stick to the plan!

Mathew shook it off and ran back to his cabin. He didn't know how much longer he could hide out there, the smell was starting to get to him. He'd just have to move along with the rest of his mission more quickly than he had hoped.

God hadn't specifically told him to dispatch the teenagers, but maybe their cabin bore his mark. Either way they would pose a problem for him. Mathew decided he would kill them no matter what before he got to Eric and his heathen friends. Then, finally, his whore sisters.

*****

"Shit, man, you ever wish we could order pizza up here?" Leo said, letting out a lung-full of pot smoke.

"Geno's Pizza down there in Lake City delivers up here, but it takes forever, and the pizza is always cold and soggy by the time it arrives," Eric replied.

"Man, I'm just high enough that even cold, soggy pizza sounds fuckin' awesome," Leo chuckled.

"Then call it in," Eric said with a laugh. "I'm good with dogs and chips.

"Hey, why don't we get this card game going?" Aaron asked. "I'm dying to win everyone's money!"

"You mean lose your money to us?!" Leo said with a laugh. "Give me a few, I'm ordering pizza!"

The words, "I'm in," rang out throughout the cabin. Everyone grabbed drinks, snacks, pot pipes, and settled around the large dining room table. Gina made it a point to sit next to Deandre. Eric and Rachel sat next to each other. Aaron divided up chips. The ante was twenty bucks each. It'd be a nice pot to the winner. Genesis had never played poker before; gambling had always been a sin. She was excited to learn and get one more freedom for herself. From what everyone had told her about the game, it sounded fun. The strategy especially sounded fun.

"Damn!" Leo exclaimed as he joined the group at the table. "The pizza place said it's too late for them to take any orders up here. Some shit about a storm coming through."

"Bummer, bro," Eric said. "But, shit, we have so much food up here."

"Yeah, but dude, pizza sounded so fuckin' good!" Leo replied.

"Maybe tomorrow night," Eric suggested.

"Yeah, maybe," Leo replied.

Aaron gathered the money and tucked it into an envelope. He shuffled the cards while he talked shit to everyone. Aaron talked a big game when it came to poker, but he was a lousy poker player. He played every hand. The man refused to fold, so he lost almost every hand and was usually one of the first players out. Aaron would buy his way back in, making that already fat pot fatter. The guys loved playing poker with Aaron for that reason.

"Aaron let's play a few practice hands without betting money so Genny and Eve can get the hang of the game," Eric suggested.

"Sounds good," Aaron said and dealt the first hand.

Genesis and Eve got the hang of the game quickly. Eve had played poker before, the strip variety a few times, but never Texas Hold 'em. The poker hands and the strategy were mostly the same and Eve caught onto Hold 'em easily.

"Is there anywhere or anything you'd all rather be doing right now?" Aaron asked as he flung cards around the table.

"Not a damn thing!" Leo said, peaking at his hole cards.

"Me neither!" Eric said and smiled at Rachel.

"A root canal would be cool but for now this'll do," Ozzy joked.

"You're a dork," Rachel said to Ozzy.

"I love it up here," Gina said glancing around the room. She smiled at Dre.

"Me too," Deandre said with a smile.

"Who's ready to play for real now?" Aaron asked, gathering up the cards.

They all agreed they were ready to wager on hands. All the cabin windows and doors were open to let in the fresh early evening air. Off in the distance, they thought they heard a woman shriek. They glanced around at each other and shook it off. Damn teenagers again. Drinks were refilled and it was time to play poker for real.

Aaron let Genesis deal the first hand. She dealt everyone some good cards and the pot got huge. Leo and Ozzy folded after the flop; it was getting too rich for their cards. Everyone else stayed in until the end. Genesis ended up winning the pot with a straight.

"Beginner's luck!" Eric chuckled.

"Or she cheated!" Aaron laughed.

Genesis blushed as she pulled in the large pile of chips. Eve collected the cards and began to shuffle them. The wind was kicking up outside, creating a nice cross breeze through the cabin. The mid-summer, early evening air was still warm, but it felt nice to have any kind of breeze. The skies were becoming overcast, and the breeze began to smell like rain was coming again.

Oh, well, they weren't going anywhere, and the porch was covered for smoke breaks. It would be a beautiful and calming setting for a night of drinks, laughter, and poker. After another thirty minutes or so, the skies opened and dumped rain. Thunder and lightning filled the dark skies. The storm created an eerie atmosphere but at the same time it was really cool.

They all took a break from cards and went outside to watch the storm. Bolts of lightning cracked over the violent waters of the lake. Thunder roared overhead. It was frightening and beautiful. Eric held Rachel close as they smoked and watched the storm. Deandre had taken Gina into his arms. Aaron had offered to hold Genesis or Eve but they both flatly said no, they were fine. Genesis was starting to get a creepy vibe from Aaron. She tried to ignore it because she knew he was one of Eric's best friends but the way he kept checking her and Eve out was beginning to bother her. Leo was stoned out of his mind and coupled with all the shots of tequila he had done; he was barely able to stand. It looked like it was going to be a rough night for him. Ozzy stood behind everyone else in awe of the storm. He loved that kind of stuff. He had his phone out and was taking photos and video of the storm.

"This is like the perfect setting for some horror flick," Ozzy said, breaking the silence. "You know like one of those slasher flicks."

"Why you always gotta say shit like that?" Eric said, chuckling.

"Just sayin'," Ozzy laughed. "None of that shit happens in real life anyway. But just in case, no one fuck tonight. The people fuckin' in those movies always die first."

"Shut the hell up you drunk bastard," Aaron said chuckling because everyone else was. He didn't like what Ozzy was saying at all.

"Does that mean I'd be first to die too cus I'm black?" Deandre asked laughing.

"Hey, man, I wasn't gonna go there," Ozzy said.

"Enough talk like that," Rachel said. "It's spooky enough out here without you guys talking about people getting killed."

Leo ran off into the woods behind the cabin and threw up. He was back there for a bit emptying his stomach. Went too hard too fast. Leo stumbled back up onto the porch. He told his friends he was going to lie down. He wandered into the cabin and crashed out on the couch. The rest of the group stayed outside and watched the storm. It was still warm out. The sound of the rain pounding the roof was loud and soothing. Lightning flashed and the thunder boomed.

They heard multiple footsteps on the wet pavement of the road. They were moving quickly. Eric put his hand to his belt for his pistol, but he didn't have it on him. The teenagers they had seen setting off fireworks earlier rounded the small bend in the road. They were soaked and looked spooked. As they got closer, everyone realized they were older teenagers, they had probably just graduated high school that year. There were four of them, two guys and two girls.

"We lost power at our cabin," one of the guys said.

"Sorry to hear that," Eric said. "You all got candles and flashlights?"

"No, we didn't bring nothin' like that," the same guy replied.

"I'll give you a couple candles and cheap flashlights but we gotta keep some in case we lose power too. Be right back," Eric said and headed into the cabin.

Eric laughed at Leo passed out on the couch as he strolled by. Leo had both arms pulled into his wet t-shirt. Eric grabbed his cheap back-up flashlights and some candlesticks. He went back outside. Eric handed the flashlights and candles to the teenagers.

"Thanks," the same guy said.

"Did you check your breaker box?" Deandre asked. "Looks like no one else lost power 'round here. Maybe you guys blew a breaker."

"We don't know how to," the same guy said.

"If your cabin is like mine," Eric began, "the breaker box is in the outbuilding with the hot water heater. Come here, I'll show you what to look for."

"We don't have an outbuilding," the guy said.

"Well, then it'll most likely be on the back of the cabin. Up near the roof," Eric said. "Doesn't matter where it is, it'll look like the same as mine."

Eric took the group of teenagers around to his outbuilding. He showed them the breaker box and how to check for flipped breakers. They thanked him and headed back to their place. Eric could tell they were waiting on an invitation to stay there, but he had no intention of doing that. They were a packed house already. He certainly did not want those immature teens hanging around. They had drama and annoying written all over them. Especially those girls. They looked like the attention hungry valley girl types. Even in the pouring rain and clearly frightened, those girls stood in a certain way to show themselves off to the guys. Probably to the girls too.

"They were hoping for an invite to stay here," Gina said as the teenagers walked away slowly.

"Hell yeah, they were," Eric said. "No way in hell I was gonna invite them though."

"Fuck that! They'd drive us nuts," Ozzy said.

"I think we should've," Aaron said, watching as the teenagers rounded the small bend.

"Yeah, of course you do," Deandre said rolling his eyes. "You just want the eye candy, you sick bastard."

"No, that ain't it, Dre!" Aaron replied defensively. "I just think it would've been nice to offer, especially if they ain't got power."

"They'll be fine," Eric said. "We don't have the room, and we sure don't want those punk teenagers hanging around."

"Whatever," Aaron said. "Anyone wanna get back to playing cards?"

"In a bit," Eric said. "I'm enjoying this storm."

They all returned their attention to the storm. They watched in silence for quite a bit. The smokers chain smoked.

*****

Mathew snuck around the back of the teenager's cabin. There was a large dent in the siding about eight feet off the ground. He smiled to himself; God had marked their cabin. He did want the teenagers dispatched after all. It made sense to Mathew those teens were clearly sinners. Mathew was relieved that he didn't have to go rogue on this one. After the fire incident he knew he was on thin ice with God already.

Mathew could hear the teens partying inside. The music was loud. As he walked around the far side of the cabin, he passed an open bedroom window. He peeked inside and saw two of the teens having relations in there. It sickened and excited him. What a perfect way to dispatch those sinners, in the middle of a sinful act.

Thunder boomed overhead and startled Mathew. He jumped back and tripped over a large rock. Mathew crashed to the ground, hitting his head on a tree. The impact knocked him out.

When Mathew came-to it was raining hard. The music inside the teenager's cabin had been turned off. Mathew stood and peeked through the bedroom window. The fornicators were gone. As the fog from being knocked out cleared more, he could hear voices out front. Shit, they were all outside. He could be discovered lurking around out back. Mathew looked around and saw a breaker box under the eve of the cabin. The box was unlocked so he opened it and flipped the main breaker. He heard the teenagers cuss and start to panic a bit. Mathew ducked into the woods and hunkered down. He waited to see what they would do.

After several minutes he watched as four teenagers wandered down the road. After they were out of sight, Mathew snuck into the cabin. Again, he waited in a bedroom closet. He knew by the time they all got back from wherever they had just gone, they'd be soaked and need to change. That's when he'd attack.

Mathew heard a noise from the bathroom. Someone was in there. He thought they had all left. The toilet flushed and the bathroom door opened. Mathew heard someone slowly walk down the hall. That someone walked into the bedroom. The cabin was dark, but he could tell it was a girl that had just walked in. She looked unsteady on her feet. Maybe the darkness? Or maybe she was drunk? Either way she looked like an easy target.

Mathew sprung from the closest and the girl shrieked. He quickly tackled her and covered her mouth with his left hand. She bit his hand hard. Mathew cried out in pain. The girl elbowed him in the ribs, and he gasped. She kicked his shin, and he let go of her. She tried to run past him back toward the door, but he sliced her leg with the knife. She screamed and fell to the floor. Mathew forced her onto her back. She was screaming and swinging her arms at him. She got a couple good hits to his face and neck. They pissed him off more than they hurt. As she swung at him, he sliced the knife through the air. He cut her arms and hands up good and she quit slapping at him.

"Be still," Mathew growled at her.

"Don't hurt me," she sobbed.

"It'll be over soon," he said to her.

"Please don't rape me," she bawled.

"What?!" Mathew yelled. "Why would I ever do such a thing? You are dirty and vile! You are a sinner, and I have been sent here by God to send you to hell!"

Mathew plunged the knife into the girl's heart. She went limp instantly. He yanked the blade out and watched as blood poured out of the wound. He was really beginning to like that part. He got off the girl. Mathew knew if the other teens came back and saw her, they'd run. He had to hide her body. He dragged her body under the bed. She gurgled and coughed, then her bowels let go. She was gone. Now he had that smell to deal with. By the time the others got home the whole place would smell of blood and defecation.

He needed a disguise. Some kind of face covering. If one, or more, of those other teens escaped, he did not want them to be able to identify him. A mask would be helpful in getting one over on Eric and his friends too. Maybe these dirty teenagers had something like that. Mathew dug a flashlight out of his pocket and started to search the closets, drawers, anywhere he thought he could find something to cover his face.

Mathew heard a large dog bark. He stopped in the middle of rummaging through one of the girls' backpacks. He hadn't seen or heard a dog all weekend. Where did that come from? Another deep, angry bark rang out, this time extremely close to the cabin. Mathew carefully went to the front window. He pulled open the curtain a crack and saw a twelve-foot-tall dog-headed man standing on the front porch. It barked, smiled, and vanished before his eyes.

Mathew suddenly felt stronger. He felt powerful and invincible. Was he even taller? Had his arms grown too? Naw, no way. He stared out the front window, frozen in shock and awe. He saw flashlights dancing up the road. The other teens were on their way back and they looked distracted. Like they were arguing with each other.

Mathew smiled and faded into the shadows of the dark cabin. This was going to be fun. Never mind the disguise, those teens looked dumb and distracted. He would have no problem releasing them to their Dark Lord.

Chapter Seven

Leo was lying on the couch. He felt a lot better. Throwing up and passing out for a bit had helped a lot. Stupid tequila! Leo looked around. He was still alone in the cabin. He thought he had heard someone come in a minute ago. He closed his eyes again. He felt like he could sleep a bit longer, even though he didn't want to sleep too long, he wanted to play more cards with his friends.

Leo felt pressure on his chest. It felt like someone was sitting on him. Suddenly he felt a knife-like stabbing pain in his side, just below his ribs. He popped his eyes open and saw a demon sitting on his chest. It had to be a demon. It had a tall, extremely skinny, man-like body but a big, ugly dog-head. It smiled at him and removed a bloody claw from his side. Leo gasped and snapped his eyes shut. The pressure went away, as did the pain in his side. When he opened his eyes, he was completely alone again. He put a shaky hand to his side. There was no wound, no pain, nothing.

"What a fucked-up dream," Leo muttered to himself.

He got up slowly and walked to the back door. Everyone else was still out on the porch watching the storm. Aaron looked annoyed and antsy. Aaron always looked like that when he wasn't getting his way. Leo assumed Aaron was done watching it rain and wanted to play cards again.

"You guys won't believe the dream I just had," Leo said to the group.

"Oh, hey! You're alive," Eric exclaimed, laughing.

"Yeah, sorry 'bout all that," Leo said embarrassed. "I went a little hard too fast. Gotta remember to pace myself."

"It's all good, bro," Deandre said. "We've all been there more times than we can count."

"What was the dream?" Rachel asked.

"Shit, it was fucked up," Leo began, "and so realistic! So, I was just lying on the couch snoozing, in my dream, that is, and it felt like someone was sitting on my chest. In my dream I thought it was one of you messing with me. Like at that point my eyes were still closed in my dream. Then I felt this stabbing pain in my side, right here under my ribs. That made me open my eyes and there was a fuckin' demon or some shit like that sitting on me. It had a head that looked like the meanest, nastiest dog ever. And the whole thing was so black. Like blacker than black itself, if that makes any sense. It's hard to explain. I still see it clear as day in my mind."

"Holy shit that sounds like a dogman!" Ozzy exclaimed. "I think a fuckin' dogman visited you!"

"Goddammit, Ozzy, quit with the horror bullshit already," Rachel scolded him. She hated that kind of talk; it freaked her out.

"Hey, I'm just saying, I've heard about shit like that," Ozzy said. He looked at Rachel, who looked pissed and scared. "But I know it was just a crazy tequila induced dream."

"Yeah, totally fucked up," Leo said shaking his head. "Sobered me up good, though!"

"I bet it did," Eric said. "That's some scary ass shit."

"I bet the drugs, tequila, and the storm all played a part in that," Rachel said, shooting Ozzy a 'shut up' look.

"Dreams are weird," Gina said. "Just last night I had a similar dream, except in mine I dreamt I was being chased by something like that. It was tall, abnormally skinny, and had a dog head."

"Fuck, I had a dream like that too," Aaron said. "It was last night too. In my dream the thing was chowing down on a really old deer carcass. I mean that deer stunk so bad in my dream that I could still smell it when I woke up this morning."

"Jesus Christ!" Rachel exclaimed. "I had a dream I was being chased by one of those things too, just like Gina."

"Has everyone had a dogman dream?" Ozzy asked with a tone of terror. "Cus, I did too last night. Mine was similar to Aaron's. The thing was eating a stank, old deer carcass. It looked up at me with blood-stained fangs and smiled. That's when I woke up sweating. Fuck, we should get the hell out of here! This isn't good. This is definitely a sign."

"I didn't dream anything like that," Eric said.

"Yeah, neither did I," Genesis said.

"Me neither," Eve added.

"Dre, how 'bout you?" Ozzy asked.

"I did too," Deandre said softly.

"Well, what was yours?" Ozzy asked after a long moment of silence.

"Same kinda thing," Dre started, "tall, stupid skinny motherfucker with a damn dog head chasing' my black ass around the woods. I tripped and fell, and the damn thing jumped on me. It raised its claw at me and that's when I woke up."

"We're getting the fuck outta here!" Ozzy exclaimed with panic in his voice.

"We ain't going anywhere," Eric said. "Besides Genny, is anyone here even sober enough to drive? Especially in this downpour?"

"Genny can drive us!" Ozzy exclaimed.

"How the fuck she gonna do that? We can't all fit in one rig and I don't think it's safe for anyone, sober or not, to be driving these mountain roads in this shit," Eric said. "Look, it's all just a weird coincidence. It's probably from that stupid horror movie you made us all go to last week. That movie had a creature just like what you're all describing."

"Then why didn't you dream about it too?" Ozzy asked. "It's weird that the only people who didn't dream about a dogman were the ones already up here."

"Why is that weird?" Eric asked. "I drank a lot last night, we were up half the night, and when we finally got to bed, I was out hard. I just didn't dream anything I guess."

"No, that ain't right," Ozzy said quietly. "It's gotta be a sign. Like a warning."

"What are you even talking about?" Eric asked. Everyone else had fallen completely silent. They all looked nervous and scared.

"I'm not even sure now," Ozzy started. "But I think we should try to leave. Something ain't right up here this time."

"He's right," Genesis said timidly. She felt put on the spot suddenly as everyone turned their attention to her. "I felt an evil presence last night."

"Genny, that was just stress and nerves from those kids fuckin' around all day yesterday," Eric said. "And pure exhaustion."

"Maybe it was," Genesis said.

"Gotta be, sis," Eve said. "I didn't dream about any creatures. I didn't feel any weird presence. The only evil up here is dad and Mathew. It feels totally normal to me."

"Look, guys, they say during lightning storms that people feel on-edge. They can even get a sense of being watched or that they're not alone. It's from the electromagnetic field getting amped up by the lightning, or some shit like that," Eric said. "We ain't going anywhere. There is no such thing as dogman, or ghosts, or demons, none of that shit's real."

"What if all that weird shit that you guys were telling us about yesterday wasn't those teenagers?" Ozzy asked. "What if there is a dogman or demon up here?"

"For fuck's sake, dude," Eric said, getting annoyed. "Lay off the weed, it's making you paranoid."

"You smoked more weed today than I have!" Ozzy exclaimed. He hated how dismissive Eric could be.

"All right, everyone enough!" Rachel snapped. "Eric, you aren't in charge. I love you but I don't think it's fair you get to say we ain't going anywhere and that's it. I do agree it's probably not safe to leave right now, but if the rain stops maybe we should consider it. I've only had two drinks, Gina's only had two, we're both fine to drive. Genesis is sober. Dre looks like he'd be good to drive. You, Aaron, and Leo aren't good, but the rest of us are. If we lay off the drinks, we'll be totally fine by the time the rain stops."

"You all tellin' me you wanna just leave over some weird dream?" Eric asked. "Dreams you all had cus you watch too many scary movies? None of this shit is real. A dogman ain't gonna come and eat us. There's no psycho out there killing people."

"We're saying we just wanna make leaving an option," Rachel said. "And if we all decide to do that, we all go."

"Fine," Eric sighed. "But I'm telling you we're safe up here. Safer here than anywhere else right now. All that weird shit yesterday *was* just punk kids fuckin' around. We all saw those shits lighting off fireworks today."

A huge, ground shaking boom of thunder cracked overhead, making everyone jump. Lightning lit up the sky. Genesis thought she saw a figure at the tree line when the lightning flashed, but she kept her mouth shut. Things were too tense already. She didn't want to add to it when she wasn't even sure she saw anything. Just her overactive imagination playing tricks on her again. Especially after all the dogman talk. Genesis knew what people called dogman was a demon. Demons could disguise themselves as whatever they wanted. She was worried that maybe they did have a demon lurking, and it presented itself to others in a form they'd recognize. Mathew accused her of inviting a demon into their lives by sinning so badly. How'd he put it? Her whore-ish ways had invited an evil that would haunt her forever? Something crazy like that.

Thunder and lightning raged above them. The lights in the cabin flickered.

"If we lose power, we're out of here, no debate," Ozzy said.

"Okay, we all need to calm down," Eric said in the calmest tone he could. "Let's go back inside, get a drink, and play some more poker. We need to relax and distract ourselves from this nonsense."

"I agree with Eric," Aaron said. He had been waiting to get back to cards for a while now.

"Sounds good to me," Deandre said. "It's starting to get chilly out here."

The group agreed it was time to head back in. The storm was beautiful and fun, but it was getting cold. The wind had picked up and was blowing moist air onto the porch. Everyone did get another drink. Rachel and Gina each grabbed a Truly, something weak in case they did have to drive later. Eric made a very strong Jack and

Coke. He was irritated with his friends, especially Rachel. Why would she call him out like that in front of everyone else? He'd have to ask her about that later. Ozzy frustrated him but Ozzy was always like that. He thought he knew everything. If he wasn't trying to school you on something, he was joking around. That's why Eric liked to call him Oswalt a lot, that was the only sure-fire way to shut the guy up for a bit. It bugged him so bad that he pouted about it for a while.

Once they all settled in around the table the heaviness they had felt outside dissipated. They all felt more comfortable and relaxed. No one talked about dogman or creepy dreams. No one mentioned the crazy happenings around the lake. They all sat around that oak table, played poker, and joked about the game. Soon, drinks started to flow more heavily and everyone, except for Genesis, started to get tipsy. That worried Genesis. If they did have to leave in a hurry, no one else in that cabin would be able to drive. Eve was tanked and that frustrated Genesis. She still didn't like seeing her sister getting drunk and smoking cigarettes. Genesis was getting used to the swearing, everyone there swore like sailors as her grandmother would've said.

It was getting late, and the rain seemed to be coming down even harder. The lightning and thunder had passed. The air in and around the cabin seemed lighter. That dark heaviness that had been out on the porch with them was gone. This was exactly what Eric had in mind when he told everyone to meet up at the cabin. Great friends sitting around a table, playing cards and shooting the shit. Drinks flowing, voices loud and happy. No tension. No animosity. Attitudes and tempers had flared earlier but that was all forgotten now. Laughter filled the room. Genesis had become quite the little card shark. She still had most of her original chips. Aaron had gone broke and bought back in twice. Both Leo and Ozzy were on their second buy in. This was what Poker Night was all about!

    Eric folded his hand before the flop. He sat back in his chair and looked around the table at his friends. They were all betting on their cards before the flop. Everyone looked so happy and relaxed. Eric saw smiles on every face at that table. Deandre looked up as Eric was looking at him. Dre smiled and nodded at his oldest friend. As if to say, "great idea, bro." Eric was pleased all that supernatural nonsense had died. After talking about religion and God with Genesis the day before and tonight the dogman BS, he was over all of it. He didn't believe any of it and he hated talking about all of it.

    Eric recalled a guy he had worked with, Corbin, who called himself spiritual. Corbin made it very clear that he wasn't religious. Spiritual was different. Corbin had said he believed in God but not like the religions do. He didn't believe God was the almighty creator of the world and everything in it. Corbin believed God was more of a force. A guiding force that made sure you got to your life's destination-what some call fate. Corbin said fate was just God getting us to where we needed to be. Corbin had said we have the illusion of free will. We convince ourselves that we are deciding what happens in our lives, but that wasn't the case at all. Corbin told Eric to think about his life up to that point. He asked Eric to give him examples of decisions he had made that impacted his life. Eric gave him a couple of examples, like taking the job at BigMart instead of a different job. That's where he met Aaron and Ozzy. He told Corbin that if he had taken the other job, he wouldn't have met some of his best friends.

Corbin told him that wasn't his decision, it had been God's. God directed him to BigMart because he was destined to meet those guys. Eric laughed at him and said it was just coincidence. He had based his decision on pay. He had actually wanted the other job more, but BigMart paid a buck-fifty more an hour. He had to take that. Eric told Corbin that he would've made friends at the other job too. Corbin said but not those guys. Those guys came into Eric's life for a reason, and they were put there by God. Eric tried to explain that he had met hundreds of people throughout his life and some stuck as friends, but most didn't. He had ex-friends that he had thought would be close friends forever. He had some friends he was surprised he even got along with. He told Corbin that he didn't believe in a God, or fate, or karma, or any of it. He said it's cool you do but it ain't the way I think. Corbin wouldn't let up though, he wasn't just telling Eric his opinion, he was trying to convince Eric that his beliefs were true. He was trying to get Eric to believe it as well, and that was precisely why Eric hated talking religion.

This group of friends all had their own beliefs and opinions. Luckily, they were all similar and mostly kept to themselves. No one in that room liked talking about religion. That's what Eric loved about these people, even though they did have different views and did argue sometimes, it never left a bitter taste in anyone's mouth. No one got their feelings hurt to a point of not wanting to be around anymore. There was a true, deep, family love amongst the group. A trust and bond that would have to be severed by a chef's knife.

An ear-piercing scream startled everyone at the table. They all looked up from their cards, glancing at each other. The screams intensified.

"Those goddamn fuckin' kids!" Eric exclaimed and banged his fist on the table.

"Let em be, babe," Rachel said. "We were all dumb kids once."

"Fine, but if they get any closer, I'm gonna go out there and tell em to knock it off. I just want some goddamn peace and quiet," Eric said and took a long sip of his drink. It was time for a refill.

*****

"I hope Chrystal isn't freaking out," Janey, one of the teenagers, said to the others.

"She's fine," Hunter, the taller of the two teenage boys, said, "it's just dark in there. It's not like she's in any danger."

"One of us shoulda stayed with her," Miley, the other girl, said.

"She said she didn't feel well," Hunter said. "She made all of us go, remember?"

"Yeah, she insisted," Conner added. "Too late now, we're already almost back."

"I just have a funny feeling," Janey said. "Like somethin' bad happened."

"It's the storm," Hunter said. "It's makes it creepy as fuck up here."

"I get that," Janey replied. "But this feeling is different. It's different than creepy storm feelings."

"You get paranoid when you drink, Janey," Hunter said, with a condescending chuckle.

"Fuck you, Hunter!" Janey snapped. "Just cus you're my older brother doesn't give you the right to talk down to me. I get sick of your shit!"

"I wasn't talking down to you. I was stating the obvious," Hunter said. "Does anyone else have a bad feeling?" The others said no. "See, Janey, it's just you. You always do this when you get drunk. You think the world is ending around you."

"Fuck off," Janey said and slowed down to fall behind her brother and the others. Miley fell back with Janey.

Hunter always said stuff like that, and it drove her nuts. He liked to pick on her in front of others. Someday she was going to knock him out. They were rounding the corner, and she could see their dad's cabin. They were lucky their dad let them use the cabin so much. It was nice to get up there and just party with their friends. Well, Hunter's friends at least. Miley was her only friend up there. Hunter was dating Chrystal and Conner went wherever Hunter went. He was like Hunter's little shadow. Janey never could figure that out. Conner was a cool dude and Hunter overpowered him all the time. The only reason Janey even bothered with any of it was to go to the cabin. Her dad wouldn't let her go unless Hunter was going too.

Janey looked up at the dark cabin and thought she saw the curtains move, as if someone had been looking out the window a second ago. Probably just Chrystal looking for them approaching. She'd be bounding out of the door any minute. She was at Hunter's side almost twenty-four-seven. Janey couldn't stand Chrystal and her overly fake, bubbly personality. That girl acted dumb so guys would do everything for her. And Hunter ate that shit up!

"Your brother's a dick," Miley said. "I know I say it a lot, but it's true."

"I know he is and worst of all, he does too! He knows you and I can't come up here without him and he uses that to control us. Sometimes I fuckin' hate him."

"He wasn't always a dick," Miley said. "When we were little, he seemed cool."

"After mom and dad split, Hunter turned into an asshole," Janey explained. "He didn't handle it well. That's when me and you couldn't hang out cus my mom moved us away."

"Yeah, that sucked."

"Well, Hunter hated her for it. Still does. She used us to get back at my dad for leaving her, but she deserved it. She was cheating on him, you know."

"No, I didn't know. You never told me that," Miley replied, surprised by the news.

"Yeah, well, once they went to court the judge said she couldn't move us away from our school and our dad. They had to have joint custody. Well, that didn't fit her lifestyle so that's how we ended up living with dad full time."

"How come you're just now telling me this?"

"I dunno, I never wanted to talk about it. I figured all anyone needed to know was that dad got custody and that's why we moved back. My point was all that fucked with Hunter. The back and forth. Mom and dad fighting all the time. Their attention wasn't on him for the first time ever. The big, bad football star wasn't getting the daily praise he needed for his fragile little ego. Turned him into the dick we now see in front of us."

"When's he leaving for college?" Miley asked.

"Two weeks, and that ain't soon enough!"

"I hear you talking shit back there!" Hunter yelled over his should.

"Fuck you!" Janey yelled.

"Quit saying that to me! I'm your older brother show some fuckin' respect!"

"You're only older by eleven months! So, fuck off!" Janey shouted at him.

Hunter didn't yell anything back. He usually didn't when she told him to "fuck off." It was about the only thing he couldn't reply to. It effectively ended his tirade. It meant I'm done. He knew there was no point in continuing to rag on her. All she would do was just say, "fuck off," over and over.

They got to the driveway of the cabin. Hunter stopped them at the road. He told the girls to wait outside while he and Conner went to make sure everything was okay.

"I thought you said there was nothing to be worried about," Janey said in a mocking tone.

"Well, I changed my mind. I have a bad feeling now," Hunter said. "I thought I saw someone looking out the window when we rounded the corner. It looked too big to be Chrystal. Just wait here," Hunter said.

"In the pouring rain?" Janey asked, irritated with him.

"You're already soaked!" Hunter exclaimed. "Ten more minutes won't kill you!"

"Fine! Hurry up!" Janey said and crossed her arms.

Janey and Miley walked to the far edge of the driveway and stood under a large tree. The tree kept most of the rain off them, but they were still getting wet. Janey was fuming. First, Hunter said she was being paranoid and now he's making her wait outside while he acts like some big old hero. He could be such a dick!

*****

Mathew stood behind the door and waited for the teenagers to open it. It wasn't going to be easy to take down four people, but he knew he had to. He needed to get the boys first. One of them looked tall and fit walking up the road. That guy looked like an athlete. He'd put up a good fight. Mathew knew he needed the element of surprise. Hopefully they would still be distracted by their bickering, and they'd all just wander in not paying attention to anything else. The smell from the back bedroom would alert them to something being wrong, but by that point Mathew would have had got at least one of them. Damn, he was looking forward to that!

The door slowly opened. A flashlight beam danced around the dark living room. Mathew's heart jumped in excitement. He clenched the handle of the knife harder. The tall guy stepped into the room, followed closely by the other guy. They were alone! Their chivalry had just made his job a whole lot easier! Those whore girls would be easy to dispatch alone.

Mathew slammed the front door shut, startling both guys. The short one swiveled around and Mathew buried the knife into his throat. The guy's eyes got huge, and he went limp. Mathew pulled the knife out and the guy crumpled to the ground.

"What the fuck?!" Hunter screamed and back-peddled away from Mathew.

Mathew stepped over Conner's body and slowly walked toward Hunter. Hunter swung his flashlight at Mathew, but he dodged it easily. Hunter stumbled and crashed into an end table, knocking a lamp off. The lamp shattered. Mathew swiped at him with the knife, grazing Hunter's forearm. Hunter let out another scream and stumbled backward again. Mathew seized his opportunity and tackled the off-balance young man.

Hunter struggled and tried to fight off Mathew. Mathew stabbed Hunter in the leg. Hunter grabbed at his throbbing leg. Mathew put a knee into Hunter's groin. He kneed Hunter over and over as Hunter gasped for air. Mathew finally put him out of his misery by burying the knife into Hunter's heart. He yanked the blade out. Mathew's favorite part followed. The last few squirts of blood leaked out of Hunter's chest as the young man's eyes glazed over.

*****

Janey watched with angry eyes as her brother and Conner tip-toed up the steps. Hunter slowly opened the unlocked front door and shined his flashlight inside. He flipped the flashlight beam around the front room before taking a cautious step inside the door. He looked back at Conner right behind him and nodded. The two walked inside.

The door slammed violently shut. Janey shook her head and looked at Miley. Those two guys were always so dramatic.

"I think they're fuckin' with us," Janey said and rolled her eyes.

"No doubt," Miley said. "They like to act all tough and shit."

"I hate it," Janey said.

They heard a loud crash and a scream from the cabin.

"Seriously guys?!" Janey yelled.

"They're making fun of you now," Miley said. "Hunter is going overboard to show you how paranoid he thinks you are."

"For sure! Fuckin' dick!"

They heard more crashing around and something shattered.

"Sounds like they're tearing the place apart," Miley said with a tone of concern.

"That doesn't sound good," Janey said softly. "Hunter wouldn't break shit just to prove a point. He knows dad wouldn't let us come back up here if we destroy the place."

The door swung open and a tall, skinny man stepped out. He was holding a bloody knife. The man looked at them with a smile that sent shivers up their spines. Janey and Miley screeched, and that made the man laugh. He bounded off the porch toward them. Janey and Miley turned and ran for the cabin they had just come from. Hopefully those people would take them in. Hopefully those people had guns!

Miley tripped and fell. Janey stopped to help her, but the man was on top of Miley before she could even get to her knees. He swung the knife at Janey, slicing her calf open. Janey screamed and stumbled backward, almost falling down. Miley was bawling and kicking at the man sitting on her mid-section. The man looked

Janey in the eyes. His eyes were dark and sinister. They looked dead, void of all light. He smiled at Janey and buried his knife all the way into Miley's chest. Miley gasped and her limbs fell still. Her chest heaved and she coughed up blood. The man looked down at that. Once he dipped his head, Janey took off running again. It hurt like hell, but she ran, nonetheless.

Janey looked back and saw the man yank the knife out of Miley. He jumped to his feet, smiling. Janey stumbled on her bum leg but kept her balance. She rounded the slight bend and started screaming. The man disappeared into a dark cabin. Janey didn't slow down.

*****

"What the fuck?!" Eric growled. "Now they're screaming right outside!"

Eric got up and went to the front door. He opened the door expecting to see those damn kids screwing around. Ungrateful little shits, after he loaned them flashlights and candles!

"Holy shit! Guys! Come quick!" Eric yelled and bolted out the front door.

One of the teenage girls was limping up the road toward his cabin screaming and crying. Even in the dark, Eric could tell her leg was bleeding badly. Eric rushed to her. As soon as she saw him coming, she quit screaming and crumpled to the ground. Eric bent down next to her.

Everyone from the cabin gathered around him and the girl. She was bawling as she clutched at her bloody leg.

"Holy fuck that looks bad!" Rachel said, as she knelt next to the girl's leg.

"What happened?" Eric asked.

"Guy stabbed Miley," the girl sobbed.

"What guy? One of your friends?" Eric asked.

"No, scary man. Dark eyes, black clothes," the girl sobbed.

"Let's get her inside," Eric said, looking up at the others.

Eric picked the girl up and Rachel carried her legs. The gash in her leg was deep. It needed stitches and a lot of them.

"Get towels and blankets," Eric told the room as they all walked into the cabin.

Gina and Deandre went to the back rooms and came back quickly with towels and blankets. Eric motioned for them to lay out the towels on the couch. Once they did that, he carefully laid the girl down on the couch. Gina draped a thick blanket over her.

"What's your name?" Rachel asked, kneeling beside the girl.

"Janey," the girl whimpered. "Miley's dead."

"Dre, guys, let's go check around," Eric said.

"Wait," Rachel said, "let's see if she can tell us anything else first. Can you do that, Janey?"

"Can I get some tissues?" Janey cried.

Gina went to the bathroom and brought back a roll of toilet paper.

"Thank you," Janey said, ripping off a chunk of toilet paper.

Janey wiped her eyes and nose. She sat up a bit and looked around. She counted nine twenty-somethings. Five strong looking men in that room. They could protect her.

"Call the police," Janey said, tears still streaming down her face. "I think that man killed my brother and his friend too."

"What happened exactly?" Rachel asked.

"When we got back my brother, Hunter, was worried so he made me and Miley wait outside. We heard all sorts of commotion and things breaking inside the cabin after he and Conner went in. At first, we thought they were fuckin' around like they always do. Then this man dressed in all black steps out of the cabin with a huge knife! Like the biggest one from a kitchen knife set. He laughed at us and then chased us," Janey paused as the tears took her over again. She sobbed for several minutes before continuing. "Miley fell. I tried to help her, but that man sliced my leg then he just stabbed her. Right in front of me, in the middle of the road, he stabbed her in the chest!" Janey wailed.

"Jesus," Eric muttered. "Come on guys! Let's go find that guy!"

"Wait! Didn't you hear what she just said?" Gina asked.

"Yeah, there's a guy with a knife stabbing people out there!" Rachel added. "Don't be heroes. Stay here where it's safe."

"I got this bad boy!" Eric exclaimed and pulled the pistol from his belt.

"Good, we'll need it if that psycho comes here!" Rachel exclaimed. "Stay here and wait for the cops with us."

"We gotta go check it out, babe!" Eric said. "Maybe we can help her friend? Dre has a gun too, right Dre?"

"You bet I do," Deandre replied, lifting his shirt to show the pistol in his waistband.

"Guys, please, stay here," Gina pleaded.

"Come on, boys, seriously, you don't gotta be heroes," Rachel said. "Eric, don't leave, please!"

"Baby, we'll be fine. I promise. I love you so much. I will come back to you. This is something we gotta do," Eric said, putting his arms around Rachel's waist.

"Please, stay," she begged.

"I have to check it out," he replied. "I can't just stay here and wait. The five of us are armed and we outnumber whatever crazy asshole is out there. We will just check it out and be right back, okay?"

Rachel knew she, nor Gina, or anyone else, could stop those guys. Once their minds were made up, they weren't getting changed.

"Fine!" Rachel snapped. "But please be careful and be quick."

"We will, baby," Eric said and gave her a kiss. "We'll be right back."

Eric and the guys walked out front, clicking on their flashlights. The rain had stopped and there was a full moon hanging in the night sky.

"Jesus, it reeks of antifreeze out here," Ozzy said.

"That's my truck," Aaron replied. "It's got a leak. I just haven't had the time to get it fixed."

They walked down the road toward the Simpson cabin. The Simpson's cabin was completely dark. They were probably asleep already. It didn't matter, none of them wanted to deal with the Simpsons. They could see Nina and Josh's cabin. Their cabin was also completely dark. Had they left already? Further down the road was yet another completely dark cabin. Maybe there had been a power outage? Maybe the Simpson cabin and the others were on a different transformer than Eric's?

"Didn't that girl say her friend was killed in the road?" Deandre asked, stopping and looking around with his flashlight.

"Yeah, I thought so," Ozzy replied.

"Then where's the body?" Deandre asked.

"Maybe it was down the road the other way," Eric said. "We need to keep an eye out for a man with a knife right now."

"Better believe we are!" Aaron replied.

"I met the people that live in the next cabin. Let's see if they're still here," Eric said.

Eric and Aaron went up to the front door. Deandre and the others waited in the road, keeping an eye out in every direction. Eric knocked on the door and it opened. He looked at Aaron who just gave him a shrug.

"Nina? Josh?" Eric hollered into the cabin. His voice bounced around the empty front room. It smelled like smoke in there. "It's Eric! We met last night! We're coming in!"

Eric and Aaron walked into the front room. There was nothing in that room except for a heavy, old, hide-a-bed couch. The smell of smoke was strong. The molding around the naked front windows was singed. Aaron and Eric walked to the bedrooms. The bedrooms were a complete disaster. Everything had been gone through and just tossed wherever.

"What the fuck?" Aaron whispered.

"Fuck if I know," Eric replied.

"I don't like this at all," Aaron said.

"Let's get outta here," Eric said. "Those people I met last night clearly moved out and just left the junk they didn't wanna take with them."

"Maybe, but this looks like it's been ransacked. And what the fuck is that smell?!"

"Mice, I think," Eric replied, regretfully sniffing the air. "Smells like dead mice."

"That wouldn't surprise me in this mess," Aaron said turning to head back into the front room.

"Come on," Eric said, "We need to check out that far cabin."

"No one home in that one?" Deandre asked after Eric and Aaron returned from Nina and Josh's cabin.

"Nope, and it's fuckin' trashed," Aaron replied.

"Like trashed how?" Deandre asked.

"Like someone broke in and just trashed the place. Shit thrown around everywhere except for the living room," Aaron said. "Broken bottles and glasses all over the counters and floor in the kitchen."

"Jesus, that isn't good," Ozzy said. "It must be the dude with the knife!"

"We still gotta find that fucker," Eric said.

"What if he's killing the girls as we speak?" Ozzy asked with panic in voice.

"Oh, for fuck's sake, Ozzy! Why would you say that?!" Eric yelled at him.

"Cus it could be happening!" Ozzy turned and ran back toward Eric's cabin.

"Dre, go with him! I have my phone, call me and let me know what's going on," Eric snapped.

"You got it!" Deandre replied and ran after Ozzy.

Eric knew everyone at the cabin was fine. Dre had a line of sight on the cabin the whole time they had been gone. Eric thought about it and decided one of them ought to stay at the cabin. Not even ten minutes later, Dre called Eric and said everything at the cabin was fine. Everyone was scared but they were all fine. He told Eric the main road had been washed out. Eric muttered a few choice words and told Dre to send Ozzy back, but to stay there. Eric wanted someone with a gun at the cabin. Minutes later Ozzy returned.

"Feel better?" Eric asked.

"Yeah, man, it just dawned on me that there's a dude with a fuckin' knife killing people and we left the girls all alone."

"Supposedly, there's a dude with a knife," Eric said. "We haven't found any bodies yet, or blood anywhere."

"That girl was sliced up good," Ozzy said. "She saw her friend get killed."

"We're all on high alert," Eric said. "If that dude's still around, he's gotta be hiding out in one of these dark cabins. Let's check out that last one."

They went to the far cabin. This time Ozzy and Leo stayed right out front. Aaron and Eric cautiously entered the cabin. It smelled like shit in there. The place was a wreck. It looked like the place had been burglarized and then trashed, worse than Nina and Josh's.

"Good God! It smells like human shit in here!" Aaron exclaimed, covering his nose with his shirt.

"Let's make this quick," Eric said, also covering his nose with his shirt.

"Make what quick?" Aaron asked, dancing his flashlight beam around the trashed front room. "Looks like no one's been here in ages. And ain't no way a murderer is hiding out in here with that smell."

"This would be *exactly* where a knife-wielding psycho would hide out. They would expect people to think precisely the way you are."

"Okay, what are we gonna do if he is in here somewhere? He's got the upper hand."

"Shoot him!" Eric replied. "I got eleven rounds locked and loaded. You can wait out front if the smell's too bad for ya."

"No, I got your back," Aaron said.

They wandered around holding their breath. The smell got worse in the back of the cabin. They found the room the smell was coming from. The carpet had shit smeared from the doorway to under the bed. Eric hesitantly got down on his knees and shined his light under the bed. There was a young woman's body crammed under the bed. Her eyes were still open, and she was staring at Eric. She was clearly dead, but it felt like she was staring at him. Eric let out a small scream and jumped to his feet.

"There's a fuckin' dead girl under that bed!"

"What?! No fuckin' way! Dude, we gotta get outta here! We gotta get the fuckin' cops up here! The state police! FBI! All of them!"

Aaron ran to the front door. He was going to puke. He didn't make it outside. He threw up in the corner of that messy front room. After he had emptied his stomach, he dashed outside. Ozzy and Leo were gone. Eric rushed outside after Aaron.

"Ozzy! Leo! Where the hell did you go?!" Aaron yelled.

"That way," Eric said pointing at footsteps in the mud with his flashlight. The footsteps went around to the back of the cabin.

Aaron and Eric ran behind the cabin. They dropped everything in their hands and screamed. Ozzy lay on the wet ground with his throat sliced wide open. His dead eyes staring into the night sky. Leo had at least a dozen stab wounds in his chest and neck area.

Aaron doubled over and vomited again. That made Eric vomit too. Their combined retching made them each fall to their knees as they continued to puke. Aaron suddenly stopped retching and went stiff. Eric looked over and saw Mathew standing there with a knife buried in Aaron's back. Mathew? Seriously, Mathew? Mathew did all this?

As Eric was trying to process what he was seeing, Mathew slowly removed the large knife from Aaron's back. Aaron fell to the ground. Mathew swiped at Eric, who dodged it. Mathew had intended to stab Eric in the back as well but only got his shoulder. Eric screamed in pain and punched Mathew in the guts. Mathew pulled the knife out as he doubled over in pain. Eric punched him in the face. Mathew went down to his hands and knees. Eric jumped to his feet and kicked Mathew in the ribs. Mathew grunted and fell to his back, holding his side. Eric took off running. He totally spaced the gun he had dropped when he saw Ozzy and Leo's bodies.

Seconds later he heard his very own gunfire. He looked over his shoulder and saw Mathew shooting at him. It was clear to Eric that Mathew had never handled a gun before. His shots were wild and didn't even come close to hitting Eric.

Except for the last one, which hit Eric in the hip, spinning him around as he fell to the wet ground. He cried out in pain again as he clutched his bleeding hip. Eric tried to get to his feet but couldn't. His hip wouldn't support his weight. He started crawling up the road toward his own place. He pulled his phone out of his pocket as he scrambled away from Mathew and called Deandre.

"Dre!" he panted. "Get everyone the fuck out of here now! Ozzy and Leo and Aaron are all dead. It's fuckin'' Mathew! Mathew killed them!"

Eric felt a cold blade slip between his shoulder blades. He dropped his phone and fell belly first onto the pavement. He lost all feeling in his body from the neck down. He couldn't move. Mathew rolled him over onto his bloody back. Mathew stood over Eric smiling.

"Matt, why?" Eric gasped.

"God told me to," Mathew calmly replied. "This is God's work." Mathew crouched down next to Eric and put the knife to his throat. "I enjoy this work, Eric. You see, my whole life I've watched sinners and heathens like you get away with anything and everything. Dirty sinners like you have the fancy cars, money, girls, alcohol, and drugs, and you think that makes you happy. You think that makes you cool or something like that. You refuse to see the light of God. Your eyes and hearts are blind to his love. You parade around this world like you aren't even sinning! It's disgusting! And now you have sinned with my sister! She was already a filthy whore, but now she is even more sullied by the likes of you." Mathew stood up and looked puzzled. "Why aren't you trying to hit me again?"

He kicked Eric's ribs. Eric groaned but didn't move. Mathew kicked him again with the same result. Mathew bent down and picked up Eric's arm. It was limp. He released the arm, and it flopped to the ground. Mathew smiled again.

"I must have severed your spine," Mathew chuckled.

"Fuck you, Matt," Eric whispered. That's all the voice he had left. He felt weightless. He couldn't see very well anymore. He could taste blood and vile in his throat.

"Yeah, yeah, 'F' Mathew. Good one, Eric. What a zinger!" Mathew crouched down again and got really close to Eric's face. "You people and your swears. You think that really hurts people, don't you? What do you think, I'll be so offended that I won't kill you and your friends? Oh, wait, I already killed three of your friends," Mathew laughed. "You know, I thought you'd be the hardest one to kill. You put up way less fight than I had anticipated. I thought you'd try to beat the life out of me. You have disappointed me. Why did you run, big bad Eric? Did you run so you could save my whore sister? If you hadn't dropped your little gun, you may have made it back to her."

Mathew jumped to his feet. He heard people running toward them. Mathew took off into the woods.

*****

Deandre burst into the cabin, completely out of breath. Everyone inside looked scared, but they were all okay. That Janey girl was asleep on the couch.

"She okay?" Deandre asked Rachel.

"No, she's gonna bleed out eventually. She's in shock too. Totally delirious. Whoever cut her, filed her calf muscle, she's bleeding badly."

"Did anyone call 911 yet?" Deandre asked.

"Yeah, they'll be on their way as soon as they can. The storm washed out the road five miles down," Rachel replied.

"Fuck! I gotta call Eric," Dre pulled out his phone. After he explained everything to Eric, Deandre said, "Eric wants you back out there, Ozzy."

"Just call him back and tell them all to come back!" Rachel said. "My shitty phone doesn't work up here or I'd call him myself."

"There ain't shit out there," Deandre said. "Eric's armed. Those guys will be fine."

Ozzy took off running back outside to meet Eric and the others.

Deandre grabbed a beer and sat at the table. He had his 9mm in his hand. No one was going to bust in on them and start any shit. Deandre was stressed, scared, and pissed. He'd have no problem blasting a crazy man. No one talked. Rachel and Gina paced the living room, both chewing on their nails. Genesis and Eve sat on the other couch, holding each other and crying.

"We gotta do something!" Rachel snapped, startling everyone. "I can't just sit in this cabin and wait it out!"

"What else can we do?" Deandre asked.

"We should be out there with Eric and the other guys," Rachel replied. "We should have never split up! God, you guys are so fuckin' bull-headed sometimes!"

"Is any of this even real?" Eve asked. "How do we even know what that chick said is even true?"

"Why wouldn't it be?" Rachel asked.

"We never did find a body out there," Deandre said.

"We don't know which way she came from," Rachel said. "You guys only looked one way."

"Look, I don't doubt there's some crazy shit going on, but what if these kids are pranking us?" Eve suggested.

"What?! That is ridiculous!" Rachel exclaimed. "Why would anyone think to do such a thing? That wound on her leg is very real and very deep. No one in their right mind would do that for a fuckin' prank!"

"Just a suggestion," Eve said, offended.

"I know, it's a valid thought, but it ain't what's going on around here. Dre, call Eric again. Get them all back here. Between Aaron's truck, My SUV, and Eric's truck we may be able to get out of here," Rachel said.

"The road's washed out, 'member?" Deandre replied.

"We have four-wheel drive," Rachel explained. "We might be able to get through."

"Or we get trapped in the middle of nowhere. At least here we have the cabin. We have all sorts of things to use as weapons. We have two guns!"

"Three," Genesis interrupted Deandre, "Eric has another one in his room."

"Okay, even better," Deandre said. "We have three guns. If this crazy knife guy comes around, he ain't going to pose much of a threat against nine people and three guns. I agree, we need to get the others back here though."

As Deandre picked up his phone to call Eric, it rang.

"Ah, shit, there he is!" Deandre said to the room.

Dre answered the phone, and a look of shock, panic, and sheer terror crept across his face. The color fell from his cheeks. Everyone looking at him knew whatever Eric was saying was very, very bad. Dre let the phone slip out of his hand and crash to the table.

"We-uh-we-holy-jee…" Deandre stammered. The fear wouldn't let him form a sentence.

"What is it?!" Rachel screamed.

"Dead, they're all dead," Deandre slowly and quietly said.

Rachel shrieked and ran for the door.

"Stop!" Deandre shouted at her. Watching Rachel bolt for the door had snapped him out of his shock. "We gotta go! Like now!"

"Not without the others! Not without Eric!" Rachel screamed.

"They're gone! Get in the rigs!" Deandre said, grabbing sets of keys off the counter.

Deandre rushed out the back door, followed closely by Rachel. The smell of motor oil and antifreeze was overpowering. Dre flipped on his flashlight. Every vehicle in the driveway had huge puddles of oil and antifreeze underneath them. Deandre dropped to the ground and slid under Aaron's truck. The brake lines were all cut too. Somebody didn't want them to try to get away.

"They're all toast," Deandre said as he stood back up.

"Then we fight that motherfucker!" Rachel yelled and started to run.

"Rachel! Wait!" Deandre hollered and chased after her. "It's Mathew!"

Rachel stopped running and let Dre catch up to her.

"What's Mathew?" she asked him.

"The killer," Dre replied.

"What?! Are you fuckin' kidding?! There's no possible way that geeky little church nut is a homicidal murderer! Did Eric tell you that?!"

"Yeah, just now. He said Mathew killed Ozzy, Leo, and Aaron. Then I..." Deandre trailed off. He didn't want to finish that sentence. He *couldn't* finish that sentence.

"Then you what?" Rachel asked quietly. She grabbed Deandre by the shirt with both hands and screamed, "Then you what?! Fuckin' tell me Dre!"

"I can't, I just can't."

Rachel let go of his shirt and took off running again. She'd killed that spineless, little fucker herself!

*****

Mathew ducked into the woods and waited. He stared at Eric's motionless body. He knew Eric was still alive, and that thrilled him. Let the nasty sinner bleed out slowly. Let him ponder his life while it slowly slipped away from him. Mathew wanted Eric to realize what a waste his life had been. Spending all his time and energy on sins of the flesh like that. Mathew knew from overhearing how Eric and Deandre talked over the years that they were both big sinners of the flesh. Drinkers too. Drug users as well. The list of sins was endless with those two.

Mathew blamed Eric for making his sisters become sinners. He knew Eric's lifestyle over the years had seeped into his sisters' heads. Eric made that life look fun and glamorous. Mathew saw how his sisters had always looked at Eric. Genesis and Eric spent a lot of time together, but it was Eve that had looked up to Eric.

Eve used to look at him like she had a crush on him. Maybe she had. Eve left the church first. She moved away and became a sinner just like Eric. Eve smoked cigarettes and drank alcohol. And Mathew knew she was having relations. Finding birth control pills in her backpack proved it.

Mathew knew Genesis was a whore, but how could she have relations with Eric? It was possibly forgivable to have premarital relations with your fiancé. There was no forgiveness for laying with a man like Eric. Mathew was seething. He was shaking with anger. Mathew had the urge to walk up to Eric and stab him a hundred times. Stab him until he couldn't physically lift the knife anymore. Screw letting him die slowly! Mathew wanted the satisfaction of stabbing him.

Mathew couldn't do that. One of Eric's whore friends ran around the corner screaming. She fell to her knees at Eric's body and just wailed. Deandre was right behind her. Mathew had seen that whore a lot of times, but he didn't know her name. He didn't care to.

Deandre stood behind the hysterical woman and yelled, "Mathew! Get your weak ass out here! You slimy motherfucker! I'm going to kill you!"

The whore screamed again. Mathew laughed. Watching people discover their friends dead was almost as fun as killing them. Almost. Mathew could see Deandre had a gun in his hand. That made Mathew wish he had been a better shot, and he wished he still had bullets in Eric's gun. The woman and Deandre were sitting ducks in the middle of the road. Mathew couldn't make a move with Deandre armed. He could tell by how Deandre held the gun that he knew how to use it. He'd drop Mathew at first sight.

Mathew watched as the woman and Deandre looked at Eric then to each other. They were in a heated discussion. Mathew couldn't hear what they were saying from his hiding spot. He smiled to himself again. All the pain, stress, and fear he had caused these people made him feel wonderful. Mathew sat up and watched as Deandre tucked his gun into his waistband. Deandre then leaned over and picked up Eric's torso while the woman picked up his legs. They started back toward Eric's cabin with Eric's arms dangling hilariously by his side.

Mathew sat back and waited. He had all the time in the world. He had these sinners right where he wanted them, panicked and distraught. They'd let their guard down at some point. Exhaustion would take them eventually. Mathew pulled the hood of his black sweatshirt up. He leaned back against a giant pine tree and closed his eyes. Mathew let himself doze for a bit.

*****

Rachel rounded the corner at a full sprint. She saw Eric lying in the road motionless. A scream she didn't even know she was capable of escaped her quivering lips. She rushed to Eric and fell to her knees beside him. Deandre came to a stop right behind her. He looked around and yelled, "Mathew! Get your weak ass out here! You slimy motherfucker! I'm going to kill you!"

Eric coughed and wiggled his head. His head was the only body part he could still move.

"I can't move," Eric croaked.

Rachel quieted herself and looked at Eric. His eyes were cloudy. Blood was pooling around his body.

"I can't move anything," Eric whispered again.

"Baby! Baby you're going to be okay!" Rachel cried.

"No, I'm not," Eric said. "Mathew ran into the woods that way." Eric pointed with his hazy eyes.

"He's no concern right now," Rachel said through tears.

"Kill him," Eric groaned.

"Dre! We gotta get him to the cabin!" Rachel cried.

"We shouldn't move him," Deandre replied.

"He's fuckin' dying, Dre! He's bleeding out!"

"We could hurt him more by moving him."

"He'll die right here in the middle of the fuckin' road if we don't move him!" Rachel screamed. "Grab his shoulders, I'll get his legs!"

Deandre tucked the pistol into his waistband. He knew Rachel was right. They had to get him back to the cabin and pack those wounds. Eric was bleeding out fast. Deandre was scared, besides himself, out of body experience scared. None of it seemed real. Everything was happening at break-neck speeds. Why did he even waste a few minutes arguing with Rachel? Eric needed them.

Deandre picked up Eric's upper body as Rachel grabbed his legs under his knees. Eric's arms flopped disturbingly at his side. Dre knew if Eric somehow lived, he'd never walk again. Tears burst out of Deandre's eyes.

When they got back to the cabin they burst into the front door.

"Get towels! Every fuckin' towel in the place!" Rachel yelled as they stepped inside. "Find every first aid kit! I don't care if it's a pinky toe band aid I fuckin' want it!"

Everyone stood in shocked silence, just staring at Deandre and Rachel holding Eric. Blood was dripping from his back and shoulder.

"Now!" Rachel screamed.

That got everyone into gear. Within precious minutes they all returned with towels, washcloths, bed sheets, and a first aid kit. Genesis quickly folded a bed sheet and put it on the floor. Rachel and Deandre carefully laid Eric down. Eric didn't make a sound or even respond to what was going on. He was in shock and letting Dre and Rachel do their thing. Eric doubted he'd live through the night, but he wasn't going to vocalize it. He had become a distraction, and he felt like that was a good thing. Eric didn't think Mathew would try to attack them all in the cabin. The cabin felt safe. Dre had a gun. Rachel had her anger and her choice of any knife or blunt object in the place. For the time being, they were safe.

Once Eric was on the floor, Rachel took off to the bedrooms. She ran back with an armload of pillows. With Deandre's help, she positioned Eric on his side so they could dress his wounds. Rachel took the scissors from the first aid kit and cut off Eric's shirt. His wounds were ghastly. His blood was already beginning to clot, which was a good sign to Rachel. Rachel and Deandre packed his wounds.

"Gina, call 911 again," Rachel said through tears.

"Everyone else just stay put," Deandre said and stood up from Eric.

He was the only man left. He knew Rachel and Gina were badassses and more than capable of putting up a good fight, but Deandre worried about Genesis and Eve. He was banking on the hope that Mathew wouldn't be dumb enough to attack them inside the cabin. If they all just stayed put and waited on the cops to get there, they should all survive this night. Eric looked terrible and it killed Dre. Part of him almost wished Mathew had finished the job. That was a horrible thought, but it had crossed his mind. At least that way Eric would be at peace already. Deandre wasn't trying to fool himself the way Rachel was. He knew Eric wasn't going to live through this.

Deandre understood why Rachel was holding onto hope. He wanted too as well, but he just couldn't. Part of him wanted to go hunt down that cowardly piece of shit and empty a clip into him. Mathew deserved to die. What would have made him do this? Did he kill the other people too and dispose of their bodies? Where were his mom and dad? Oh, shit, did he kill them too?

"911 said the state's working on the washout now. They should have the road cleared within the hour. Sherriff, state patrol, fire and rescue are all standing by at the washout," Gina told everyone.

"Fuckin' A that's great news," Deandre said. "Now we can just lock the doors and wait."

Deandre locked the doors and sat down at the table again. Gina sat next to him and took his hand. He gave her hand a loving squeeze and she burst into tears.

Rachel was still crouched next to Eric, who was out cold. He seemed to be breathing normally. That was at least a little reassuring.

"Who would do something like this?" Genesis asked.

"Yeah, this is like horror movie shit," Eve added. "I didn't think people actually did this kinda stuff."

Rachel and Deandre exchanged glances. Should they tell them who? Gina noticed Rachel and Dre exchange those glances.

"Do you guys know?" Gina asked slowly and quietly.

"I don't think 'who' matters right now," Rachel said. "What matters now is staying inside and waiting for the cops."

"If you know who it is we can tell the cops!" Gina exclaimed.

"And we will," Rachel replied.

"Eric and I met some people last night that seemed off," Genesis said. "It was a married couple and the husband's brother. The brother was creepy. I got a bad vibe from him. Eric didn't like him either."

"That could be it," Rachel lied. She didn't want to tell Genesis and Eve it was Mathew.

"Like Rachel said, we just gotta wait on the cops. I never thought I'd be excited to see cops," Deandre said and forced himself to chuckle at his joke.

It was not the time for jokes, but it was a bit of a relief as everyone else forced a chuckle too. Dre knew Eric would've liked that one.

"I think we are finally safe and that's all that matters right now," Rachel said. "I don't think whoever is doing this would take the chance of busting in on five people. They gotta know we're armed."

They were all still very much on edge, but a feeling of security had settled on them. The air was less heavy. No one was jovial by any means, but they were all a little more relaxed. Knowing the authorities would be up within an hour helped out a lot. As long as they stayed inside, they should be safe.

Chapter Eight

Mathew awoke from his catnap in a panic. He knew those sinners had called the authorities. He didn't know how he knew that, but he was certain of it. Mathew was also quite aware that they would lock themselves in their cabin until the cavalry arrived. There was no way he could finish his mission with them all locked inside that cabin. If he tried to break in, Deandre would shoot him dead, no doubt. Mathew stood up. His backside was soaked from sitting on the wet forest floor.

"Lord, help me finish those sinners off," Mathew said to the cool night air.

"Fire," God responded.

"Fire?"

"Yes, my son, fire," God replied.

"But you said that would bring too much attention," Mathew said timidly.

"Help is already on the way. You must flush the sinners out and end them before help arrives."

Mathew smiled, that made perfect sense. An idea crept into his head. He'd start his own cabin, where he hid all the bodies, on fire first. Get that raging, then start

Eric's cabin ablaze. Those dirty sinners would have to leave the cabin. Then he could pluck them off one by one. That was a solid plan. He'd have to get Deandre first. The women would be easy, but Deandre was armed.

Mathew walked back to his cabin. He went out to the utility shed and got one of the gas cans. He went inside and doused the pile of bodies with gasoline. He emptied the rest of the can around the cabin. On his way out the door, Mathew lit the gas on fire. It went up in flames immediately. He rushed back out to the shed and fetched the other gas can. There wasn't much left in that can. He hoped it would be enough to start a fire at Eric's cabin. Mathew snuck over to the cabin. Every light inside and out was on. There was no way he could sneak around that cabin without someone inside seeing him. He knew Eric had told everyone it was him doing all of this. They would all be on the lookout for him.

Eric's cabin didn't have a fuse box on the backside like his and the others did. Mathew noticed the outbuilding tucked into a patch of pine trees. He went inside and found the fuse box. He killed the power and everything went dark. Perfect, now he could hopefully get the fire going unnoticed. Plus, the power suddenly going out on the sinners would distract them. They would panic and assume he had done it. That would heighten their defenses and make them want to stay inside even more.

Maybe he'd get lucky, and they'd all die in the fire. He had really wanted to kill them personally, but the end game was for them all to die. It didn't really matter how. He was getting tired. He needed to figure out an escape plan. Every vehicle up there was traceable. No way could he just drive off in his parents' car or any other car out there. Mathew needed to find a way out of there.

"Lord? What do I do now?" Mathew asked after he started the fire. It didn't catch as quickly as the one he had set in his own cabin.

"Wait, My Son," God replied. "They will run away from the fire."

"How do I get out of here?"

"You must finish your mission."

"I'm tired, Lord."

"You will find the strength, My Son."

"You will give me the strength to finish them off?"

"I will. Go forth and complete your mission. All else will fall into place."

"Thank you, Lord."

Mathew hid behind one of the trucks in Eric's driveway. He could see both doors from there. He waited. The fire was petering out. He didn't have enough gas to get it hot enough to combat the wet ground. He saw flashlight beams bouncing around the inside of the house. Maybe Deandre would head out to check the fuse box. If Mathew could sneak up on him, he could possibly finish Deandre off before he even knew what happened. Then the women would be alone and scared.

Mathew had an anxious feeling in his stomach. He felt like something wasn't quite right. Something wasn't sitting well with him. God had been vague, as he usually was, but the tone was different. Mathew didn't get that feeling of divine presence this time. He had gotten more of an evil feeling. Mathew felt guilty for the first time. Even killing his mom and dad hadn't made him feel an ounce of guilt. In fact, he had thoroughly enjoyed killing each person he had that day. It had all been thrilling to him. He had had an excitement running through his entire body leading up to each kill. Especially Eric, even though he knew Eric wasn't dead yet.

He was nervous. His guts were churning, and he felt like he was going to throw up. His hands were shaking. Mathew looked down at the bloody knife in his trembling hand. An hour ago, the sight of that bloody knife had thrilled him. Now, it sickened him. Where was that thrilling feeling? What had changed between stabbing Eric and now? Was it his sisters? They were so close now. They were basically next on the list. He knew he had to kill them, but deep down was there a part of him that didn't want to? Or, maybe, couldn't do it? Was that why he was suddenly so nervous and anxious?

Mathew had always loved his sisters. They had meant so much to him. He didn't in any way approve of their behavior of late, but they used to be good souls. They had been good, God-fearing Christians at one point, logic suggests they could be again. What if they were savable? What if he murdered them and they could have found God again? Maybe he could spare them and show them the errors of their ways? What if he showed them exactly what happened to dirty fornicators and helped them get back in the good graces of the Lord?

He'd still have to dispatch the rest. Mathew couldn't imagine his sisters just sitting there and watching it all happen. He knew Eve well enough to know she'd fight for those sinners. Genesis might too. She had some sort of misguided love for Eric. She probably cared for the others as well. That would be a problem. Mathew didn't want to fight off his sisters. He'd have to somehow mount a surprise attack. Kill the others before his sisters even knew what was happening. They'd have to be last.

"You will complete your mission as originally assigned," God said, interrupting Mathew's train of thought.

The nervousness and anxiety tripled inside him. He was going to puke, he knew it.

"Do you hear me?"

Mathew doubled over and vomited.

"My Son, you have been given a gift. Do not squander the power I have instilled in you. You will not like what happens to you if you do not complete your mission."

Mathew retched again and burst into tears. It was the first time he could remember crying since he was in grade school. The tears felt so alien and burned his flushed cheeks. Mathew curled up into a ball on the gravel driveway and just bawled.

"My Son!" God's voice boomed inside his head. It felt like his head was going to explode. "Get up! Go do your task. No more of this cowardice."

"Lord," Mathew sobbed, "I'm scared. I'm tired. I'm sick."

"None of that will last, My Son. You want to inherit the kingdom with me, don't you?"

"Yes, Lord."

"You want to live eternity bathed in my love, don't you?"

"Yes, Lord."

"You want to eradicate sin, don't you?"

"Yes, Lord."

"Then get up and finish your mission!" God screamed inside Mathew's head.

With that, the voice of God was gone again. He could feel it. Mathew did stand up. He dusted himself off and wiped his face. The bloody knife caught his attention, and he smiled. There was that feeling of excitement again. There was that strength again. Those sinners were going to be sent to hell one way or the other.

*****

Time seemed to stand still for everyone inside the cabin. Rachel was sitting next to Eric with her hand on his good shoulder. He was in and out of consciousness. His breathing had become more labored and had a wetness to it. Rachel was terrified. She was beside herself with fear, anxiety, and emotion. One minute she was furious, the next she was in tears, another moment she was emotionless. Rachel prayed to a God she didn't believe existed, but if he did, Eric needed his help. Eric was all but dead already. It killed her to be literally watching him die. They had had such an up and down relationship through the years, but they had always loved each other no matter what. Rachel couldn't imagine a life without Eric in it somehow. How would she ever be able to live on without him? One day you're having fun with someone, the next day they're just gone. Totally gone, never to be seen or heard again. There was no living on after that. There's just surviving it. You can't move on from a sudden death like that, especially a violent one like this.

Eric was still alive, yes, but everyone in that cabin knew he wouldn't be for long. Maybe he'd make it through the night. Even that was looking a lot less likely. Eric knew he was dying too. He could feel it. He had no feeling from the neck down, but he could still feel that his organs weren't running right. Eric could barely feel Rachel's hand on his shoulder. He wasn't sure if he was *actually* feeling it, or he simply knew her hand was there, and his mind was giving him the sensation of her touch. Either way, it felt nice and if he were to die at least he would do it with her by his side. Eric had imagined one day one of them would be saying goodbye to the other forever, but he assumed that wouldn't be for another sixty years.

Goddamn fuckin' Mathew! He did all of this. He, for whatever reason, decided to go on a killing spree? What? In the name of God? That was horseshit! There was no God and Eric knew that. He also knew Mathew had snapped and is now saying God told him to do it all. Eric wished he could move. He wished he could get his hands on Mathew. He knew between Deandre, Rachel, and the others, they'd all tune Mathew up pretty well, but he really wanted to be a part of that. Mathew wasn't going to survive the night either.

The lights went out and everyone screamed. Rachel jumped to her feet and looked around the dark room. She heard Deandre going through drawers. He soon clicked on a couple of flashlights. He handed one to Rachel, one to Gina, and held on to one for himself.

"You all go hide in the bathroom," Deandre said, bouncing his light at each of them. "I'm going to go check the fuse box."

"Don't, Dre," Gina said and wrapped her arms around him. "Stay with us."

"Yeah, Dre, don't go out there," Rachel agreed. "You know Mathew did that to get us out of the cabin." As soon as his name came out of her mouth, she regretted it, but it just slipped out in the panic.

"Mathew?" Genesis said softly. "What's Mathew gotta do with all of this?"

"Holy fuck!" Eve yelled. "It's him! It's fuckin' him, isn't it?!"

Deandre and Rachel exchanged looks again. Dre knew they had to tell them. Gina, Eve, and Genesis needed to know who was after them.

"Sorry, but, yes, it is him," Deandre said with a tone of sadness.

"Fuckin' A! Why the fuck would he being doing this?!" Eve cried. "Why am I not more surprised?"

"It can't be Mathew," Genesis whimpered as tears ran down her face. "He would never do anything like this."

"The whys and hows don't matter right now," Deandre said. "What matters is we know who and we have to be on the lookout for him. He's close and we know it. I'm sure he killed the lights to flush us out."

"That's exactly why you aren't going out there!" Rachel exclaimed.

"Me and Mr. 9mm here *are* going out there. I'm finishing this now. That little fucker is out there waiting, I can feel it."

Genesis and Eve sobbed harder. How could it be Mathew? What would ever possess him to do anything like this? It slowly dawned on Genesis. That was it! He was possessed! That was the only logical explanation.

"Wait, maybe we don't have to kill him," Genesis said. "I think he's possessed. We could cast the demon out and get the old Mathew back."

"Genesis," Rachel began, "he's killed God-knows how many people already. He's after us now. We won't go hunt him down," she shot Deandre a look, "but we will protect ourselves."

"I'm going out and getting those lights back on," Deandre said. "He won't break in on us if the house is lit up. Now, please go hide in the bathroom and I'll be right back."

"Not a chance," Rachel said. "If you insist then I'm coming with you."

"No fuckin' way!" Deandre exclaimed. "We all know he shut the main power off. It'll take me two minutes to run out there and turn everything back on. I don't wanna sound like a dick but I'm doing it. That's final."

"Well, then I'm staying out with here Eric," Rachel said defiantly.

"Fine, you all stick together out here. I'll be back in two minutes, promise," Deandre said.

He removed the 9mm from his waistband and headed for the back door. Deandre opened the door and shone his light around. He couldn't see anything out of the ordinary. He knew Mathew was hiding out there somewhere. Deandre raised the pistol with his right hand and pointed the flashlight around with his left. He made a beeline for the outbuilding. Deandre ran inside and flipped the breaker. He turned back to head out when he felt a hot burning feeling in his guts. His hands dropped the gun and flashlight as if they had a mind of their own. Deandre had turned right into Mathew and his knife. Mathew was six inches from Deandre's face.

"You motherfucker!" Deandre gurgled. "Ima kill you!"

Mathew pulled the knife out. Deandre clutched his stomach and fell, hitting his head on a shelf. The impact knocked him out and he crumpled to the floor.

Back in the cabin, Rachel told Gina to call 911 again. Deandre had been gone too long after the lights had come back on. Gina went to the dining room table where she had left her phone. Gina nervously paced between the table and back door, waiting for 911 to answer.

The back door was kicked open and Mathew buried his knife into Gina's side. Her eyes bugged out and she dropped her phone. He stabbed her two more times, and she went to the floor in a heap. Genesis and Eve screeched. Rachel jumped to her feet and ran to the knife block. She grabbed a knife and lunged at Mathew. He laughed and swatted her attack away.

"Mathew!" Genesis yelled as she jumped to her feet. "Stop this right now! Jesus, rid my brother of this demon!"

"Sister, sister," Mathew began, "I have no demon. God himself set me on this mission."

Mathew glanced at his sisters. Rachel took advantage of him being distracted for a second. She lunged at him with the small kitchen knife. Her sudden movement caught Mathew's eye. At the last second, he stepped back and Rachel was only able to graze him with the knife. She cut his forearm; it bled nicely but was only a superficial wound. She lunged at him again, this time slicing his shoulder. He let out a groan and turned to face her. Mathew was flipping his knife back and forth in his hand. He was dancing on his toes. Rachel stepped back a few feet to square up to him. He'd have to step over Gina to get to Rachel. That would be her chance to stab him. He'd have to look down as he stepped over her cousin.

Mathew glanced at his sisters again and smiled. He returned his stare to Rachel, still smiling. Rachel braced herself for a fight. Mathew's knife was three times the size of hers. His arms were a good foot longer than hers. Mathew had the upper hand, no doubt. Mathew looked down and stepped over Gina. Rachel squatted down and lunged at Mathew as he stepped over Gina. He saw her coming and side-stepped her at the last minute. Rachel missed him completely. Mathew buried his knife into her shoulder blade. Rachel screamed out in pain and fell to the floor. Mathew's knife was still in her shoulder. When he bent down to pull it out, Rachel stabbed him in the shoulder. He grunted and stood up straight. He stared at the little kitchen knife sticking out of his shoulder and laughed. He had a huge, evil smile on his face. His eyes were dark and hateful.

"Mathew Josiah Simpson!" Genesis screamed. Eve was on her feet too, side-by-side with her sister.

"Hush," Mathew said, not even looking at Genesis and Eve.

Everything narrowed for Rachel. The room was growing dark. Her mind raced. Everyone she had loved in her life was now dead or almost dead. Even if the ambulance showed up that second, Eric wasn't going to survive his wounds. Not a chance. Mathew reached down and pulled his knife out of her shoulder. She shrieked. Pulling it out hurt worse than when he stabbed her. She felt her warm, sticky blood flood out of the wound. Mathew stabbed her again and again. Rachel swatted and kicked at him, but it was useless.

Mathew plunged his knife into Rachel's throat, and she was gone. Eve and Genesis shrieked. Mathew looked up from his handy work and smiled at his sisters. He pulled out a chair from the dining room table. He turned it to face his sisters and sat down. He rested his hands, still clutching the blood-soaked knife, in his lap.

"Sit. Let's chat," Mathew smiled.

"Fuck you!" Eve screamed at him.

"Quiet!" Mathew shouted. He tilted his head back and forth.

Mathew could hear what sounded like a woman's voice behind him. He turned around in his chair and saw Gina's phone on the floor under the table. Mathew got up and grabbed the phone. As he had expected, it was 911 on the other end. He put the phone to his ear.

"Hello? Help is on the way," the woman said on the other end. "Thirty minutes out."

"We are fine," Mathew calmly replied. "Call em off." He disconnected the line. He knew they were coming no matter what.

"Well, sisters, we don't have as much time as I had hoped we would. We gotta get to it right away."

"Get to what?" Genesis asked. "What the hell are you doing, Mathew? Why would you do all of this?"

"Where's mom and dad?" Eve asked, slowly realizing he didn't need to answer that.

"They're in hell, where they belong," Mathew answered with a smile. "Same place you two whores will be shortly."

"Fuck off!" Eve screamed. "You didn't?!"

"Oh, I very much did. Mother, father, that dirty, disgusting three-some next door to us. Those filthy whore teenagers. Your nasty, drug-riddled friends here. All of them dispatched to hell."

"But why, Mathew?" Genesis said, hoping if they kept him talking the police would show up before he tried to kill them as well.

"You know why," he replied.

"No, we don't. They were all good people," Genesis replied.

Eve was slowly moving away from Genesis toward the front door. In the corner behind where the door swung open was a wooden baseball bat. Eric had kept one there for protection, although it seemed more likely that if someone ever broke in, they'd use that bat on him.

Mathew threw his head back and laughed. A full volume, hysterical laugh.

"They certainly were not," Mathew said between chuckles. He was still standing, the knife in his right hand and Gina's phone in his left. "And neither are either of you. Eve? What are you doing? Trying to make a run for it? Not surprising you'd leave Genesis behind and try to make your escape. You have always been the coward of the family."

Eve stopped in her tracks and stared at her brother. Was he even her brother anymore? Or were they looking at Satan himself? She doubted that, but it was easier to imagine him possessed than doing all of this of his own free will.

"They were all sinners, just like you two are," Mathew said and sat back down. "Again, sisters, sit. You aren't going to get away from me. You are my sisters, and I want to give you a chance to repent before you die. Maybe God will look kindly on your souls if you confess your many, many sins."

"What good comes of all that if you're just gonna kill us anyway?" Eve asked.

"Mathew, you don't have to do this. You're our brother. We're family," Genesis pleaded, still just trying to keep him talking.

"Sisters, you have disappointed me time and time again."

Rage was building up inside of Eve and Genesis. Mathew was standing there like nothing had happened. He was acting contentiously and righteously.

"I spent my life in service of the Lord," Mathew continued. "I have had my wants and desires. I've had my temptations, but not once have I strayed from his love. You two, on the other hand, have given into all temptations. You two have laid with men. You have sullied yourselves with sins of the flesh. You have become cohorts with fools like these. You have let yourselves stray from the church and God's love. He told me he still loves you, but you're too far gone to be saved. That's why I want to give you a chance to repent. I know he loves you. I believe he may still let you into Heaven. It's a long shot but we must try, sisters."

Eve bolted for the door and grabbed the bat. Mathew remained didn't move as he watched her pick up that bat. She turned to him. Mathew had a huge smile on his face. He dropped Gina's phone. He had forgotten he was still holding it. Mathew moved the knife to his left hand and reached around his back. He pulled Eric's gun out and pointed it at his sisters. They didn't know it was empty.

"Eve, put the bat away," Mathew said calmly. She did. "Now, please sit," Mathew motioned to the couch they had been sitting on with the pistol. They obeyed and sat down on the edge of the couch. He sat back down on the kitchen chair and kept the empty pistol pointed at them. "You sinners ready to repent? Or do you want to go straight to hell? I don't know why I'm even giving you a chance. Maybe because you're my sisters and I've always looked out for you? Maybe it's because I feel guilty that I let you stray so far from the church?"

"Shut up, Mathew!" Genesis hissed. "You never looked out for us! You controlled us like dad did! You berated us every fuckin' chance you got!" The 'F' word had slipped out, but it had certainly gotten a reaction from Mathew. "Now you're doing it again. Look at you, Mathew! You are pointing a gun at us! I'm pregnant Mathew! Are you seriously considering killing an unborn baby?!" She paused and breathed deeply for a second. "We're your sisters! *If* you ever honestly loved us, put the gun and knife down. You repent your sins! You're going to jail forever no matter what. Do you really need to kill us too? Your own sisters?"

Mathew pondered all of that and smiled, "yes, I do. God told me to. He said you'd argue with me about it. He said you'd pull the sister card. 'Oh, Mathew, spare us, your poor, misguided sisters.' Not a chance. Not an option at this stage of the game."

"Game?! This is all a game to you?!" Genesis said, seething with rage. She wasn't scared; she had a feeling that he couldn't do it. "You're scared, aren't you, Mathew?"

"Not in the least," Mathew replied, smugly. "God has my back. This is my mission and once complete, I will take my place in paradise with him."

"I think you're listening to Satan, not God," Genesis said.

Eve was sitting quietly next to her sister. She had figured out what Genesis was doing by making Mathew talk. It was genius, they both knew how Mathew liked to carry on.

"Satan has no power over me," Mathew replied, triumphantly. "I am God's sword. God protects me from all evil. You and all these other pathetic sinners are the ones who have listened to Satan. He has tempted you with sin and you have all taken the bait. I feel sorry for you that you cannot see that. Why would Satan want me to kill his people?" Mathew paused and chuckled, shaking his head. "You and the rest if this scum keep evil in the world. Satan loves people like you. God has tapped me to get rid of sin and evil. Together we will rid the world of people like you."

Genesis glanced at the clock on the wall. Help had to be close by now. A movement on the ground outside the open back door caught her eye. She quickly looked away from it. She didn't want Mathew to see her staring outside.

"Okay, if we are all sinners of the flesh and all that, then why mom and dad? They were good Christians, weren't they?" Genesis asked, sneaking a look out back again.

"Not at all, sister," Mathew replied. "Mother was a pill-popper and father was a drunk. Mother and Mr. Bilster had an inappropriate relationship. I don't think they ever laid together, but they were far too close. Father had his rage and was prone to violence, as you well know. They were both fakes. I call them Sunday Christians. They acted the part at church and were sinners the rest of the time."

Genesis looked past Mathew at the back door. She grabbed Eve and pulled her to the floor. Mathew spun around and saw Deandre standing in the doorway. Dre was clutching his bleeding side with his left hand and pointing his 9mm at Mathew's head with his right. Deandre squeezed the trigger and blew Mathew's brains out the back of his head. Mathew's body slumped to the floor in a wet thud. Deandre fell to the ground and passed out.

Chapter Nine

Genesis and Eve sat in the back of an ambulance, wrapped in itchy, wool blankets. Two ambulances had already whisked Deandre and Eric away. It seemed like Deandre had a fighting chance, Eric not so much. He was unresponsive when help finally arrived. He barely had a pulse, and Eve had overheard one paramedic say he'd be dead before they even got to the hospital. Eve didn't think Genesis had heard that and had no intention of telling her. The others were all dead, including Janey, who had bled out during all the pandemonium. They already knew Rachel and Gina were dead, they'd seen them die.

They'd also seen their own brother die. They hadn't wanted to, but they saw it, nonetheless. Why weren't they hysterical after everything they had witnessed? The sight of Mathew's head exploding seared into their memory forever. The smell of blood, guts, and gunpowder forever lodged in their nostrils. The silent screams they saw in Eric's dying eyes. All of it now a permanent memory. A nightmare they'd never wake from.

They were in shock, no doubt. The cries and the hysterics would come later. The night sweats and sleepless nights were coming too. Guilt and grief would plague them for years, possibly forever. Genesis didn't know how she'd raise a baby in this world. How could she be an effective mother when she had seen what she had? She would never let that kid out of her sight. Genesis knew the threat had ended when Deandre shot Mathew, but she'd never feel completely safe. If her own brother could do such heinous things, anybody could.

From the back of the ambulance, they could see crime scene techs hauling burnt bodies out their own cabin. They were told the fire did some damage and the bodies were badly burned but identifiable. Genesis and Eve knew who at least two of those bodies were. Their mom, dad, and brother were all gone. Violently and needlessly ripped from them. The same people they had been desperate to get away from just a day ago.

The sisters had almost not come up for their dad's birthday weekend. Would any of this have happened if they hadn't? Would Mathew still have killed everyone else? Had them coming up there and then refusing to stay at the cabin set him off?

A detective approached them slowly. He looked familiar to Genesis. He stopped at the back of the ambulance.

"I'm Detective Drew Wilkerson," the man said.

"Have we met?" Genesis asked. "You look familiar."

"I think we have," he replied. "You look familiar as well."

"I don't remember for sure," Genesis said and dropped her head.

"It doesn't matter right now," he replied. "I want you two to call me Drew, just Drew, no Detective Wilkerson stuff, okay?" They both nodded. "I am deeply sorry for what you have been through. What you have witnessed and how it all went down is frankly horrifying. Please, if you aren't ready to talk about any of it, let me know. I do not want to force you to."

"Tom's Diner, a while back," Genesis said, looking back up at Drew. "You asked me out."

"Oh, shit, that's right," Drew said and turned red. "I go there every day for coffee with my partner. I had never seen you before. I just felt a need to say hello. I am terribly sorry if I came off as being too forward."

"Honestly, you creeped me out a bit," Genesis said unapologetically.

"Again, I do apologize. I did not mean to seem anything but genuine. Are you comfortable talking to me or should I get my partner?"

"I'm fine," Genesis said. "Thinking back on it now, it was flattering. Especially after the morning I had had that day. It meant enough to stick in my memory after all this time and everything I've been through since. No worries, Drew."

"I appreciate you saying that," Drew said, the embarrassment dropping from his cheeks.

"I want to talk," Genesis said. "I can't just sit here and let what happened tonight just run through my mind over and over again."

"I can't talk about it," Eve said. "I don't wanna relive it."

"Sis, we have to," Genesis said calmly as she put an arm around Eve. "It happened. Not telling the detective what happened won't make it go away. Talking about it will help, I promise."

"If you two need a minute, I'll come back in a bit," Drew said.

"No, we're good, Drew," Genesis replied. Eve buried her face into Genesis's shoulder.

"Okay," Drew said and pulled out his phone. He opened a recording app and started recording. "What happened first?"

"What do you mean first?" Genesis asked. "We've been up here a few days now."

Genesis wasn't trying to be short; he seemed like a nice man just trying to do his job. All she wanted to do was get this part over with as soon as possible. She could feel Eve sobbing onto her shoulder.

"What I'd like to know is when this all started." Drew replied.

"Well, weird things were happening all weekend. I felt like there was evil up here, something dark and sinister. Now I know there was. Most won't believe it, but Mathew didn't do this on his own. I'm sure this will go down in your books as a troubled young man who broke. Mathew was troubled but not in the way you all will spin it. And I get that. You can't write a report saying he was possessed. You guys will write up that he went insane, crumbled under the pressure of a stifling Christian upbringing. What you all believe to be insanity is the same we believe to be possession. Whatever it's referred to as, the end result was the same. Mathew didn't just snap, he's been shutting himself off for years now. He has become more and more withdrawn and quiet. I thought it was because Eve left the church, then I did, and it was just him and our parents. Am I surprised he did this? Oh, yes, I am. I would've never thought he would be capable of murder. He was bull-headed and selfish. He was rude and nasty to Eve and me especially. Controlling, domineering, abusive, all of those, but a murderer? Never.

"Make no mistake, Mathew did do all of this, and he died because of it. If Deandre hadn't shot Mathew, Eve and I would be dead and one of *you* would've ended up killing Mathew. Either way he wouldn't have survived this nightmare, and he knew it. He had this illusion that he was going to ascend to heaven to sit with God. Personally, I think the devil lied to him and used him to carry out heinous things. I can tell by the look on your face you think I'm crazy and frankly, I feel crazy. I don't know what's real anymore. Just a few hours ago we were sitting around a table eating food and playing poker. Now every one of our friends and family are dead. Brutally murdered by our own brother." That made Eve wail. Genesis patted her back and pulled her in tighter. "I hate to say it, but Mathew got what he deserved. I just wish someone had killed him sooner. So many people lost their lives today. I don't know what Eve and I will do moving forward."

"You guys will make it through this," Drew said, trying to be as reassuring as possible. It didn't work.

"That's all anyone will ever say to us moving forward. That's all they can say. Not too many people can put themselves in our shoes."

"There's help available to you. I'll give you some numbers."

"Thank you. What else do you need to know?" Genesis asked.

"Did you witness any of it?" he asked.

"We did, we saw him kill Gina and Rachel. I feel bad. We just stood there and watched him do it. It was like I couldn't make my body move." Eve nodded her head in agreement. "I've never even seen anything like it in movies. I don't watch those types of movies. I can't even put it into words. We knew we may have to fight for our lives when this all started happening. He tried to kill our friend Eric, but he didn't die right away. Eric told us everyone else was dead. As I'm sure Eric himself is by now." Genesis paused and looked past Drew. She wasn't focused on anything in particular. She just stared for a bit. "I should be more upset. Why aren't I more upset?"

"You're in shock," Drew said. "Your brain is keeping you from feeling the full scope of what happened to you."

"Will it always be like this?"

"Unfortunately, no. Someday soon it will hit you and it won't be pretty."

"Well, until that moment, I want to give you as much information as possible."

"I'd appreciate that, Ms. Simpson."

"Please, call me Genesis. I don't want to hear my last name," Genesis felt tears in her eyes. The mention of her last name reminded her that she and Eve were the last of their Simpson family.

"I will," Drew said, wringing his fingers together. "Did Mathew ever say anything to you that might make you think he'd be capable of this?"

"Not until tonight," Genesis said. Eve's tears had soaked through her shirt.

"What did he say tonight?"

"What didn't he say, is a shorter answer," Genesis said with a sigh. "He told us, along with everyone else, that we were sinners. The greatest sinners possible. We had sinned so much and so greatly that he was instructed by God Himself to eradicate us. To put an end to sin forever, in his words. He wanted us to repent our sins before he killed us. He told us maybe we had a shot of going to heaven if we repented. I'm telling you that was not our brother. Not totally anyway. He had a dark passenger steering the ship. I could see it in his eyes. They weren't Mathew's eyes. Everything else was my brother, but not those eyes. This won't make it out of here, but I'm telling you he was possessed. Write it up however you want to, but I know in my heart he was."

"Did he confess to any of the other murders?"

"Yes, every one of them. He seemed to have thoroughly enjoyed each one as well. I never liked my brother much, he was an asshole through and through, but I still loved him. You don't have to like someone to love them. He was still a person. I know deep down he was a good person. He battled a lot of inner demons, both figuratively and now literally. He was deeply troubled, Drew. We all knew it. Mom and dad never did much to help him. Dad would give Mathew small praises, but more often he berated him. Mathew lived for those small praises. That's why Mathew was so hard on Eve and I. Dad praised him for being tough on us. He praised Mathew for calling us whores. For telling us we were sinners and scum. How dare we lie with men. How dare we smoke or drink. How dare we do anything but what he and dad told us to.

"I honestly think Mathew was possessed but this was a longtime in the making. Dad did this to Mathew. Dad sheltered him. Dad put him down every chance he got. Dad introduced Mathew to self-doubt. He made Mathew feel small and inconsequential. No wonder when the devil came around, masquerading as God, Mathew fell for it. I'm sure Satan promised Mathew the world. Promised him love and admiration. Promised him a kingdom he had no right promising. All things Mathew would literally die for. All things my dad kept from him. All Mathew ever wanted was to be validated and loved. That's all we ever wanted. Eve and I wised up. We moved out of my dad's house- my mom lived there but it was in no way her house. We found validation in friends, work, and partners. We found love in all those same people. We were treated as equals and as valuable members of a group. These people up here treated us more like family in two days than our family ever did in two decades. That's why Mathew did all of this. That's why he's got a bullet hole in his head now."

Genesis burst into tears.

*****

Deandre awoke in the ICU. He felt groggy and loopy, but he didn't feel any pain. They must have had him on some good drugs. Everything was a blur. He knew he was in the hospital, but he couldn't remember how he got there. Or how long he had been there. Deandre remembered shooting Mathew, one shot to the head. He remembered passing out after that. Next thing he knew was waking up in the ICU. He wondered if Eric had made it. That whole trip was Eric's idea. If Eric did live, he would carry a lot of guilt over what happened. He would surely blame himself. No one would have been up there if not for him inviting everyone to meet him at the cabin.

Deep down Deandre knew Eric was dead. He could feel it. That made Deandre feel a little better. It tore him up to lose his best friend, but he knew Eric would never walk again. He would have put that whole nightmare on himself. Deandre knew Eric well enough to know he'd spend the rest of his life drinking himself stupid in a wheelchair, especially with Rachel dead. Sometimes it's better to let someone go than to watch them live like that. If you can even call the way Eric would have lived living.

Deandre had lost everyone that mattered to him. Why did he ever turn his back when he was in that out building? He should have paid better attention to his surroundings. If he had seen Mathew coming, he would have saved Gina and Rachel as well. Deandre owned that guilt, and he would carry it forever. One different move here or there and that whole night could have ended differently. He should've hunted Mathew down. All Mathew had was a knife. Why didn't he ignore the girls and find that little fucker and shoot him between the eyes before he could kill anyone else.

Instead, Deandre got a knife to the belly and Rachel and Gina got murdered. That was on him. He did save Genesis and Eve though. And Genny's baby. Deandre shuddered to think that Mathew would not only kill his own sisters, but his sister's baby as well. What kind of monster would even consider that? The same monster that would stab you in the guts and laugh about it. The same monster that stabbed his own mom countless times. The same monster that ate lunch at a table his dad was bleeding out on.

Deandre felt delirious. The room was spinning, and he wanted to puke. He was strapped to the bed. He felt something in his right hand. It was the call button. Deandre pushed it and a middle-aged woman rushed into his room. The nurse looked concerned but confident. She looked like a sweet lady.

"I don't feel good," Deandre whimpered.

"Oh, dear, I'm sorry," the nurse replied. "Do you need a pail?"

"Maybe, I'm dizzy."

The nurse went to his other side. She took a syringe from her pocket and delivered its contents to his veins through his IV. Within minutes, Deandre felt one hundred percent better.

"Thank you," he said to the nurse. "What was that?"

"Something for the nausea," she replied. "Rest up."

"Am I going to be, okay?"

"Yes, you will make a full recovery. The doctor will be in sometime today to talk to you about it."

"Okay, thank you," Deandre said. His eyes felt heavy.

"You're welcome," the nurse replied but Deandre was fast asleep already.

Deandre woke up several hours later feeling better. The dizziness was gone, so was the nausea. The delirium had passed. He could think straight again. He was no longer strapped to the bed. How had they unstrapped him without waking him? Again, they must have him on some good drugs. That was kind of scary. Deandre had dabbled with drugs in his life, but these hospitals had the really good stuff. The stuff that'll knock you out for hours. What else had they done to him while he was out?

There was a knock on his door and then it opened. A small, squatty man pushed a stretcher into Deandre's room.

"It's moving day," the man said with a smile.

The man helped Deandre slide onto the stretcher. The man loosely strapped Dre to the stretcher. He wheeled Deandre out of the room and down to a large elevator. After what felt like five or six floors, the elevator dinged, and Dre was wheeled out and down another hall. The man pushed him into a room and helped him get into bed. After the man got Deandre settled, a tall, dark-skinned doctor walked in.

"Mr. Wilson you are looking much better."

"How much longer will I be here?" Deandre asked.

"A couple more days at the most," the doctor replied. He pulled Deandre's gown aside and examined his wound. "Your injury was serious but not life-threatening. You are lucky, Mr. Wilson. We're talking centimeters either way and you wouldn't have made it. The surgery went well and you're healing nicely."

"That's good," Deandre said. "I'm ready to go home."

"We have to get you on your feet first. We need to make sure you can move around without causing internal damage. As I said, you were very lucky. That knife went between your liver and kidney, but it did nick your kidney. We got you all stitched up inside, but you need to take it easy. By the time you got here you already had some infection. That's why you ended up in ICU. But you're out of the woods now and well on your way to a full recovery."

"So, everything will be normal again?"

"Yes, eventually the only way you'll know it ever happened will be the scar on your abdomen."

"I guess I am lucky," Deandre said sadly as tears welled up in his eyes.

"You are," the doctor said. "The police have been waiting to speak with you. Are you up for that?"

"Sure, I feel fine," Deandre replied.

"Okay, I'll send them in. After you speak with them, I want you to rest. I have you scheduled for light physical therapy this afternoon."

"Okay, thank you."

The doctor left and minutes later two detectives walked in. They were both young. They didn't look old enough to even be cops, much less detectives.

"Mr. Wilson?" one of the detectives said as he pulled up a chair next to Deandre's bed. The other detective stayed standing and hung back a bit. "I'm Detective Drew Wilkerson but just call me Drew. And this is Detective Rob Miller." Detective Miller nodded at Deandre. Neither of them were the least bit intimidating. "We are very sorry for what you endured last week."

"Last week?!" Deandre exclaimed. "How long have I been here?"

"Five days, Mr. Wilson," Drew said.

"Holy shit! How has it been so long? Did Eric make it? How's Genny and Eve?"

"Sir, I know it's a shock, but they had to put you in a coma for a couple days. Don't ask why because I ain't your doctor. If this is all too stressful right now, we can come back later."

"Am I in any trouble for, well, for, you know?"

"No, Mr. Wilson, you are not. You did what had to be done and you saved two lives, your own too probably, and who knows how many more if that man had gotten away before we arrived."

"Okay, I'm fine to talk now," Deandre said. The shock of being in the hospital for five days was wearing off. "Did Eric make it?"

Drew glanced at Rob. They exchanged a look, and Drew returned his attention to Deandre.

"I'm sorry to say…"

Deandre began to cry.

"I'm sorry, Mr. Wilson," Drew said.

"Thank you for telling me," Deandre sobbed. "I already knew it, but I just needed to hear it."

"It's a tragedy and that's not even a strong enough word for it," Drew offered.

"It is," Dre agreed. "What do you wanna know? How can I be of any help? Seems like things are pretty obvious at this point."

"We want to know what you saw and how you ended up shooting him."

"Well, none of us saw much. That little fucker was sneaky. He got people alone and attacked them from behind. He snuck up on me and stabbed me in the guts. Goddamn I wish that shock and pain hadn't made me drop my gun. He was like a foot away. I coulda blasted him right there in that goddamn shed! I coulda saved Gina and Rachel."

"No need for could haves or should haves right now," Drew said. "What happened after he stabbed you?"

"I fell," Dre replied. "I got knocked out. I must've hit my head when I fell. I don't know how long I was out, but it was long enough for him to kill Gina and Rachel. When I finally woke up, I crawled out of the shed. I could see the back door was open and I knew he was inside. I just fuckin' knew it! I peeked over the porch and saw him facing away from the door rambling on and on about something to Genesis and Eve. Bad move on his part but good for me. Genny almost blew my cover though." Dre smiled at that. "So, I crawled back to the shed and found my nine. I pulled myself up onto the porch and stood up. I almost passed out right there from the pain in my side. I kept it together though. I crept around the corner of the porch to the doorway. I almost lost it when I saw Gina and Rachel lying on the floor covered in blood. Rage filled my entire body. Rage fueled me and gave me that last bit of energy I needed to shoot that fucker. Genny saw me, grabbed Eve, and pulled her to the floor. Mathew swiveled around and I shot. Got him in the forehead. He fell to the floor, and I passed out again."

    Rob was hurriedly scribbling notes onto a pad of paper. Drew looked at Rob then back to Deandre.

    "You did the right thing, Mr. Wilson," Drew said. "You're a hero."

    "Part of me wishes I had only wounded him. I wish he would have to spend the rest of his life in prison thinking about what he did. Death was too easy for him. But in that moment, everything inside of me said kill him. If he ain't dead he's able to kill. That motherfucker saddled me with being a killer for the rest of my life. He killed everyone I know and love and he's dead. I'm the one living with being a killer."

    "Don't think of it in those terms," Drew said. "Think of yourself as a hero not a killer. Sometimes heroes have to do things they never thought they would even be capable of. You did just that."

    "Still, I took a life," Deandre dropped his head. He was feeling tired and sick again.

    "You saved countless more, three for sure."

"I know," Dre sobbed.

Deandre looked up at Drew, then to Rob. He glanced around the room. They had given him a private room, probably so he could talk to the cops. What would have happened if that knife got him centimeters either way and he had died there on the shed floor? Would Mathew have killed his sisters and bolted? Would he have kept killing people? What had even possessed him to do it all in the first place? Deandre imagined someone capable of killing his own family probably would have kept killing until he was caught or killed by someone else. Deandre thought maybe he should be proud of what he did. That fucker killed kids that had just graduated high school, he wouldn't have had any qualms with killing God-knows who else.

"What else can I help you with?" Deandre asked.

"Do you have any idea why he would do this?" Drew asked.

"No, I don't," Deandre replied. "I know he was mad at his sisters. He called them whores and sinners. He was mad at us for letting the girls stay with us. He called us heathens and sinners. To me that is motive but why kill anyone else? I don't wanna try to get in his head. I couldn't tell you what possessed him to do it."

"We know that's a tough question, but sometimes we get a good idea of why from it," Drew said. "Anything else stand out to you?"

"Eric told us that there were these teenagers up there making a ruckus all weekend. Maybe that's why Mathew killed them?"

"Could be," Drew said. "Anything about his behavior leading up to that night? His sisters told us there had been a confrontation between him and you guys."

"Oh, yeah," Deandre recalled. "His dad too. His dad came to Eric's cabin spitting mad that we had Genesis and Eve over. He demanded we return them immediately. We told him they were grown women, and they'll go home when they're good and ready. His dad called us sinners and heathens as well. Eric about beat the guy. I had to pull Eric away from him. Mathew was standing there the whole time but didn't say anything. I do remember he looked like shit."

"How so?"

"Like tired and weathered. Like he'd pulled an all-nighter or something. His eyes were dodgy too, like he was watching someone pace to his left. He was more skittish than normal that day."

"Was that the day of?"

"Yes, it was. He did it the first day we were all up there. Mathew had come by that morning too, while Eric was making breakfast. They got into it pretty good. Eric scared him away. You think all of that set him off?"

"Maybe," Drew replied. "We'll never know for sure since we can't ask him."

"I'm getting sleepy and don't feel well," Deandre said. Reliving that night by talking about it was taking the life out of him.

"Okay, well you have given us a lot of valuable information. If you need anything or think of anything else, please call me." Drew stood up and handed Deandre a business card. "Take care, Mr. Wilson."

"Thank you."

Drew and Rob left the room. Deandre closed his eyes and fell asleep. He saw Mathew's face. He then watched as the back of Mathew's head blew away. Mathew stared at him with a big smile. Mathew moved toward Deandre, still missing half his head. He was cocking his head back and forth. That smile widened. His eyes were black as at night.

"You did this," Mathew said and pointed to the hole in his head. "You shot me." His smile widened even more, now far too big for his face. "Well played, sir, well played. If only I hadn't tried to get my whore sisters to repent. I could've finished my mission before you even woke up. I thought you were dead. Stupid me, I should have stabbed you a few more times to be sure. That's on me. And look what that one mistake got me. A hole in the head." Mathew laughed and blood spurted out the back of his head. "You know what it was? I got cocky. I should've just listened to God and carried out my mission. He told me those whores weren't worth saving. He told me they were not going to be welcomed to heaven. I should have listened. Dang-it, Mathew, always listen to God! Maybe this," he pointed to the hole again, "was part of His plan all along. I want you to know, I forgive you. I must forgive you. God has not lifted me to heaven yet and you're the only reason I can think of why he hasn't. When you shot me, I was angry. I was holding on to ill intentions. I blame you for failing my mission. I must get right with the Lord so I can assume my place in Heaven and bask in all His glory."

Mathew stared at Deandre. Those black eyes gleaming. Shimmering.

"Well?" Mathew asked. "Do you accept my forgiveness?"

"Fuck no!" Deandre snapped.

"But you must. I need to get to Heaven."

"You ain't going to heaven, Matt. Murderers go to hell."

"I am not a murderer!" Mathew exclaimed greatly offended. "I am an instrument of God! God's instruments go to Heaven to be with Him. He promised me."

"You're fucked, little man," Deandre said and laughed in Mathew's face. "I would never accept your forgiveness, and I would never forgive you! You killed everyone I loved. You took my life-long best friend from me! You took *all* of my friends from me. I have no one left thanks to you! I hate you and I always will 'til the day I die!"

Mathew's face changed. It morphed into a huge dog-like head. The eyes were still black and shimmering. Razor-sharp teeth glistened. The dog head lunged at Deandre and he awoke with a scream.

*****

Genesis and Eve sat in the hospital waiting room, aimlessly scrolling on their phones. They were told Deandre was at physical therapy and they could see him in thirty minutes. That was forty-five minutes ago. They hadn't seen or talked to him since that night almost a week ago. The stress of that night and the following days had caused Genesis to go into false labor. She was hospitalized for one night. Thanks to medication and observation, her and the baby were fine. She found out she was going to have a boy.

Toby and Elijah were long gone. Genesis hadn't heard from him in months. She tried to get ahold of him after the night at the cabin, but he changed his number. Genesis called his mother and was told to never to call again. Toby's mom said that Genesis had sullied her boy's good name and that she was not welcome with their family anymore. Somehow in their minds the pregnancy was all her fault, as if she had done it on purpose to make him look bad. It was frustrating and infuriating, but Genesis couldn't do anything about it. Except despise Toby and his entire family. Eve had been told that Toby and Elijah ran off together under the guise of a mission trip.

Genesis tried to keep her mind off Toby and his family. They didn't want anything to do with her or the baby, there was no reason to fret about it anymore. It was just her and Eve now. Neither of them wanted to be alone anymore so they were in the process of getting a place together. They wanted an apartment or condo, somewhere a lot of other people lived. A place where people would always be around. Everything was happening too fast, yet time seemed to drag on. They had so much to deal with and handle before the baby came in a few weeks. Eve's landlord said she could get out of her lease as long as she stayed in the complex. They would write her and Genesis a new lease. They would be able to move in within a week.

Eve and her boyfriend split up. He couldn't handle her emotions, and she didn't want a man in her life anymore. They had been on the fritz before anything had happened, that was the main reason he never ended up at the cabin that weekend. They had been fighting for a while; she just hadn't told anyone yet. Not even Genesis. Eve was glad to be out of a relationship. She didn't have the patience, mental fortitude, or emotional stability to be in a relationship. She hadn't slept for more than an hour or two straight since that fateful night. Every time she fell asleep, she'd have nightmares. Mathew stalked her dreams. She knew it was him and not just her subconscious reminding her of that night.

Mathew was different in her dreams. His presence was dark and heavy. His eyes were darker than the night. His breath smelled of fire with a sour, death note to it. He would always face her and smile that creepy smile he had that night in Eric's cabin. Except the smile was far too big for his face. His face looked hollow, as if it was decomposing from the inside. Or as if his facial bones were shrinking. He always asked her for forgiveness. He would tell her he forgave her for being a whore. He forgave her for resisting him all those years. Eve always told him to fuck off. His head would morph into a huge dog's head. The eyes stayed black and that smile never wavered. He'd lunge at her with that gigantic muzzle, and she'd awake in a sweat, her heart beating out of her chest. Every damn night.

Genesis had nightmares too. In her dreams she was giving birth to her son. A nurse would hand her a crying baby boy. He was tiny and beautiful. Her heart was happy. The happiness never lasted long. As she looked at her baby his cute little face would slowly turn into Mathew's devilish smiling face. The back of his head was gone. His eyes were blacker than black. His teeth were jagged and fang-like. He never spoke to her, but she knew what he wanted. He wanted her forgiveness. Not a chance, Mathew, no way, never. She would deal with these nightmares before she ever gave him her forgiveness. He didn't deserve it.

Deandre's nurse stepped into the waiting room and let them know Deandre was ready for company. Eve and Genesis were excited and nervous. They were surprised at how good he looked when they entered his room. He was smiling and in good spirits.

"You look good!" Genesis exclaimed giving him a hug.

"Thank you. I feel good. They say I can leave tomorrow."

"That's great news!" Genesis said, sitting down in a chair next to his bed.

"You really do look good, my man," Eve said hugging him and then sitting down.

"Thanks," Deandre said. "You guys do too. How have you been?"

"We're fine," Genesis said. "Living day-to-day, you know? We're getting a place together soon. Neither of us want to live alone anymore."

"That's a good idea," Deandre said. "I'm going to stay with my mom for a bit when I get out of here. They want me to take it easy and not lift too much. Plus, mom's a stellar cook and after hospital food I'm ready for mom's cooking!"

"That's a good idea," Genesis said. "How is your family handling all of this?"

"Best they can. They were all close to Eric and Rachel. They're obviously shocked and devastated, but carrying on."

"How are you handling everything?" Genesis asked.

"Same, best I can. Being stuck here is tough because I have no distractions outside PT and TV. TV is useless to me, even if I find something I actually wanna watch it doesn't keep my mind off of things for very long."

"I know what you mean," Eve said. "Even watching my favorite shows isn't enough to keep my mind from wandering."

"I can't even watch one show without being reminded of everyone. The commercials always show these happy groups of friends having a good time. It's too much," Genesis said, tearing up.

"I don't think things will ever be the same again," Eve said.

"They can't be," Deandre said. "Our old life is totally gone. Replaced with this new nightmare of an existence. I'm hoping once I'm out of here, I will feel better. Never the same, but at least better."

"I hope so too," Genesis said. "I feel so bad for you. I want to thank you for saving us. Thank you for finding the courage to do what you did. I can't imagine what that was like."

"You don't wanna know," Deandre said. "You are welcome. It had to be done. I wasn't gonna just lie there in that damn shed and bleed to death. I knew Mathew was in that cabin. I just hoped I wasn't too late. I'm glad you two survived. I wish everyone could have." Tears streamed down his face. Eve and Genesis began to cry as well.

"We miss them all too," Genesis sobbed. "We are so, so sorry Mathew did all this."

"Don't be sorry on that motherfucker's behalf!" Dre snapped through tears. "Don't you guys dare feel an ounce of guilt about what he did. Your brother or not, that was all on him. Do not feel bad about any of it. Feel sorrow and remorse for our friends but not for that piece of shit brother of yours."

They all fell quiet for a while, silently crying.

"What do you think the others would do if they survived instead of us?" Eve asked through sniffles.

"Same as we are. Get along the best they could." Deandre replied. "I know em all well, they'd feel the same as we do."

"We should say a few words for them," Genesis suggested.

"I ain't ready for any of that," Deandre said. "I can't even let myself think about them. I saw them every day of my life and they're just gone. Poof! I'll never see them again. I know you grew up seeing Eric every summer for a weekend here and there. I saw him every damn day! For most of my life. Now I'll never see him again. No more smoke breaks. No more drinks at the bar. No more poker night. It's all gone, and it was all ripped away for no fuckin' reason!"

Deandre was crying and he was steaming mad. There was so much more he wanted to say but not to those two. Their brother took his best friend from him. Their brother took all of his friends, people he considered family. He wanted to rail on Mathew. In the end it was mostly pointless, Mathew was dead too. Going on and on about what a piece of shit the guy was would feel good but served no other purpose.

"Mathew is a piece of shit!" Eve exclaimed through tears. "You don't have to censor yourself because of us. I hated my brother long before he did this. I don't know what made him do it, but he did it and you're right- that's on him. I've wished him dead many times. It is still strange that he is in fact gone. Mom and dad too. But I didn't see them every day. I didn't look forward to seeing them or talking to them. One doesn't tend to look forward to talking to people who call them a whore." Eve looked over at Genesis. "Why are we beating ourselves up over this? Deandre saved our lives. We should be celebrating that. We should be honoring Deandre by living our best life possible."

"I feel like we are," Genesis said. "We're still in shock and we're still grieving, but I don't feel like we're moping around."

"I get that, but we still let this get to us all the damn time," Eve said. "Shit, we dream about Mathew every night! I don't wanna dream about him or think about him or even talk about him anymore. We're giving him what he always wanted, attention. He's gone and frankly good-fuckin'-riddance!"

"I dream about him too," Deandre said.

"Oh, yeah? What do you dream?" Eve asked.

"It's fucked up and it's every damn night," Deandre said. They had all stopped crying but were still very down. "He has a hole in his head and he's telling me he forgives me. That's right, forgives me. He's basically begging me for forgiveness so he can get into heaven. I always shut him down and then he turns into a dog-headed creature who tries to bite me. Then I wake up all sweaty."

"Holy shit!" Eve exclaimed. "That's almost exactly like my nightly dream. Are his eyes super black and his smile too big for his face?"

"Yes!" Deandre replied. "Way blacker than should be possible."

"Tell him yours, sis," Eve said turning to Genesis.

"I don't want to," Genesis said and shifted nervously in her chair.

"Can I?" Eve asked.

"Knock yourself out," Genesis replied, standing up. "I'm going to go get some water while you do. Anyone want anything?"

"Could you get me a root beer? Like a full-sized bottle? All they give me 'round here are those baby cans."

"You bet," Genesis said. "Sis?" Eve shook her head no. Genesis left Deandre's room.

Genesis heard Eve start to tell Deandre about the dreams. She didn't want to hear her own dream told. Genesis wished she had never even told Eve. She shouldn't have told anyone. Oh well, no big deal, now. There were bigger things to worry about than stupid dreams. They weren't stupid, though. They were vivid and all too real. Mathew was physically gone but he didn't seem like he was totally gone. Hopefully he wouldn't haunt them forever.

Genesis got her water and Deandre's root beer. She hadn't had root beer in years, it looked good. She returned to Dre's room; he and Eve were talking about baseball. Thankfully the subject of conversation was no longer on Mathew and nightmares. Genesis couldn't take much more of those topics. She handed Deandre his root beer and he lit up. He looked like a kid whose grandma just gave him his favorite candy bar.

"Thank you so much!" Deandre exclaimed, opening the soda and taking a drink.

"You're welcome," Genesis smiled.

The three chatted for another half hour. They chatted about sports, life, Genesis's baby. They talked about living arrangements a bit more. Deandre told them they shouldn't give up Genesis's house. They should move into it together. He explained they shouldn't let what happened make them live in constant fear. Something like that would never happen again. Besides, they lived in the city, in a good neighborhood, help was always less than ten minutes away- if even that long. As everything Deandre was saying sunk in, the girls realized he was absolutely right. Why live in an apartment when Genesis already had a nice house? It was a rental, but it was in a nice neighborhood. Genesis knew a couple of her neighbors and they were extremely nice people. It was settled right there in Deandre's hospital room that they were moving into Genesis's place. A solid, lifelong friendship between the three of them was solidified in that hospital room as well.

*****

When the time came, Genesis had no doubt she was in labor. Being a nurse, she knew the signs well and she felt them deeply that day. She had never felt such pain before. The uncontrollable bearing-down feeling in her groin, the immense back pain, it was all so intense and foreign. Eve took Genesis to the hospital. They got her set up and called her doctor.

Genesis was indeed in labor. Her baby boy was on his way into this world. Everything became a blur of emotions and pain for Genesis. She wasn't ready to have the baby yet. She still had so much to do. That baby had different plans. It took almost six hours, but her beautiful, healthy baby boy was born that day. And he was a beautiful boy. Genesis wept when the nurse handed her bundled up baby to her. Eve burst into tears as well. He was perfect. Perfect in every way. He had a head full of dark, curly hair. His little nose and mouth were perfect and adorable. At one point he opened his eyes, and they were a beautiful light brown color. So much life and innocence in those tiny eyes.

She named him Jonathan Eric Simpson. Jonathan was Deandre's middle name. That baby boy grew up being called Johnny. Johnny was a happy, healthy, energetic little boy. He had no care in the world. He brought life and happiness to Genesis, Eve, and Deandre. The boy didn't seem to care or miss having extended family. Not even when he got old enough to know other kids had grandparents and cousins and siblings. When Johnny was five, Eve gave him his first and only cousin. Eve married a wonderful man named Richard. He was a police officer and a hell of a guy. He treated Eve and everyone else like gold. Richard was a beautiful soul and a tremendous father and uncle.

Deandre met a wonderful, spirited woman named Keisha. They eventually married and had twin boys within a year. Those boys were spitfires. They were rambunctious, sweet little guys. Deandre was a proud father. He loved those boys more than anything in the world. Every spare moment he had was spent outside playing football or basketball with his sons. Keisha was a loving, devoted mother and a dynamite wife and partner. Deandre adored her, and she did him.

Genesis met a good man named Ryan. They moved into together quickly and got married. Ryan was a tremendous stepfather to Johnny. He got along great with Eve, Richard, and especially Deandre. Those two hit it off from day one. It was as if they'd been friends forever. Ryan and Genesis would eventually give Johnny a little sister and then a little brother. Ryan was a firefighter and Genesis continued working as a nurse. She got a great job in a doctor's office, no more crazy hospital hours. Genesis would wake up every day and look at her beautiful family. The family she had always dreamed of. Ryan helped her learn how to be an equal partner. All Genesis had ever known was how her parents had operated. Ryan said he wanted a partner, not a docile woman. Genesis grew and blossomed into a strong, passionate, grounded woman. Her and Ryan were a perfect match. Thank God Toby had flipped out and disappeared. Genesis knew if he had reacted differently, she would've married him and would have been absolutely miserable.

The memory of that night at the cabin faded as life went on. As good things happened and new lives came around, that night seemed to be more and more distant. Every once in a while, especially after a stressful day, the nightmares would return. Mathew would appear with a hole in his head. He'd say his Mathew things and then turn into that dog-headed creature. It was always the same, so it became less frightening each time, until the dreams were so few and far between, they didn't even matter anymore.

Genesis, Eve, and Deandre didn't let themselves feel guilty anymore. They had been chosen to survive for a reason. Their children were that reason.

Made in the USA
Columbia, SC
08 April 2025